# THE
# EXPLORER

# THE
# EXPLORER

# W. SOMERSET
# MAUGHAM

Carroll & Graf Publishers, Inc.
New York

To my dear Mrs. G. W. Steevens

First Carroll & Graf edition 1991

Carroll & Graf Publishers, Inc.
260 Fifth Avenue
New York, N.Y. 10001

ISBN: 0-88184-654-6

Manufactured in the United States of America

# I

THE sea was very calm. There was no ship in sight, and the sea-gulls were motionless upon its even greyness. They sky was dark with lowering clouds, but there was no wind. The line of the horizon was clear and delicate. The shingly beach, no less deserted, was thick with tangled seaweed, and the innumerable shells crumbled under the feet that trod them. The breakwaters, which sought to prevent the unceasing encroachment of the waves, were rotten with age and green with the sea-slime. It was a desolate scene, but there was a restfulness in its melancholy; and the great silence, the suave monotony of colour, might have given peace to a heart that was troubled. They could not assuage the torment of the woman who stood alone upon that spot. She did not stir; and, though her gaze was steadfast, she saw nothing. Nature has neither love nor hate, and with indifference smiles upon the light at heart and to the heavy brings a deeper sorrow. It is a great irony that the old Greek, so wise and prudent, who fancied that the gods lived utterly apart from human passions, divinely unconscious in their high palaces of the grief and joy, the hope and despair, of the turbulent crowd of men, should have gone down to posterity as the apostle of brutish pleasure.

But the silent woman did not look for solace.  She
had a vehement pride which caused her to seek comfort only in her own heart; and when, against her
will, heavy tears rolled down her cheeks, she shook
her head impatiently.  She drew a long breath and set
herself resolutely to change her thoughts.

But they were too compelling, and she could not drive
from her mind the memories that absorbed it.  Her
fancy, like a homing bird, hovered with light wings
about another coast; and the sea she looked upon reminded her of another sea.  The Solent.  From her
earliest years that sheet of water had seemed an essential part of her life, and the calmness at her feet
brought back to her irresistibly the scenes she knew
so well.  But the rippling waves washed the shores of
Hampshire with a persuasive charm that they had not
elsewhere, and the broad expanse of it, lacking the il-
limitable majesty of the open sea, could be loved like
a familiar thing.  Yet there was in it, too, something
of the salt freshness of the ocean, and, as the eye followed its course, the heart could exult with a sense of
freedom.  Sometimes, in the dusk of a winter afternoon, she remembered the Solent as desolate as the
Kentish sea before her; but her imagination presented it to her more often with the ships, outward bound or homeward bound, that passed continually.  She loved them all.  She loved the great
liners that sped across the ocean, unmindful of
wind or weather, with their freight of passengers;
and at night, when she recognised them only by
the long row of lights, they fascinated her by the
mystery of their thousand souls going out strangely
into the unknown.  She loved the little panting ferries

that carried the good folk of the neighbourhood across the water to buy their goods in Southampton, or to sell the produce of their farms; she was intimate with their sturdy skippers, and she delighted in their airs of self-importance. She loved the fishing boats that went out in all weathers, and the neat yachts that fled across the bay with such a dainty grace. She loved the great barques and the brigantines that came in with a majestic ease, all their sails set to catch the remainder of the breeze; they were like wonderful, stately birds, and her soul rejoiced at the sight of them. But best of all she loved the tramps that plodded with a faithful, grim tenacity from port to port; often they were squat and ugly, battered by the tempest, dingy and ill-painted; but her heart went out to them. They touched her because their fate seemed so inglorious. No skipper, new to his craft, could ever admire the beauty of their lines, nor look up at the swelling canvas and exult he knew not why; no passengers would boast of their speed or praise their elegance. They were honest merchantmen, laborious, trustworthy, and of good courage, who took foul weather and peril in the day's journey and made no outcry. And with a sure instinct she saw the romance in the humble course of their existence and the beauty of an unboasting performance of their duty; and often, as she watched them, her fancy glowed with the thought of the varied merchandise they carried, and their long sojourning in foreign parts. There was a subtle charm in them because they went to Southern seas and white cities with tortuous streets, silent under the blue sky.

Striving still to free herself of a passionate regret,

the lonely woman turned away and took a path
that led across the marshes. But her heart sank, for
she seemed to recognise the flats, the shallow dykes,
the coastguard station, which she had known all her
life. Sheep were grazing here and there, and two
horses, put out to grass, looked at her listlessly as she
passed. A cow heavily whisked its tail. To the indifferent, that line of Kentish coast, so level and
monotonous, might be merely dull, but to her it was
beautiful. It reminded her of the home she would
never see again.

And then her thoughts, which had wandered around
the house in which she was born, ever touching the
fringe as it were, but never quite settling with the
full surrender of attention, gave themselves over to it
entirely.

Hamlyn's Purlieu had belonged to the Allertons for
three hundred years, and the recumbent effigy, in stone,
of the founder of the family's fortunes, with his two
wives in ruffs and stiff martingales, was to be seen in
the chancel of the parish church. It was the work of
an Italian sculptor, lured to England in company of
the craftsmen who made the lady-chapel of Westminster Abbey; and the renaissance delicacy of its work
was very grateful in the homely English church. And
for three hundred years the Allertons had been men
of prudence, courage, and worth, so that the walls of
the church by now were filled with the lists of their vir-
tues and their achievements. They had intermarried
with the great families of the neighbourhood, and with
the help of these marble tablets you might have made
out a roll of all that was distinguished in Hampshire.

The Maddens of Brise, the Fletchers of Horton Park, the Daunceys of Malden Hall, the Garrods of Penda, had all, in the course of time, given daughters to the Allertons of Hamlyn's Purlieu; and the Allertons of Hamlyn's Purlieu had given in exchange richly dowered maidens to the Garrods of Penda, the Daunceys of Malden Hall, the Fletchers of Horton Park, and the Maddens of Brise.

And with each generation the Allertons grew prouder. The peculiar situation of their lands distinguished them a little from their neighbours; for, whereas the Garrods, the Daunceys, and the Fletchers lived within walking distance of each other, and Madden of Brise, because of his rank and opulence the most distinguished person in the county, within six or seven miles, Hamlyn's Purlieu was near the sea and separated by forest land from other places. The seclusion in which its owners were thus forced to dwell differentiated their characters from those of the neighbouring gentlemen. They found much cause for self-esteem in the number of their acres, and, though many of these consisted of salt marshes, and more of wild heath, others were as good as any in Hampshire; and the grand total made a formidable array in works of reference. But they found greater reason still for self-congratulation in their culture. No pride is so great as the pride of intellect, and the Allertons never doubted that their neighbours were boors beside them. Whether it was due to the peculiar lie of the land on which they were born and bred, that led them to introspection, or whether it was due to some accident of inheritance, the Allertons had all an interest in the things of the mind which had never troubled the Fletchers or the

Garrods of Penda, the Daunceys or my lords Madden
of Brise. They were as good sportsmen as the others,
and hunted or shot with the best of them, but they
read books as well, and had a subtlety of intelligence
which was no less unexpected than pleasing. The fat
squires of the county looked up to them as miracles
of learning, and congratulated themselves over their
port on possessing in their midst persons who combined, in such excellent proportions, gentle birth and
a good seat in the saddle with adequate means and
an encyclopedic knowledge. Everything conspired to
give the Allertons a good opinion of themselves. They
not only looked down from superior heights on the
persons with whom they habitually came in contact
—that is common enough—but these very persons without question looked up to them.

The Allertons made the grand tour in a style be-
fitting their dignity; and the letters which each son
of the house wrote in turn, describing Paris, Vienna,
Dresden, Munich, and Rome, with the persons of consequence who entertained him, were preserved with
scrupulous care among the family papers. They tes-
tified to an agreeable interest in the arts; and each
of them had made a point of bringing back with him,
according to the fashion of his day, beautiful things
which he had purchased on his journey. Hamlyn's
Purlieu, a fine stone house goodly to look upon, was
thus filled with Italian pictures, French cabinets of
delicate workmanship, bronzes of all kinds, tapestries,
and old Eastern carpets. The gardens had been tended
with a loving care, and there grew in them trees
and flowers which were unknown to other parts of England. Each Allerton in his time cherished the place

with a passionate pride, looking upon it as his greatest privilege that he could add a little to its beauty and hand on to his successor a more magnificent heritage.

But at length Hamlyn's Purlieu came into the hands of Fred Allerton; and the gods, blind for so long to the prosperity of this house, determined now, it seemed, to wreak their malice. Fred Allerton had many of the characteristics of his race, but in him they took a sudden turn which bore him swiftly to destruction. They had been marked always by good looks, a persuasive manner, and a singular liberality of mind; and he was perhaps the handsomest, and certainly the most charming of them all. But the freedom from prejudice which had prevented the others from giving way too much to their pride had in him degenerated into a singular unscrupulousness. His parents died when he was twenty, and a year later he found himself master of a great estate. The times were hard then for those who depended upon their land, and Fred Allerton was not so rich as his forebears. But he flung himself extravagantly into the pursuit of pleasure. He was the only member of his family who had failed to reside habitually at Hamlyn's Purlieu. He seemed to take no interest in it, and except now and then to shoot, never came near his native county. He lived much in Paris, which in the early years of the third republic had still something of the wanton gaiety of the Empire; and here he soon grew notorious for his prodigality and his adventures. He was an unlucky man, and everything he did led to disaster. But this never impaired his cheerfulness. He boasted that he had lost money in every gambling hell in Europe, and vowed that he would give up racing in disgust if ever a horse of his won a race. His charm of manner was irresistible, and no one had more friends than he. His generosity was great, and he was willing to lend money to everyone who asked. But it is even more expensive to be a man whom everyone likes than to keep a stud, and Fred Allerton found himself in due course much in need of ready money. He did not hesitate to mortgage his lands, and till he came to the end of these resources also, continued gaily to lead a life of splendour.

At length he had raised on Hamlyn's Purlieu every penny that he could, and was crippled with debt besides; but he still rode a fine horse, lived in expensive chambers, dressed better than any man in London, and gave admirable dinners to all and sundry. He realised then that he could only retrieve his fortunes by a rich marriage. Fred Allerton was still a handsome man, and he knew from long experience how easy it was to say pleasant things to a woman. There was a peculiar light in his blue eyes which persuaded everyone of the goodness of· his heart. He was amusing and full of spirits. He fixed upon a Miss Boulger, one of the two daughters of a Liverpool manufacturer, and succeeded after a surprisingly short time in assuring her of his passion. There was a convincing air of truth in all he said, and she returned his flame with readiness. It was clear to him that her sister was equally prepared to fall in love with him, and he regretted with diverting frankness to his more intimate friends that the laws of the land prevented him from marrying them both and acquiring two fortunes instead of one. He married the younger Miss Boulger, and on her dowry paid off the mortgages on Hamlyn's Purlieu, his own debts, and succeeded for several years in having an excellent time. The poor woman, happily blind to his defects, adored him with all her soul. She trusted him entirely with the management of her money and only regretted that the affairs connected with it kept him so much in town. With marriage and his new connection with commerce Fred Allerton had come to the conclusion that he had business abilities, and he occupied himself thenceforward with all manner of financial schemes. With unwearied enthusiasm he entered upon some new affair which was going to bring him untold wealth as soon as the last had finally sunk into the abyss of bankruptcy. Hamlyn's Purlieu had never known such gaieties as during the fifteen years of Mrs. Allerton's married life. All kinds of people were brought down by Fred ; and the dignified dining-room, which for centuries had witnessed discussions, learned or flippant, on the merits of Greek and Latin authors, or the excellencies of Italian masters, now heard strange talk of stocks and shares, companies, syndicates, options and holdings. When Mrs. Allerton died suddenly she was entirely unconscious that her husband had squandered every penny of the money which had been settled on her children, had mortgaged once more the broad fields of his ancestors, and was head over ears in debt. She expired with his name upon her lips, and blessed the day on which she had first seen him. She had one son and one daughter. Lucy was a girl of fifteen when her mother died, and George, the boy, was ten.

It was Lucy, now a woman of twenty-five, who turned her back upon the Kentish sea and slowly walked across the marsh. And as she walked, the recollection of the ten years that had passed since then was placed before her as it were in a single flash.

At first her father had seemed the most wonderful being in the world, and she had worshipped him with all her childish heart. The love that bound her to her mother was pale in comparison, for Lucy could not divide her affections, giving part here, part there; her father, with his wonderful gift of sympathy, his indescribable charm, conquered her entirely. It was her greatest delight to be with him. She was entertained and exhilarated by his society, and she hated the men of business who absorbed so much of his time.

When Mrs. Allerton died George was sent to school, but Lucy, in charge of a governess, remained year in, year out, at Hamlyn's Purlieu with her books, her dogs, and her horses. And gradually, she knew not how, it was borne in upon her that the father who had seemed such a paragon of chivalry, was weak, unreliable, and shifty. She fought against the suspicions that poisoned her mind, charging herself bitterly with meanness of spirit, but one small incident after another brought the truth home to her. She recognised with a shiver of anguish that his standard of veracity was utterly different from hers. He was not very careful to keep his word. He was not scrupulous in money matters. With her, honesty, truthfulness, exactness in all affairs, were not only instinctive, but deliberate; for the pride of her birth was so great that she felt it incumbent upon her to be ten times more careful in these things than the ordinary run of men.

And then, from a word here and a word there, by horrified guesses and by a kind of instinctive surmise, she realised presently the whole truth of her father's life. She found out that Hamlyn's Purlieu was mort-gaged for every penny it was worth, she found out that there was a bill of sale on the furniture, that money had been raised on the pictures; and, at last, that her mother's money, left in her father's trust to her and George, had been spent. And still Fred Allerton lived with prodigal magnificence.

It was only very gradually that Lucy discovered these things. There was no one whom she could con-sult, and she had to devise some mode of conduct by herself. It was all a matter of supposition, and she knew almost nothing for certain. She made up her mind that she would probe no deeper. But since such knowledge as she had came to her only by degrees, she was able the better to adapt her behaviour to it. The pride which for so long had been a characteristic of the Allertons, but had unaccountably missed Fred, in her enjoyed all its force; and what she knew now served only to augment it. In the ruin of her ideals she had nothing but that to cling to, and she cherished it with an unreasoning passion. She had a cult for the ances-tors whose portraits looked down upon her in one room after another of Hamlyn's Purlieu, and from their names and the look of them, which was all that re-mained, she made them in her fancy into personalities whose influence might somehow counteract the weak-ness of her father. In them there was so much up-rightness, strength, and simple goodness; the sum total of it must prevail in the long run against the unruly in-stincts of one man. And she loved her old home, with all its exquisite contents, with its rich gardens, its broad, fertile fields, above all with its wild heath and flat sea-marshes, she loved it with a hungry devotion, saddened and yet more vehement because her hold on it was jeopardised. She set the whole strength of her will on preserving the place for her brother. Her greatest desire was to fill him with the determination to reclaim it from the foreign hands that had some hold upon it, and to restore it to its ancient freedom.

Upon George were set all Lucy's hopes. He could restore the fallen fortunes of their race, and her part must be to train him to the glorious task. He was growing up, and she made up her mind to keep from him all knowledge of her father's weakness. To George he must seem to the last an honest gentleman.

Lucy transferred to her brother all the love which she had lavished on her father. She watched his growth fondly, interesting herself in his affairs, and seeking to be to him not only a sister, but the mother he had lost, and the father who was unworthy. When he was of a fit age she saw that he was sent to Winchester. She followed his career with passion and entered eagerly into all his interests.

But if Lucy had lost her old love for her father, its place had been taken by a pitying tenderness; and she did all she could to conceal from him the change in her feelings. It was easy when she was with him, for then it was impossible to resist his charm; and it was only afterwards, when he was no longer there to explain things away, that she could not crush the horror and resentment with which she regarded him. But of this no one knew anything; and she set herself deliberately not only to make such headway as she could in the tangle of their circumstances, but to conceal from everyone the actual state of things.

For presently Fred Allerton seemed no longer to have an inexhaustible supply of ready money, and Lucy had to resort to a very careful economy. She reduced expenses in every way she could, and when left alone in the house, lived with the utmost frugality. She hated to ask her father for money, and since often he did not pay the allowance that was due to her, she was obliged to exercise a good deal of self-denial. As soon as she was old enough, Lucy had taken the household affairs into her own hands and had learned to conduct them in such a way as to hide from the world how difficult it was to make both ends meet. Now, feeling that things were approaching a crisis, she sold the horses and dismissed most of the servants. A great fear seized her that it would be impossible to keep Hamlyn's Purlieu, and she was stricken with panic. She was willing to make every sacrifice but that, and if she were only allowed to remain there, did not care how penuriously she lived.

But the struggle was growing harder. None knew what she had endured in her endeavour to keep their heads above water. And she had borne everything with perfect cheerfulness. Though she saw a good deal of the neighbouring gentry, connected with her by blood or long friendship, not one of them divined her great anxiety. She felt vaguely that they knew how things were going, but she held her head high and gave no one an opportunity to pity her. Her father was now absent from home more frequently and seemed to avoid being alone with her. They had never discussed the state of their affairs, for he assumed with Lucy a determined flippancy which prevented any serious conversation. On her twenty-first birthday he had made some facetious observation about the money of which she was now mistress, but had treated the matter with such an airy charm that she had felt unable to proceed with it. Nor did she wish to, for if he had spent her money nothing could be done, and it was better not to know for certain. Notwithstanding settlements and wills, she felt that it was really his to do what he liked with, and she made up her mind that nothing in her behaviour should be construed as a reproach.

At length the crash came.

She received a telegram one day—she was nearly twenty-three then—from Richard Lomas, an old friend of her mother's, to say that he was coming down for luncheon. She walked to the station to meet him. She was very fond of him, not only for his own sake, but because her mother had been fond of him, too; and the affection which had existed between them, drew her nearer to the mother whom she felt now she had a little neglected. Dick Lomas was a barrister, who, after contesting two seats unsuccessfully, had got into Parliament at the last general election and had made already a certain name for himself by the wittiness of his speeches and the bluntness of his common sense. He had neither the portentous gravity nor the dogmatic airs which afflicted most of his legal colleagues in the house. He was a man who had solved the difficulty of being sensible without tediousness and pointed without impertinence. He was wise enough not to speak too often, and if only he had not possessed a sense of humour—which his countrymen always regard with suspicion in an English politician—he might have looked forward to a brilliant future. He was a wiry little man, with a sharp, good-humoured face and sparkling eyes. He carried his seven and thirty years with gaiety.

But on this occasion he was unusually grave. Lucy, already surprised at his sudden visit, divined at once from the uneasiness of his pleasant, grey eyes that something was amiss. Her heart began to beat more quickly. He forced himself to smile as he took her hand, congratulating her on the healthiness of her appearance; and they walked slowly from the station. Dick spoke of indifferent things, while Lucy distractedly turned over in her mind all that could have happened. Luncheon was ready for them, and Dick sat down with apparent gusto, praising emphatically the good things she set before him; but he ate as little as she did. He seemed impatient for the meal to end, but unwilling to enter upon the subject which oppressed him. They drank their coffee.

' Shall we go for a turn in the garden? ' he suggested.

' Certainly.'

After his last visit, Dick had sent down an old sundial which he had picked up in a shop in Westminster, and Lucy took him to the place which they had before decided needed just such an ornament. They discussed it at some length, but then silence fell suddenly upon them, and they walked side by side without a word. Dick slipped his arm through hers with a caressing motion, and Lucy, unused to any tenderness, felt a sob rise to her throat. They went in once more and stood in the drawing-room. From the walls looked down the treasures of the house. There was a portrait by Reynolds, and another by Hoppner, and there was a beautiful picture of the Grand Canal by Guardi, and there was a portrait by Goya of a General Allerton who had fought in the Peninsular War. Dick gave them a glance, and his blood tingled with admiration. He leaned against the fireplace.

'Your father asked me to come down and see you, Lucy. He was too worried to come himself.'

Lucy looked at him with grave eyes, but made no reply.

'He's had some very bad luck lately. Your father is a man who prides himself on his business ability, but he has no more knowledge of such matters than a child. He's an imaginative man, and when some scheme appeals to his feeling for romance, he loses all sense of proportion.'

Dick paused again. It was impossible to soften the blow, and he could only put it bluntly.

'He's been gambling on the Stock Exchange, and he's been badly let down. He was bulling a number of South American railways, and there's been a panic in the market. He's lost enormously. I don't know if any settlement can be made with his creditors, but if not he must go bankrupt. In any case, I'm afraid Hamlyn's Purlieu must be sold.'

Lucy walked to the window and looked out. But she could see nothing. Her eyes were blurred with tears. She breathed quickly, trying to control herself.

'I've been expecting it for a long time,' she said at last. 'I've refused to face it, and I put the thought away from me, but I knew really that it must come to that.'

'I'm very sorry,' said Dick helplessly.

She turned on him fiercely, and the colour rose to her cheeks. But she restrained herself and left unsaid the bitter words that had come to her tongue. She made a pitiful gesture of despair. He felt how poor were his words of consolation, and how inadequate to her great grief, and he was silent.

'And what about George?' she asked.

George was then eighteen, and on the point of leaving Winchester. It had been arranged that he should go to Oxford at the beginning of the next term.

'Lady Kelsey has offered to pay his expenses at the 'Varsity,' answered Dick, 'and she wants you to go and stay with her for the present.'

'Do you mean to say we're penniless?' asked Lucy, desperately.

'I think you cannot depend on your father for much regular assistance.'

Lucy was silent again.

Lady Kelsey was the elder sister of Mrs. Allerton, and some time after that lady's marriage had accepted a worthy merchant whose father had been in partnership with hers; and he, after a prosperous career crowned by surrendering his seat in Parliament to a defeated cabinet-minister—a patriotic act for which he was rewarded with a knighthood—had died, leaving her well off and childless. She had but one other nephew, Robert Boulger, her brother's only son, but he was rich with all the inherited wealth of the firm of Boulger & Kelsey; and her affections were placed chiefly upon the children of the man whom she had loved devotedly and who had married her sister.

'I was hoping you would come up to town with me now,' said Dick. 'Lady Kelsey is expecting you, and I cannot bear to think of you by yourself here.'

'I shall stay till the last moment.'

Dick hesitated again. He had wished to keep back the full brutality of the blow, but sooner or later it must be given.

'The place is already sold. Your father accepted an offer from Jarrett—you remember him, he has been down here; he is your father's broker and chief creditor—and everything else is to go to Christy's at once.'

'Then there is no more to be said.'

She gave Dick her hand.

'You won't mind if I don't come to the station with you?'

'Won't you come up to London?' he asked again.

She shook her head.

'I want to be alone. Forgive me if I make you go so abruptly.'

'My dear girl, it's very good of you to make sure that I don't miss my train,' he smiled drily.

'Good-bye and thank you.'

# II

WHILE Lucy wandered by the seashore, occupied with painful memories, her old friend Dick, too lazy to walk with her, sat in the drawing-room of Court Leys, talking to his hostess.

Mrs. Crowley was an American woman, who had married an Englishman, and on being left a widow, had continued to live in England. She was a person who thoroughly enjoyed life; and indeed there was every reason that she should do so, since she was young, pretty, and rich; she had a quick mind and an alert tongue. She was of diminutive size, so small that Dick Lomas, by no means a tall man, felt quite large by the side of her. Her figure was exquisite, and she had the smallest hands in the world. Her features were so good, regular and well-formed, her complexion so perfect, her agile grace so enchanting, that she did not seem a real person at all. She was too delicate for the hurly-burly of life, and it seemed improbable that she could be made of the ordinary clay from which human beings are manufactured. She had the artificial grace of those dainty, exquisite ladies in the *Embarquement pour Cithère* of the charming Watteau; and you felt that she was fit to saunter on that sunny strand, habited in satin of delicate colours, with a witty, decadent cavalier by her side. It was preposterous to talk to her of serious things, and nothing but an airy badinage seemed possible in her company.

Mrs. Crowley had asked Lucy and Dick Lomas to

stay with her in the house she had just taken for a term of years. She had spent a week by herself to arrange things to her liking, and insisted that Dick should admire all she had done. After a walk round the park he vowed that he was exhausted and must rest till tea-time.

' Now tell me what made you take it. It's so far from anywhere.'

' I met the owner in Rome last winter. It belongs to a Mrs. Craddock, and when I told her I was looking out for a house, she suggested that I should come and see this.'

' Why doesn't she live in it herself? '

' Oh, I don't know. It appears that she was passionately devoted to her husband, and he broke his neck in the hunting-field, so she couldn't bear to live here any more.'

Mrs. Crowley looked round the drawing-room with satisfaction. At first it had borne the cheerless look of a house uninhabited, but she had quickly made it pleasant with flowers, photographs, and silver ornaments. The Sheraton furniture and the chintzes suited the style of her beauty. She felt that she looked in place in that comfortable room, and was conscious that her frock fitted her and the circumstances perfectly. Dick's eye wandered to the books that were scattered here and there.

' And have you put out these portentous works in order to improve your mind, or with the laudable desire of impressing me with the serious turn of your intellect? '

' You don't think I'm such a perfect fool as to try and impress an entirely flippant person like yourself? '

On the table at his elbow were a copy of the *Revue des Deux Mondes* and one of the *Fortnightly Review*. He took up two books, and saw that one was the *Fröhliche Wissenschaft* of Nietzsche, who was then beginning to be read in England by the fashionable world and was on the eve of being discovered by men of letters, while the other was a volume of Mrs. Crowley's compatriot, William James.

'American women amaze me,' said Dick, as he put them down. 'They buy their linen at Doucet's and read Herbert Spencer with avidity. And what's more, they seem to like him. An Englishwoman can seldom read a serious book without feeling a prig, and as soon as she feels a prig she leaves off her corsets.'

'I feel vaguely that you're paying me a compliment,' returned Mrs. Crowley, 'but it's so elusive that I can't quite catch it.'

'The best compliments are those that flutter about your head like butterflies around a flower.'

'I much prefer to fix them down on a board with a pin through their insides and a narrow strip of paper to hold down each wing.'

It was October, but the autumn, late that year, had scarcely coloured the leaves, and the day was warm. Mrs. Crowley, however, was a chilly being, and a fire burned in the grate. She put another log on it and watched the merry crackle of the flames.

'It was very good of you to ask Lucy down here,' said Dick, suddenly.

'I don't know why. I like her so much. And I felt sure she would fit the place. She looks a little like a Gainsborough portrait, doesn't she? And I like to see her in this Georgian house.'

' She's not had much of a time since they sold the family place. It was a great grief to her.'

' I feel such a pig to have here the things I bought at the sale.'

When the contents of Hamlyn's Purlieu were sent to Christy's, Mrs. Crowley, recently widowed and without a home, had bought one or two pictures and some old chairs. She had brought these down to Court Leys, and was much tormented at the thought of causing Lucy a new grief.

' Perhaps she didn't recognise them,' said Dick.

' Don't be so idiotic. Of course she recognised them. I saw her eyes fall on the Reynolds the very moment she came into the room.'

' I'm sure she would rather you had them than any stranger.'

' She's said nothing about them. You know, I'm very fond of her, and I admire her extremely, but she would be easier to get on with if she were less reserved. I never shall get into this English way of bottling up my feelings and sitting on them.'

' It sounds a less comfortable way of reposing oneself than sitting in an armchair.'

' I would offer to give Lucy back all the things I bought, only I'm sure she'd snub me.'

' She doesn't mean to be unkind, but she's had a very hard life, and it's had its effect on her character. I don't think anyone knows what she's gone through during these ten years. She's borne the responsibilities of her whole family since she was fifteen, and if the crash didn't come sooner, it was owing to her. She's never been a girl, poor thing; she was a child, and then suddenly she was a woman.'

'But has she never had any lovers?'

'I fancy that she's rather a difficult person to make love to. It would be a bold young man who whispered sweet nothings into her ear; they'd sound so very foolish.'

'At all events there's Bobbie Boulger. I'm sure he's asked her to marry him scores of times.'

Sir Robert Boulger had succeeded his father, the manufacturer, as second baronet; and had promptly placed his wealth and his personal advantages at Lucy's feet. His devotion to her was well known to his friends. They had all listened to the protestations of undying passion, which Lucy, with gentle humour, put smilingly aside. Lady Kelsey, his aunt and Lucy's, had done all she could to bring the pair together; and it was evident that from every point of view a marriage between them was desirable. He was not unattractive in appearance, his fortune was considerable, and his manners were good. He was a good-natured, pleasant fellow, with no great strength of character perhaps, but Lucy had enough of that for two; and with her to steady him, he had enough brains to make some figure in the world.

'I've never seen Mr. Allerton,' remarked Mrs. Crowley, presently. 'He must be a horrid man.'

'On the contrary, he's the most charming creature I ever met, and I don't believe there's a man in London who can borrow a hundred pounds of you with a greater air of doing you a service. If you met him you'd fall in love with him before you'd got well into your favourite conversation on bimetallism.'

'I've never discussed bimetallism in my life,' protested Mrs. Crowley.

'All women do.'

'What?'

'Fall in love with him. He knows exactly what to talk to them about, and he has the most persuasive voice you ever heard. I believe Lady Kelsey has been in love with him for five and twenty years. It's lucky they've not yet passed the deceased wife's sister's bill, or he would have married her and run through her money as he did his first wife's. He's still very good-looking, and there's such a transparent honesty about him that I promise you he's irresistible.'

'And what has happened to him since the catastrophe?'

'Well, the position of an undischarged bankrupt is never particularly easy, though I've known men who've cavorted about in motors and given dinners at the *Carlton* when they were in that state, and seemed perfectly at peace with the world in general. But with Fred Allerton the proceedings before the Official Receiver seem to have broken down the last remnants of his self-respect. He was glad to get rid of his children, and Lady Kelsey was only too happy to provide for them. Heaven only knows how he's lived during the last two years. He's still occupied with a variety of crackbrained schemes, and he's been to me more than once for money to finance them with.'

'I hope you weren't such a fool as to give it.'

'I wasn't. I flatter myself that I combined frankness with good-nature in the right proportion, and in the end he was always satisfied with the nimble fiver. But I'm afraid things are going harder with him. He has lost his old alert gaiety, and he's a little down at heel in character as well as in person. There's a furtive

look about him, as though he were ready for undertakings that were not quite above board, and there's a
shiftiness in his eye which makes his company a little
disagreeable.'

' You don't think he'd do anything dishonest?' asked
Mrs. Crowley quickly.

' Oh, no. I don't believe he has the nerve to sail
closer to the wind than the law allows, and really, at
bottom, notwithstanding all I know of him, I think he's
an honest man. It's only behind his back that I have
any doubts about him; when he's there face to face with
me I succumb to his charm. I can believe nothing to
his discredit.'

At that moment they saw Lucy walking towards
them. Dick Lomas got up and stood at the window.
Mrs. Crowley, motionless, watched her from her chair.
They were both silent. A smile of sympathy played
on Mrs. Crowley's lips, and her heart went out to the
girl who had undergone so much. A vague memory
came back to her, and for a moment she was puzzled;
but then she hit upon the idea that had hovered about
her mind, and she remembered distinctly the admirable
picture by John Furse at Millbank, which is called
*Diana of the Uplands*. It had pleased her always, not
only because of its beauty and the fine power of the
painter, but because it seemed to her as it were a syn-
thesis of the English spirit. Her nationality gave her
an interest in the observation of this, and her wide,
systematic reading the power to compare and analyse.
This portrait of a young woman holding two hounds in
leash, the wind of the northern moor on which she
stands, blowing her skirts and outlining her lithe
figure, seemed to Mrs. Crowley admirably to follow in

the tradition of the eighteenth century. And as Reynolds and Gainsborough, with their elegant ladies in powdered hair and high-waisted gowns, standing in leafy, woodland scenes, had given a picture of England in the age of Reason, well-bred and beautiful, artificial and a little airless, so had Furse in this represented the England of to-day. It was an England that valued cleanliness above all things, of the body and of the spirit, an England that loved the open air and feared not the wildness of nature nor the violence of the elements. And Mrs. Crowley had lived long enough in the land of her fathers to know that this was a true England, simple and honest; narrow perhaps, and prejudiced, but strong, brave, and of great ideals. The girl who stood on that upland, looking so candidly out of her blue eyes, was a true descendant of the ladies that Sir Joshua painted, but she had a bath every morning, loved her dogs, and wore a short, serviceable skirt. With an inward smile, Mrs. Crowley acknowledged that she was probably bored by Emerson and ignorant of English literature; but for the moment she was willing to pardon these failings in her admiration for the character and all it typified.

Lucy came in, and Mrs. Crowley gave her a nod of welcome. She was fond of her fantasies and would not easily interrupt them. She noted that Lucy had just that frank look of *Diana of the Uplands,* and the delicate, sensitive face, refined with the good-breeding of centuries, but strengthened by an athletic life. Her skin was very clear. It had gained a peculiar freshness by exposure to all manner of weather. Her bright, fair hair was a little disarranged after her walk, and she went to the glass to set it right. Mrs. Crowley observed with delight the straightness of her nose and the delicate curve of her lips. She was tall and strong, but her figure was very slight; and there was a charming litheness about her which suggested the good horse-woman.

But what struck Mrs. Crowley most was that only the keenest observer could have told that she had endured more than other women of her age. A stranger would have delighted in her frank smile and the kindly sympathy of her eyes; and it was only if you knew the troubles she had suffered that you saw how much more womanly she was than girlish. There was a self-possession about her which came from the responsibilities she had borne so long, and an unusual reserve, unconsciously masked by a great charm of manner, which only intimate friends discerned, but which even to them was impenetrable. Mrs. Crowley, with her American impulsiveness, had tried in all kindliness to get through the barrier, but she had never succeeded. All Lucy's struggles, her heart-burnings and griefs, her sudden despairs and eager hopes, her tempestuous angers, took place in the bottom of her heart. She would have been as dismayed at the thought of others seeing them as she would have been at the thought of being discovered unclothed. Shyness and pride combined to make her hide her innermost feelings so that no one should venture to offer sympathy or commiseration.

'Do ring the bell for tea,' said Mrs. Crowley to Lucy, as she turned away from the glass. 'I can't get Mr. Lomas to amuse me till he's had some stimulating refreshment.'

'I hope you like the tea I sent you,' said Dick.

'Very much. Though I'm inclined to look upon it as a slight that you should send me down only just enough to last over your visit.'

'I always herald my arrival in a country house by a little present of tea," said Dick. 'The fact is it's the only good tea in the world. I sent my father to China for seven years to find it, and I'm sure you will agree that my father has not lived an ill-spent life.'

The tea was brought and duly drunk. Mrs. Crowley asked Lucy how her brother was. He had been at Oxford for the last two years.

'I had a letter from him yesterday,' the girl answered. 'I think he's getting on very well. I hope he'll take his degree next year.'

A happy brightness came into her eyes as she talked of him. She apologised, blushing, for her eagerness.

'You know, I've looked after George ever since he was ten, and I feel like a mother to him. It's only with the greatest difficulty I can prevent myself from telling you how he got through the measles, and how well he bore vaccination.'

Lucy was very proud of her brother. She found a constant satisfaction in his good looks, and she loved the openness of his smile. She had striven with all her might to keep away from him the troubles that oppressed her, and had determined that nothing, if she could help it, should disturb his radiant satisfaction with the world. She knew that he was apt to lean on her, but though she chid herself sometimes for fostering the tendency, she could not really prevent the intense pleasure it gave her. He was young yet, and would soon enough grow into manly ways; it could not matter if now he depended upon her for everything. She rejoiced in the ardent affection which he gave her; and the implicit trust he placed in her, the complete reliance on her judgment, filled her with a proud humility. It made her feel stronger and better capable of affronting the difficulties of life. And Lucy, living much in the future, was pleased to see how beloved George was of all his friends. Everyone seemed willing to help him, and this seemed of good omen for the career which she had mapped out for him.

The recollection of him came to Lucy now as she had last seen him. They had been spending part of the summer with Lady Kelsey at her house on the Thames. George was going to Scotland to stay with friends, and Lucy, bound elsewhere, was leaving earlier in the afternoon. He came to see her off. She was touched, in her own sorrow at leaving him, by his obvious emotion. The tears were in his eyes as he kissed her on the platform. She saw him waving to her as the train sped towards London, slender and handsome, looking more boyish than ever in his whites; and she felt a thrill of gratitude because, with all her sorrows and regrets, she at least had him.

' I hope he's a good shot,' she said inconsequently, as Mrs. Crowley handed her a cup of tea. ' Of course it's in the family.'

' Marvellous family!' said Dick, ironically. ' You would be wiser to wish he had a good head for figures.'

' But I hope he has that, too,' she answered.

It had been arranged that George should go into the business in which Lady Kelsey still had a large interest. Lucy wanted him to make great sums of money, so that he might pay his father's debts, and perhaps buy back the house which her family had owned so long.

'I want him to be a clever man of business—since business is the only thing open to him now—and an excellent sportsman.'

She was too shy to describe her ambition, but her fancy had already cast a glow over the calling which George was to adopt. There was in the family an innate tendency toward the more exquisite things of life, and this would colour his career. She hoped he would become a merchant prince after the pattern of those Florentines who have left an ideal for succeeding ages of the way in which commerce may be ennobled by a liberal view of life. Like them he could drive hard bargains and amass riches—she recognised that riches now were the surest means of power—but like them also he could love music and art and literature, cherishing the things of the soul with a careful taste, and at the same time excel in all sports of the field. Life then would be as full as a man's heart could wish; and this intermingling of interests might so colour it that he would lead the whole with a certain beauty and grandeur.

'I wish I were a man,' she cried, with a bright smile. 'It's so hard that I can do nothing but sit at home and spur others on. I want to do things myself.'

Mrs. Crowley leaned back in her chair. She gave her skirt a little twist so that the line of her form should be more graceful.

'I'm so glad I'm a woman,' she murmured. 'I want none of the privileges of the sex which I'm delighted to call stronger. I want men to be noble and heroic and self-sacrificing; then they can protect me from a trouble-

some world, and look after me, and wait upon me. I'm
an irresponsible creature with whom they can never be
annoyed however exacting I am—it's only pretty
thoughtlessness on my part—and they must never lose
their tempers however I annoy—it's only nerves. Oh,
no, I like to be a poor, weak woman.'

' You're a monster of cynicism,' cried Dick. ' You
use an imaginary helplessness with the brutality of a
buccaneer, and your ingenuousness is a pistol you put
to one's head, crying: your money or your life.'

' You look very comfortable, dear Mr. Lomas,' she retorted. ' Would you mind very much if I asked you to
put my footstool right for me ? '

' I should mind immensely,' he smiled, without
moving.

' Oh, please do,' she said, with a piteous little expression of appeal. ' I'm so uncomfortable, and my
foot's going to sleep. And you needn't be horrid to
me.'

' I didn't know you really meant it,' he said, getting up obediently and doing what was required of
him.

' I didn't,' she answered, as soon as he had finished.
' But I know you're a lazy creature, and I merely wanted
to see if I could make you move when I'd warned you
immediately before that—I was a womanly woman.'

' I wonder if you'd make Alec MacKenzie do that? '
laughed Dick, good-naturedly.

' Good heavens, I'd never try. Haven't you discovered that women know by instinct what men they can
make fools of, and they only try their arts on them?
They've gained their reputation for omnipotence only
on account of their robust common-sense, which leads

them only to attack fortresses which are already half demolished.'

'That suggests to my mind that every woman is a Potiphar's wife, though every man isn't a Joseph,' said Dick.

'Your remark is too blunt to be witty,' returned Mrs. Crowley, 'but it's not without its grain of truth.'

Lucy, smiling, listened to the nonsense they talked. In their company she lost all sense of reality; Mrs. Crowley was so fragile, and Dick had such a whimsical gaiety, that she could not treat them as real persons. She felt herself a grown-up being assisting at some childish game in which preposterous ideas were bandied to and fro like answers in the game of consequences.

'I never saw people wander from the subject as you do,' she protested. 'I can't imagine what connection there is between whether Mr. MacKenzie would arrange Julia's footstool, and the profligacy of the female sex.'

'Don't be hard on us,' said Mrs. Crowley. 'I must work off my flippancy before he arrives, and then I shall be ready to talk imperially.'

'When does Alec come?' asked Dick.

'Now, this very minute. I've sent a carriage to meet him at the station. You won't let him depress me, will you?'

'Why did you ask him if he affects you in that way?' asked Lucy, laughing.

'But I like him—at least I think I do—and in any case, I admire him, and I'm sure he's good for me. And Mr. Lomas wanted me to ask him, and he plays bridge extraordinarily well. And I thought he would be interesting. The only thing I have against him is that he never laughs when I say a clever thing, and looks so uncomfortably at me when I say a foolish one.'

' I'm glad I laugh when you say a clever thing,' said Dick.

' You don't. But you roar so heartily at your own jokes that if I hurry up and slip one in before you've done, I can often persuade myself that you're laughing at mine.'

' And do you like Alec MacKenzie, Lucy?' asked Dick.

She paused for a moment before she answered, and hesitated.

' I don't know,' she said. ' Sometimes I think I rather dislike him. But I'm like Julia, I certainly admire him.'

' I suppose he is rather alarming,' said Dick. ' He's difficult to know, and he's obviously impatient with other people's affectations. There's a certain grimness about him which disturbs you unless you know him intimately.'

' He's your greatest friend, isn't he? '

' He is.'

Dick paused for a little while.

' I've known him for twenty years now, and I look upon him as the greatest man I've ever set eyes on. I think it's an inestimable privilege to have been his friend.'

' I've not noticed that you treated him with especial awe,' said Mrs. Crowley.

' Heaven save us! ' cried Dick. ' I can only hold my own by laughing at him persistently.'

' He bears it with unexampled good-nature.'

' Have I ever told you how I made his acquaintance?

It was in about fifty fathoms of water, and at least a
thousand miles from land.'

' What an inconvenient place for an introduction!'

' We were both very wet. I was a young fool in those
days, and I was playing the giddy goat—I was just
going up to Oxford, and my wise father had sent me
to America on a visit to enlarge my mind—I fell over-
board and was proceeding to drown, when Alec jumped
in after me and held me up by the hair of my head.'

' He'd have some difficulty in doing that now,
wouldn't he?' suggested Mrs. Crowley, with a glance
at Dick's thinning locks.

' And the odd thing is that he was absurdly grateful
to me for letting myself be saved. He seemed to think
I had done him an intentional service, and fallen into
the Atlantic for the sole purpose of letting him pull
me out.'

Dick had scarcely said these words when they heard
the carriage drive up to the door of Court Leys.

' There he is,' cried Dick eagerly.

Mrs. Crowley's butler opened the door and announced
the man they had been discussing. Alexander Mac-
Kenzie came in.

He was just under six feet high, spare and well-made.
He did not at the first glance give you the impression of
particular strength, but his limbs were well-knit, there
was no superfluous flesh about him, and you felt immediately that he had great powers of endurance. His
hair was dark and cut very close. His short beard and
his moustache were red. They concealed the squareness
of his chin and the determination of his mouth. His
eyes were not large, but they rested on the object that
attracted his attention with a peculiar fixity. When he

talked to you he did not glance this way or that, but looked straight at you with a deliberate steadiness that was a little disconcerting. He walked with an easy swing, like a man in the habit of covering a vast number of miles each day, and there was in his manner a self-assurance which suggested that he was used to command. His skin was tanned by exposure to tropical suns.

Mrs. Crowley and Dick chattered light-heartedly, but it was clear that he had no power of small-talk, and after the first greetings he fell into silence; he refused tea, but Mrs. Crowley poured out a cup and handed it to him.

'You need not drink it, but I insist on your holding it in your hand. I hate people who habitually deny themselves things, and I can't allow you to mortify the flesh in my house.'

Alec smiled gravely.

'Of course I will drink it if it pleases you,' he answered. 'I got in the habit in Africa of eating only two meals a day, and I can't get out of it now. But I'm afraid it's very inconvenient for my friends.' He looked at Lomas, and though his mouth did not smile, a look came into his eyes, partly of tenderness, partly of amusement. 'Dick, of course, eats far too much.'

'Good heavens, I'm nearly the only person left in London who is completely normal. I eat my three square meals a day regularly, and I always have a comfortable tea into the bargain. I don't suffer from any disease. I'm in the best of health. I have no fads. I neither nibble nuts like a squirrel, nor grapes like a bird—I care nothing for all this jargon about pepsins and proteids and all the rest of it. I'm not a vegetarian, but a carnivorous animal; I drink when I'm thirsty, and I decidedly prefer my beverages to be alcoholic.'

'I was thinking at luncheon to-day,' said Mrs. Crowley, 'that the pleasure you took in roast-beef and ale showed a singularly gross and unemotional nature.'

'I adore good food as I adore all the other pleasant things of life, and because I have that gift I am able to look upon the future with equanimity.'

'Why?' asked Alec.

'Because a love for good food is the only thing that remains with man when he grows old. Love? What is love when you are five and fifty and can no longer hide the disgraceful baldness of your pate. Ambition? What is ambition when you have discovered that honours are to the pushing and glory to the vulgar. Finally we must all reach an age when every passion seems vain, every desire not worth the trouble of achieving it; but then there still remain to the man with a good appetite three pleasures each day, his breakfast, his luncheon, and his dinner.'

Alec's eyes rested on him quietly. He had never got out of the habit of looking upon Dick as a scatter-brained boy who talked nonsense for the fun of it; and his expression wore the amused disdain which one might have seen on a Saint Bernard when a toy-terrier was going through its tricks.

'Please say something,' cried Dick, half-irritably.

'I suppose you say those things in order that I may contradict you. Why should I? They're perfectly untrue, and I don't agree with a single word you say. But if it amuses you to talk nonsense, I don't see why you shouldn't.'

' My dear Alec, I wish you wouldn't use the mailed
fist in your conversation. It's so very difficult to play a
game with a spillikin on one side and a sledge-hammer
on the other.'

Lucy, sitting back in her chair, quietly, was observ-
ing the new arrival. Dick had asked her and Mrs.
Crowley to meet him at luncheon immediately after his
arrival from Mombassa. This was two months ago now,
and since then she had seen much of him. But she felt
that she knew him little more than on that first day,
and still she could not make up her mind whether she
liked him or not. She was glad that they were staying
together at Court Leys; it would give her an opportunity of really becoming acquainted with him, and
there was no doubt that he was worth the trouble. The
fire lit up his face, casting grim shadows upon it, so
that it looked more than ever masterful and determined. He was unconscious that her eyes rested
upon him. He was always unconscious of the attention
he aroused.

Lucy hoped that she would induce him to talk of
the work he had done, and the work upon which he was
engaged. With her mind fixed always on great endeavours, his career interested her enormously; and it
gained something mysterious as well because there were
gaps in her knowledge of him which no one seemed
able to fill. He knew few people in London, but was
known in one way or another of many; and all who had
come in contact with him were unanimous in their
opinion. He was supposed to know Africa as no
other man knew it. During fifteen years he had
been through every part of it, and had traversed districts which the white man had left untouched. But

he had never written of his experiences, partly from
indifference to chronicle the results of his undertakings,
partly from a natural secrecy which made him hate to
recount his deeds to all and sundry. It seemed that reserve was a deep-rooted instinct with him, and he was
inclined to keep to himself all that he discovered. But
if on this account he was unknown to the great public,
his work was appreciated very highly by specialists.
He had read papers before the Geographical Society,
(though it had been necessary to exercise much pres-
sure to induce him to do so), which had excited
profound interest; and occasionally letters appeared
from him in *Nature,* or in one of the ethnographical
publications, stating briefly some discovery he had
made, or some observation which he thought necessary
to record. He had been asked now and again to make
reports to the Foreign Office upon matters pertaining
to the countries he knew; and Lucy had heard his per-
spicacity praised in no measured terms by those in
power.

She put together such facts as she knew of his
career.

Alec MacKenzie was a man of considerable means.
He belonged to an old Scotch family, and had a fine
place in the Highlands, but his income depended chiefly
upon a colliery in Lancashire. His parents died during
his childhood, and his wealth was much increased by a
long minority. Having inherited from an uncle a
ranch in the West, his desire to see this occasioned
his first voyage from England in the interval between
leaving Eton and going up to Oxford; and it was then
he made acquaintance with Richard Lomas, who had
remained his most intimate friend. The unlikeness of

the two men caused perhaps the strength of the tie between them, the strenuous vehemence of the one finding a relief in the gaiety of the other. Soon after leaving Oxford, MacKenzie made a brief expedition into Algeria to shoot, and the mystery of the great continent seized him. As sometimes a man comes upon a new place which seems extraordinarily familiar, so that he is almost convinced that in a past state he has known it intimately, Alec suddenly found himself at home in the immense distances of Africa. He felt a singular exhilaration when the desert was spread out before his eyes, and capacities which he had not suspected in himself awoke in him. He had never thought himself an ambitious man, but ambition seized him. He had never imagined himself subject to poetic emotion, but all at once a feeling of the poetry of an adventurous life welled up within him. And though he had looked upon romance with the scorn of his Scottish common sense, an irresistible desire of the romantic surged upon him, like the waves of some unknown, mystical sea.

When he returned to England a peculiar restlessness took hold of him. He was indifferent to the magnificence of the bag, which was the pride of his companions. He felt himself cribbed and confined. He could not breathe the air of cities.

He began to read the marvellous records of African exploration, and his blood tingled at the magic of those pages. Mungo Park, a Scot like himself, had started the roll. His aim had been to find the source and trace the seaward course of the Niger. He took his life in his hands, facing boldly the perils of climate, savage pagans, and jealous Mohammedans, and discovered the upper portions of that great river. On a second expedition he undertook to follow it to the sea. Of his party some died of disease, and some were slain by the natives. Not one returned; and the only trace of Mungo Park was a book, known to have been in his possession, found by British explorers in the hut of a native chief.

Then Alec MacKenzie read of the efforts to reach Timbuktu, which was the great object of ambition to the explorers of the nineteenth century. It exercised the same fascination over their minds as did El Dorado, with its golden city of Monoa, to the adventurers in the days of Queen Elizabeth. It was thought to be the capital of a powerful and wealthy state; and those ardent minds promised themselves all kinds of wonders when they should at last come upon it. But it was not the desire for gold that urged them on, rather an irresistible curiosity, and a pride in their own courage. One after another desperate attempts were made, and it was reached at last by another Scot, Alexander Gordon Laing. And his success was a symbol of all earthly endeavours, for the golden city of his dreams was no more than a poverty-stricken village.

One by one Alec studied the careers of these great men; and he saw that the best of them had not gone with half an army at their backs, but almost alone, sometimes with not a single companion, and had depended for their success not upon the strength of their arms, but upon the strength of their character. Major Durham, an old Peninsular officer, was the first European to cross the Sahara. Captain Clapperton, with his servant, Richard Lander, was the first who traversed Africa from the Mediterranean to the Guinea Coast. And he died at his journey's end. And there was something fine in the devotion of Richard Lander, the faithful servant, who went on with his master's work and cleared up at last the great mystery of the Niger. And he, too, had no sooner done his work than he died, near the mouth of the river he had so long travelled on, of wounds inflicted by the natives. There was not one of those early voyagers who escaped with his life. It was the work of desperate men that they undertook, but there was no recklessness in them. They counted the cost and took the risk; the fascination of the unknown was too great for them, and they reckoned death as nothing if they could accomplish that on which they had set out.

Two men above all attracted Alec MacKenzie's interest. One was Richard Burton, that mighty, enigmatic man, more admirable for what he was than for what he did; and the other was Livingstone, the greatest of African explorers. There was something very touching in the character of that gentle Scot. MacKenzie's enthusiasm was seldom very strong, but here was a man whom he would willingly have known; and he was strangely affected by the thought of his lonely death, and his grave in the midst of the Dark Continent he loved so well. On that, too, might have been written the epitaph which is on the tomb of Sir Christopher Wren.

Finally he studied the works of Henry M. Stanley. Here the man excited neither admiration nor affection, but a cold respect. No one could help recognising the greatness of his powers. He was a man of Napoleonic instinct, who suited his means to his end, and ruthlessly fought his way until he had achieved it. His books were full of interest, and they were practical. From them much could be learned, and Alec studied them with a thoroughness which was in his nature.

When he arose from this long perusal, his mind was made up. He had found his vocation.

He did not disclose his plans to any of his friends till they were mature, and meanwhile set about seeing the people who could give him information. At last he sailed for Zanzibar, and started on a journey which was to try his powers. In a month he fell ill, and it was thought at the mission to which his bearers brought him that he could not live. For ten weeks he was at death's door, but he would not give in to the enemy. He insisted in the end on being taken back to the coast, and here, as if by a personal effort of will, he recovered. The season had passed for his expedition, and he was obliged to return to England. Most men would have been utterly discouraged, but Alec was only strengthened in his determination. He personified in a way that deadly climate and would not allow himself to be beaten by it. His short experience had shown him what he needed, and as soon as he was back in England he proceeded to acquire a smattering of medical knowledge, and some acquaintance with the sciences which were wanted by a traveller. He had immense powers of concentration, and in a year of tremendous labour acquired a working knowledge of botany and geology, and the elements of surveying; he learnt how to treat the maladies which were likely to attack people in tropical districts, and enough surgery to set a broken limb or to conduct a simple operation. He felt himself ready now for a considerable undertaking; but this time he meant to start from Mombassa.

So far Lucy was able to go, partly from her own imaginings, and partly from what Dick had told her. He had given her the proceedings of the Royal Geographical Society, and here she found Alec MacKenzie's account of his wanderings during the five years that followed. The countries which he explored then, became afterwards British East Africa.

But the bell rang for dinner, and so interrupted her meditations.

# III

THEY played bridge immediately afterwards. Mrs. Crowley looked upon conversation as a fine art, which could not be pursued while the body was engaged in the process of digestion; and she was of opinion that a game of cards agreeably diverted the mind and prepared the intellect for the quips and cranks which might follow when the claims of the body were satisfied. Lucy drew Alec MacKenzie as her partner, and so was able to watch his play when her cards were on the table. He did not play lightly as did Dick, who kept up a running commentary the whole time, but threw his whole soul into the game and never for a moment relaxed his attention. He took no notice of Dick's facetious observations. Presently Lucy grew more interested in his playing than in the game; she was struck, not only by his great gift of concentration, but by his boldness. He had a curious faculty for knowing almost from the beginning of a hand where each card lay. She saw, also, that he was plainly most absorbed when he was playing both hands himself; he was a man who liked to take everything on his own shoulders, and the division of responsibility irritated him.

At the end of the rubber Dick flung himself back in his chair irritably.

'I can't make it out,' he cried. 'I play much better than you, and I hold better hands, and yet you get the tricks.'

Dick was known to be an excellent player, and his annoyance was excusable.

'We didn't make a single mistake,' he assured his partner, ' and we actually had the odd in our hands, but not one of our finesses came off, and all his did.' He turned to Alec. ' How the dickens did you guess I had those two queens? '

' Because I've known you for twenty years,' answered Alec, smiling. ' I know that, though you're impulsive and emotional, you're not without shrewdness; I know that your brain acts very quickly and sees all kinds of remote contingencies; then you're so pleased at having noticed them that you act as if they were certain to occur. Given these data, I can tell pretty well what cards you have, after they've gone round two or three times.'

' The knowledge you have of your opponents' cards is too uncanny,' said Mrs. Crowley.

' I can tell a good deal from people's faces. You see, in Africa I have had a lot of experience; it's apparently so much easier for the native to lie than to tell the truth that you get into the habit of paying no attention to what he says, and a great deal to the way he looks."

While Mrs. Crowley made herself comfortable in the chair, which she had already chosen as her favourite, Dick went over to the fire and stood in front of it in such a way as effectually to prevent the others from getting any of its heat.

' What made you first take to exploration? ' asked Mrs. Crowley suddenly.

Alec gave her that slow, scrutinising look of his, and answered, with a smile:

'I don't know. I had nothing to do and plenty of money.'

'Not a bit of it,' interrupted Dick. 'A lunatic wanted to find out about some district that people had never been to, and it wouldn't have been any use to them if they had, because, if the natives didn't kill you, the climate made no bones about it. He came back crippled with fever, having failed in his attempt, and, after asserting that no one could get into the heart of Rofa's country and return alive, promptly gave up the ghost. So Alec immediately packed up his traps and made for the place.'

'I proved the man was wrong,' said Alec quietly. 'I became great friends with Rofa, and he wanted to marry my sister, only I hadn't one.'

'And if anyone said it was impossible to hop through Asia on one foot, you'd go and do it just to show it could be done,' retorted Dick 'You have a passion for doing things because they're difficult or dangerous, and, if they're downright impossible, you chortle with joy.'

'You make me really too melodramatic,' smiled Alec.

'But that's just what you are. You're the most transpontine person I ever saw in my life.' Dick turned to Lucy and Mrs. Crowley with a wave of the hand. 'I call you to witness. When he was at Oxford, Alec was a regular dab at classics; he had a gift for writing verses in languages that no one except dons wanted to read, and everyone thought that he was going to be the most brilliant scholar of his day.'

'This is one of Dick's favourite stories,' said Alec. 'It would be quite amusing if there were any truth in it.'

But Dick would not allow himself to be interrupted.

' At mathematics, on the other hand, he was a perfect ass. You know, some people seem to have that part of their brains wanting that deals with figures, and Alec couldn't add two and two together without making a hexameter out of it. One day his tutor got in a passion with him and said he'd rather teach arithmetic to a brick wall. I happened to be present, and he was certainly very rude. He was a man who had a precious gift for making people feel thoroughly uncomfortable. Alec didn't say anything, but he looked at him; and, when he flies into a temper, he doesn't get red and throw things about like a pleasant, normal person—he merely becomes a little paler and stares at you.'

' I beg you not to believe a single word he says,' remonstrated Alec.

' Well, Alec threw over his classics. Everyone concerned reasoned with him; they appealed to his common sense; they were appealing to the most obstinate fool in Christendom. Alec had made up his mind to be a mathematician. For more than two years he worked ten hours a day at a subject he loathed; he threw his whole might into it and forced out of nature the gifts she had denied him, with the result that he got a first class. And much good it's done him.'

Alec shrugged his shoulders.

' It wasn't that I cared for mathematics, but it taught me to conquer the one inconvenient word in the English language.'

' And what the deuce is that? '

' I'm afraid it sounds very priggish,' laughed Alec. ' The word *impossible*.'

Dick gave a little snort of comic rage.

'And it also gave you a ghastly pleasure in doing things that hurt you. Oh, if you'd only been born in the Middle Ages, what a fiendish joy you would have taken in mortifying your flesh, and in denying yourself everything that makes life so good to live! You're never thoroughly happy unless you're making yourself thoroughly miserable.'

'Each time I come back to England I find that you talk more and greater nonsense, Dick,' returned Alec drily.

'I'm one of the few persons now alive who can talk nonsense,' answered his friend, laughing. 'That's why I'm so charming. Everyone else is so deadly earnest.'

He settled himself down to make a deliberate speech.

'I deplore the strenuousness of the world in general. There is an idea abroad that it is praiseworthy to do things, and what they are is of no consequence so long as you do them. I hate the mad hurry of the present day to occupy itself. I wish I could persuade people of the excellence of leisure.'

'One could scarcely accuse you of cultivating it yourself,' said Lucy, smiling.

Dick looked at her for a moment thoughtfully.

'Do you know that I'm hard upon forty?'

'With the light behind, you might still pass for thirty-two,' interrupted Mrs. Crowley.

He turned to her seriously.

'I haven't a grey hair on my head.'

'I suppose your servant plucks them out every morning?'

'Oh, no, very rarely; one a month at the outside.'

'I think I see one just beside the left temple.'

He turned quickly to the glass.

' Dear me, how careless of Charles! I shall have to give him a piece of my mind.'

' Come here, and let me take it out,' said Mrs. Crowley.

' I will let you do nothing of the sort. I should consider it most familiar.'

' You were giving us the gratuitous piece of information that you were nearly forty,' said Alec.

' The thought came to me the other day with something of a shock, and I set about a scrutiny of the life I was leading. I've worked at the bar pretty hard for fifteen years now, and I've been in the House since the general election. I've been earning two thousand a year, I've got nearly four thousand of my own, and I've never spent much more than half my income. I wondered if it was worth while to spend eight hours a day settling the sordid quarrels of foolish people, and another eight hours in the farce of governing the nation.'

' Why do you call it that? '

Dick Lomas shrugged his shoulders scornfully.

' Because it is. A few big-wigs rule the roost, and the rest of us are only there to delude the British people into the idea that they're a self-governing community.'

' What is wrong with you is that you have no absorbing aim in politics,' said Alec gravely.

' Pardon me, I am a suffragist of the most vehement type," answered Dick, with a thin smile.

' That's the last thing I should have expected you to be,' said Mrs. Crowley, who dressed with admirable taste. ' Why on earth have you taken to that? '

Dick shrugged his shoulders.

' No one can have been through a parliamentary election without discovering how unworthy, sordid, and narrow are the reasons for which men vote. There are very few who are alive to the responsibilities that have been thrust upon them. They are indifferent to the importance of the stakes at issue, but make their vote a matter of ignoble barter. The parliamentary candidate is at the mercy of faddists and cranks. Now, I think that women, when they have votes, will be a trifle more narrow, and they will give them for motives that are a little more sordid and a little more unworthy. It will reduce universal suffrage to the absurd, and then it may be possible to try something else.'

Dick had spoken with a vehemence that was unusual to him. Alec watched him with a certain interest.

' And what conclusions have you come to? '

For a moment he did not answer, then he gave a deprecating smile.

' I feel that the step I want to take is momentous for me, though I am conscious that it can matter to nobody else whatever. There will be a general election in a few months, and I have made up my mind to inform the whips that I shall not stand again. I shall give up my chambers in Lincoln's Inn, put up the shutters, so to speak, and Mr. Richard Lomas will retire from active life.'

' You wouldn't really do that? ' cried Mrs. Crowley.

' Why not? '

' In a month complete idleness will simply bore you to death.'

' I doubt it. Do you know, it seems to me that a

great deal of nonsense is talked about the dignity of work. Work is a drug that dull people take to avoid the pangs of unmitigated boredom. It has been adorned with fine phrases, because it is a necessity to most men, and men always gild the pill they're obliged to swallow. Work is a sedative. It keeps people quiet and contented. It makes them good material for their leaders. I think the greatest imposture of Christian times is the sanctification of labour. You see, the early Christians were slaves, and it was necessary to show them that their obligatory toil was noble and virtuous. But when all is said and done, a man works to earn his bread and to keep his wife and children; it is a painful necessity, but there is nothing heroic in it. If people choose to put a higher value on the means than on the end, I can only pass with a shrug of the shoulders, and regret the paucity of their intelligence.'

' It's really unfair to talk so much all at once,' said Mrs. Crowley, throwing up her pretty hands.

But Dick would not be stopped.

' For my part I have neither wife nor child, and I have an income that is more than adequate. Why should I take the bread out of somebody else's mouth? And it's not on my own merit that I get briefs—men seldom do—I only get them because I happen to have at the back of me a very large firm of solicitors. And I can find nothing worthy in attending to these foolish disputes. In most cases it's six of one and half a dozen of the other, and each side is very unjust and pig-headed. No, the bar is a fair way of earning your living like another, but it's no more than that; and, if you can exist without, I see no reason why Quixotic

motives of the dignity of human toil should keep you
to it. I've already told you why I mean to give up
my seat in Parliament.'

'Have you realised that you are throwing over a
career that may be very brilliant? You should get
an under-secretaryship in the next government.'

'That would only mean licking the boots of a few
more men whom I despise.'

'It's a very dangerous experiment that you're making.'

Dick looked straight into Alec MacKenzie's eyes.

'And is it you who counsel me not to make it on
that account?' he said, smiling. 'Surely experiments
are only amusing if they're dangerous.'

'And to what is it precisely that you mean to devote
your time?' asked Mrs. Crowley.

'I should like to make idleness a fine art,' he laughed.
'People, nowadays, turn up their noses at the dilettante.
Well, I mean to be a dilettante. I want to devote
myself to the graces of life. I'm forty, and for all I
know I haven't so very many years before me: in the
time that remains, I want to become acquainted with
the world and all the graceful, charming things it
contains.'

Alec, fallen into deep thought, stared into the fire.
Presently he took a long breath, rose from his chair,
and drew himself to his full height.

'I suppose it's a life like another, and there is no
one to say which is better and which is worse. But, for
my part, I would rather go on till I dropped. There
are ten thousand things I want to do. If I had ten
lives I couldn't get through a tithe of what, to my
mind, so urgently needs doing.'

'And what do you suppose will be the end of it?' asked Dick.

'For me?'

Dick nodded, but did not otherwise reply. Alec smiled faintly.

'Well, I suppose the end of it will be death in some swamp, obscurely, worn out with disease and exposure; and my bearers will make off with my guns and my stores, and the jackals will do the rest.'

'I think it's horrible,' said Mrs. Crowley, with a shudder.

'I'm a fatalist. I've lived too long among people with whom it is the deepest rooted article of their faith, to be anything else. When my time comes, I cannot escape it.' He smiled whimsically. 'But I believe in quinine, too, and I think that the daily use of that admirable drug will make the thread harder to cut.'

To Lucy it was an admirable study, the contrast between the man who threw his whole soul into a certain aim, which he pursued with a savage intensity, knowing that the end was a dreadful, lonely death; and the man who was making up his mind deliberately to gather what was beautiful in life, and to cultivate its graces as though it were a flower garden.

'And the worst of it is that it will all be the same in a hundred years,' said Dick. 'We shall both be forgotten long before then, you with your strenuousness, and I with my folly.'

'And what conclusion do you draw from that?' asked Mrs. Crowley.

'Only that the psychological moment has arrived for a whisky and soda.'

# IV

THERE was some rough shooting on the estate which Mrs. Crowley had rented, and next day Dick went out to see what he could find. Alec refused to accompany him.

'I think shooting in England bores me a little,' he said. 'I have a prejudice against killing things unless I want to eat them, and these English birds are so tame that it seems to me rather like shooting chickens.'

'I don't believe a word of it,' said Dick, as he set out. 'The fact is that you can't hit anything smaller than a hippopotamus, and you know that there is nothing here to suit you except Mrs. Crowley's cows.'

After luncheon Alec MacKenzie asked Lucy if she would take a stroll with him. She was much pleased.

'Where would you like to go?' she asked.

'Let us walk by the sea.'

She took him along a road called Joy Lane, which ran from the fishing town of Blackstable to a village called Waveney. The sea there had a peculiar vastness, and the salt smell of the breeze was pleasant to the senses. The flatness of the marsh seemed to increase the distances that surrounded them, and unconsciously Alec fell into a more rapid swing. It did not look as if he walked fast, but he covered the ground with the steady method of a man who has been used to long journeys, and it was good for Lucy that she was accustomed to much walking. At first they spoke of trivial things, but presently silence fell upon them. Lucy saw that he was immersed in thought, and she did not interrupt him. It amused her that, after asking her to walk with him, this odd man should take no pains to entertain her. Now and then he threw back his head with a strange, proud motion, and looked out to sea. The gulls, with their melancholy flight, were skimming upon the surface of the water. The desolation of that scene—it was the same which, a few days before, had rent poor Lucy's heart—appeared to enter his soul; but, strangely enough, it uplifted him, filling him with exulting thoughts. He quickened his pace, and Lucy, without a word, kept step with him. He seemed not to notice where they walked, and presently she led him away from the sea. They tramped along a winding road, between trim hedges and fertile fields; and the country had all the sweet air of Kent, with its easy grace and its comfortable beauty. They passed a caravan, with a shaggy horse browsing at the wayside, and a family of dinglers sitting around a fire of sticks. The sight curiously affected Lucy. The wandering life of those people, with no ties but to the ramshackle carriage which was their only home, their familiarity with the fields and with strange hidden places, filled her with a wild desire for freedom and for vast horizons. At last they came to the massive gates of Court Leys. An avenue of elms led to the house.

'Here we are,' said Lucy, breaking the long silence.

'Already?' He seemed to shake himself. 'I have to thank you for a pleasant stroll, and we've had a good talk, haven't we?'

'Have we?' she laughed. She saw his look of sur-

prise. ' For two hours you've not vouchsafed to make
an observation.'

' I'm so sorry,' he said, reddening under his tan.
' How rude you must have thought me! I've been alone
so much that I've got out of the way of behaving
properly.'

' It doesn't matter at all,' she smiled. ' You must
talk to me another time.'

She was subtly flattered. She felt that, for him, it
was a queer kind of compliment that he had paid her.
Their silent walk, she did not know why, seemed to
have created a bond between them; and it appeared
that he felt it, too, for afterwards he treated her with
a certain intimacy. He seemed to look upon her no
longer as an acquaintance, but as a friend.

A day or two later, Mrs. Crowley having suggested
that they should drive into Tercanbury to see the
cathedral, MacKenzie asked her if she would allow him
to walk.

He turned to Lucy.

' I hardly dare to ask if you will come with me,' he
said.

' It would please me immensely.'

' I will try to behave better than last time.'

' You need not,' she smiled.

Dick, who had an objection to walking when it
was possible to drive, set out with Mrs. Crowley in
a trap. Alec waited for Lucy. She went round to
the stable to fetch a dog to accompany them, and,
as she came towards him, he looked at her. Alec
was a man to whom most of his fellows were ab-
stractions. He saw them and talked to them, not-

ing their peculiarities, but they were seldom living persons to him. They were shadows, as it were, that had to be reckoned with, but they never became part of himself. And it came upon him now with a certain shock of surprise to notice Lucy. He felt suddenly a new interest in her. He seemed to see her for the first time, and her rare beauty strangely moved him. In her serge dress and her gauntlets, with a motor cap and a flowing veil, a stick in her hand, she seemed on a sudden to express the country through which for the last two or three days he had wandered. He felt an unexpected pleasure in her slim erectness and in her buoyant step. There was something very charming in her blue eyes.

He was seized with a great desire to talk. And, without thinking for an instant that what concerned him so intensely might be of no moment to her, he began forthwith upon the subject which was ever at his heart. But he spoke as his interest prompted, of each topic as it most absorbed him, starting with what he was now about and going back to what had first attracted his attention to that business; then telling his plans for the future, and to make them clear, finishing with the events that had led up to his determination. Lucy listened attentively, now and then asking a question; and presently the whole matter sorted itself in her mind, so that she was able to make a connected narrative of his life since the details of it had escaped from Dick's personal observation.

For some years Alec MacKenzie had travelled in Africa with no object beyond a great curiosity, and no ambition but that of the unknown. His first important expedition had been, indeed, occasioned by the failure of a fellow-explorer. He had undergone the common vicissitudes of African travel, illness and hunger, incredible difficulties of transit through swamps that seemed never ending, and tropical forest through which it was impossible to advance at the rate of more than one mile a day; he had suffered from the desertion of his bearers and the perfidy of native tribes. But at last he reached the country which had been the aim of his journey. He had to encounter then a savage king's determined hostility to the white man, and he had to keep a sharp eye on his followers who, in abject terror of the tribe he meant to visit, took every opportunity to escape into the bush. The barbarian chief sent him a warning that he would have him killed if he attempted to enter his capital. The rest of the story Alec told with an apologetic air, as if he were ashamed of himself, and he treated it with a deprecating humour that sought to minimise both the danger he had run and the courage he had displayed. On receiving the king's message, Alec MacKenzie took up a high tone, and returned the answer that he would come to the royal kraal before midday. He wanted to give the king no time to recover from his astonishment, and the messengers had scarcely delivered the reply before he presented himself, unarmed and unattended.

'What did you say to him?' asked Lucy.

'I asked him what the devil he meant by sending me such an impudent message,' smiled Alec.

'Weren't you frightened?' said Lucy.

'Yes,' he answered.

He paused for a moment, and, as though unconsciously he were calling back the mood which had then seized him, he began to walk more slowly.

' You see, it was the only thing to do. We'd about come to the end of our food, and we were bound to get some by hook or by crook. If we'd shown the white feather they would probably have set upon us without more ado. My own people were too frightened to make a fight of it, and we should have been wiped out like sheep. Then I had a kind of instinctive feeling that it would be all right. I didn't feel as if my time had come.'

But, notwithstanding, for three hours his life had hung in the balance; and Lucy understood that it was only his masterful courage which had won the day and turned a sullen, suspicious foe into a warm ally.

He achieved the object of his expedition, discovered a new species of antelope of which he was able to bring back to the Natural History Museum a complete skeleton and two hides; took some geographical observations which corrected current errors, and made a careful examination of the country. When he had learnt all that was possible, still on the most friendly terms with the ferocious ruler, he set out for Mombassa. He reached it in one month more than five years after he had left it.

The results of this journey had been small enough, but Alec looked upon it as his apprenticeship. He had found his legs, and believed himself fit for much greater undertakings. He had learnt how to deal with natives, and was aware that he had a natural influence over them. He had confidence in himself. He had surmounted the difficulties of the climate, and felt himself more or less proof against fever and heat. He returned to the coast stronger than he had ever been in his life, and his enthusiasm for African travel increased tenfold. The siren had taken hold of him, and no escape now was possible.

He spent a year in England, and then went back to Africa. He had determined now to explore certain districts to the northeast of the great lakes. They were in the hinterland of British East Africa, and England had a vague claim over them; but no actual occupation had taken place, and they formed a series of independent states under Arab emirs. He went this time with a roving commission from the government, and authority to make treaties with the local chieftains. Spending six years in these districts, he made a methodical survey of the country, and was able to prepare valuable maps. He collected an immense amount of scientific material. He studied the manners and customs of the inhabitants, and made careful observations on the political state. He found the whole land distracted with incessant warfare, and broad tracts of country, fertile and apt for the occupation of white men, given over to desolation. It was then that he realised the curse of slave-raiding, the abolition of which was to become the great object of his future activity. His strength was small, and, anxious not to arouse at once the enmity of the Arab slavers, he had to use much diplomacy in order to establish himself in the country. He knew himself to be an object of intense suspicion, and he could not trust even the petty rulers who were bound to him by ties of gratitude and friendship. For some time the sultan of the most powerful state kept him in a condition bordering on captivity, and at one period his life was for a year in the greatest danger. He never knew from day to day whether he would see the setting of the sun. The Arab, though he treated him with honour, would not let him go; and, at last, Alec, seizing an opportunity when the sultan was engaged in battle with a brother who sought to usurp his sovereignty, fled for his life, abandoning his property, and saving only his notes, his specimens, and his guns.

When MacKenzie reached England, he laid before the Foreign Office the result of his studies. He pointed out the state of anarchy to which the constant slave-raiding had reduced this wealthy country, and implored those in authority, not only for the sake of humanity, but for the prestige of the country, to send an expedition which should stamp out the murderous traffic. He offered to accompany this in any capacity; and, so long as he had the chance of assisting in a righteous war, agreed to serve under any leader they chose. His knowledge of the country and his influence over its inhabitants were indispensable. He guaranteed that, if they gave him a certain number of guns with three British officers, the whole affair could be settled in a year.

But the government was crippled by the Boer War; and though, appreciating the strength of his arguments, it realised the necessity of intervention, was disinclined to enter upon fresh enterprises. These little expeditions in Africa had a way of developing into much more important affairs than first appeared. They had been taught bitter lessons before now, and could not risk, in the present state of things, even an insignificant rebuff. If they sent out a small party, which was defeated, it would be a great blow to the prestige of the country through Africa—the Arabs would carry the news to India—and it would be necessary, then, to despatch such a force that failure was impossible. To supply this there was neither money nor men.

Alec was put off with one excuse after another. To him it seemed that hindrances were deliberately set in his way, and in fact the relations of England with the rest of Europe made his small schemes appear an intolerable nuisance. At length he was met with a flat refusal.

But Alec MacKenzie could not rest with this, and opposition only made him more determined to carry his business through. He understood that it was hard at second hand to make men realise the state of things in that distant land. But he had seen horrors beyond description. He knew the ruthless cruelty of the slave-raiders, and in his ears rang, still, the cries of agony when a village was set on fire and attacked by the Arabs. Not once, nor twice, but many times he had left some tiny kraal nestling sweetly among its fields of maize, an odd, savage counterpart to the country hamlet described in prim, melodious numbers by the gentle Goldsmith: the little naked children were playing merrily; the women sat in groups grinding their corn and chattering; the men worked in the fields or lounged idly about the hut doors. It was a charming scene. You felt that here, perhaps, one great mystery of life had been solved; for happiness was on every face, and the mere joy of living was a sufficient reason for existence. And, when he returned, the village was a pile of cinders, smoking still; here and there were lying the dead and wounded; on one side he recognised a chubby boy with a great spear wound in his body;

on another was a woman with her face blown away by some clumsy gun; and there a man in the agony of death, streaming with blood, lay heaped upon the ground in horrible disorder. And the rest of the inhabitants had been hurried away pellmell on the cruel journey across country, brutally treated and half starved, till they could be delivered into the hands of the slave merchant.

Alec MacKenzie went to the Foreign Office once more. He was willing to take the whole business on himself, and asked only for a commission to raise troops at his own expense. Timorous secretaries did not know into what difficulties this determined man might lead them, and if he went with the authority of an official, but none of his responsibilities, he might land them in grave complications. The spheres of influence of the continental powers must be respected, and at this time of all others it was necessary to be very careful of national jealousies. Alec MacKenzie was told that if he went he must go as a private person. No help could be given him, and the British Government would not concern itself, even indirectly, with his enterprise. Alec had expected the reply and was not dissatisfied. If the government would not undertake the matter itself, he preferred to manage it without the hindrance of official restraints. And so this solitary man made up his mind, single handed, to crush the slave traffic in a district larger than England, and to wage war, unassisted, with a dozen local chieftains and against twenty thousand fighting men. The attempt seemed Quixotic, but Alec had examined the risks and was willing to take them. He had on his side a thorough knowledge of the country, a natural power over the natives, and some skill in managing them. He was accustomed now to the diplomacy which was needful, and he was well acquainted with the local politics.

He did not think it would be hard to collect a force on the coast, and there were plenty of hardy, adventurous fellows who would volunteer to officer the native levies, if he had money to pay them. Ready money was essential, so he crossed the Atlantic and sold his estate in Texas; he made arrangements to raise a further sum, if necessary, on the income which his colliery in Lancashire brought him. He engaged a surgeon, whom he had known for some years, and could trust in an emergency, and then sailed for Zanzibar, where he expected to find white men willing to take service under him. At Mombassa he collected the bearers who had been with him during his previous expeditions, and, his fame among the natives being widely spread, he was able to take his pick of those best suited for his purpose. His party consisted altogether of over three hundred.

When he arrived upon the scene of his operations, everything for a time went well. He showed great skill in dividing his enemies. The petty rulers were filled with jealousy of one another and eager always to fall upon their friends, when slave-raiding for a season was unsuccessful. Alec's plan was to join two or three smaller states in an attack upon the most powerful of them all, to crush this completely, and then to take his old allies one by one, if they would not guarantee to give up their raids on peaceful tribes. His influence with the natives was such that he felt certain it was possible to lead them into action against

their dreaded foes, the Arabs, if he was once able to
give them confidence. Everything turned out as he
had hoped.

The great state which had aimed at the hegemony
of the whole district was defeated; and Alec, with
the method habitual to him, set about organising each
strip of territory which was reclaimed from barbarism. He was able to hold in check the emirs who
had fought with him, and a sharp lesson given to one
who had broken faith with him, struck terror in the
others. The land was regaining its old security. Alec
trusted that in five years a man would be able to travel
from end to end of it as safely as in England. But
suddenly everything he had achieved was undone. As
sometimes happens in countries of small civilisation, a
leader arose from among the Arabs. None knew from
where he sprang, and it was said that he had been a
camel driver. He was called Mohammed the Lame,
because a leg badly set after a fracture had left him
halting, and he was a shrewd man, far-seeing, ruthless, and ambitious. With a few companions as desperate as himself, he attacked the capital of a small
state in the North which was distracted by the
death of its ruler, seized it, and proclaimed himself
king.

In a year he had brought under his sway all those
shadowy lands which border upon Abyssinia, and was
leading a great rabble, mad with the lust of conquest,
fanatic with hatred of the Christian, upon the South.
Consternation reigned among the tribes to whom Mac-
Kenzie was the only hope of salvation. He pointed
out to the Arabs who had accepted his influence, that
their safety, as well as his, lay in resistance to the

Lame One; but the war cry of the Prophet prevailed
against the call of reason, and he found that they
were against him to a man. His native allies were
faithful, with the fidelity of despair, and these he
brought up against the enemy. A pitched battle was
fought, but the issue was undecided. The losses were
great on both sides, and Alec was himself badly
wounded.

Fortunately the wet season was approaching, and
Mohammed the Lame, with a wholesome respect for
the white man who for the moment, at least, had
checked his onward course, withdrew to the Northern
regions where his power was more secure. Alec knew
that he would resume the attack at the first opportunity,
and he knew also that he had not the means to withstand a foe who was astute and capable. His only
chance was to get back to the coast, return to England,
and try again to interest the government in the undertaking; if they still refused help he determined to go
out once more himself, taking this time Maxim guns
and men capable of handling them. He knew that
his departure would seem like flight, but he could
not help that. He was obliged to go. His wound
prevented him from walking, but he caused himself to be carried; and, firing his caravan with his
own indomitable spirit, he reached the coast by forced
marches.

His brief visit to England was already drawing to
its close, and, in less than a month now, he proposed
to set out for Africa once more. This time he meant
to finish the work. If only his life were spared, he
would crush for ever the infamous trade which turned
a paradise into a wilderness.

Alec stopped speaking as they entered the cathedral close, and they paused for a moment to look at the stately pile. The trim lawns that surrounded it, in a manner enhanced its serene majesty. They entered the nave. There was a vast and solemn stillness. And there was something subtly impressive in the naked space; it uplifted the heart, and one felt a kind of scorn for all that was mean and low. The soaring of the Gothic columns, with their straight simplicity, raised the thoughts to a nobler standard. And, though that place had been given for three hundred years to colder rites, the atmosphere of an earlier, more splendid faith seemed still to cling to it. A vague odour of a spectral incense hung about the pillars, a sweet, sad smell, and the shadows of ghostly priests in vestments of gold, and with embroidered copes, wound in a long procession through the empty aisles.

Lucy was glad that they had come there, and the restful grandeur of the place fitted in with the emotions that had filled her mind during the walk from Blackstable. Her spirit was enlarged, and she felt that her own small worries were petty. The consciousness came to her that the man with whom she had been speaking was making history, and she was fascinated by the fulness of his life and the greatness of his undertakings. Her eyes were dazzled with the torrid African sun which had shone through his words, and she felt the horror of the primeval forest and the misery of the unending swamps. And she was proud because his outlook was so clear, because he bore his responsibilities so easily, because his plans were so vast. She looked at him. He was standing by her side, and his eyes were upon her. She felt the colour rise to her cheeks, she knew not why, and in embarrassment looked down.

By some chance they missed Dick Lomas and Mrs. Crowley. Neither was sorry. When they left the cathedral and started for home, they spoke for a while of indifferent things. It seemed that Alec's tongue was loosened, and he was glad of it. Lucy knew instinctively that he had never talked to anyone as he talked to her, and she was curiously flattered.

But it seemed to both of them that the conversation could not proceed on the strenuous level on which it had been during the walk into Tercanbury, and they fell upon a gay discussion of their common acquaintance. Alec was a man of strong passions, hating fools fiercely, and he had a sardonic manner of gibing at persons he despised, which caused Lucy much amusement.

He described interviews with the great ones of the land in a broadly comic spirit; and, when telling an amusing story, he had a way of assuming a Scottish drawl that added vastly to its humour.

Presently they began to speak of books. Being strictly limited as to number, he was obliged to choose for his expeditions works which could stand reading an indefinite number of times.

'I'm like a convict,' he said. 'I know Shakespeare by heart, and I've read Boswell's *Johnson* till I think you couldn't quote a line which I couldn't cap with the next.'

But Lucy was surprised to hear that he read the Greek classics with enthusiasm. She had vaguely imagined that people recognised their splendour, but did not read them unless they were dons or schoolmasters, and it was strange to find anyone for whom they were living works. To Alec they were a deliberate inspiration. They strengthened his purpose and helped him to see life from the heroic point of view. He was not a man who cared much for music or for painting; his whole æsthetic desires were centred in the Greek poets and the historians. To him Thucydides was a true support, and he felt in himself something of the spirit which had animated the great Athenian. His blood ran faster as he spoke of him, and his cheeks flushed. He felt that one who lived constantly in such company could do nothing base. But he found all he needed, put together with a power that seemed almost divine, within the two covers that bound his Sophocles. The mere look of the Greek letters filled him with exultation. Here was all he wanted, strength and simplicity, and the greatness of life, and beauty.

He forgot that Lucy did not know that dead language and could not share his enthusiasm. He broke suddenly into a chorus from the *Antigone:* the sonorous, lovely words issued from his lips, and Lucy, not understanding, but feeling vaguely the beauty of the sounds, thought that his voice had never been more fascinating. It gained now a peculiar and entrancing softness. She had never dreamed that it was capable of such tenderness.

At last they reached Court Leys and walked up the avenue that led to the house. They saw Dick hurrying towards them. They waved their hands, but he did not reply, and, when he approached, they saw that his face was white and anxious.

'Thank God, you've come at last! I couldn't make out what had come to you.'

'What's the matter?'

The barrister, all his flippancy gone, turned to Lucy.

'Bobbie Boulger has come down. He wants to see you. Please come at once.'

Lucy looked at him quickly. Sick with fear, she followed him into the drawing-room.

# V

MRS. CROWLEY and Robert Boulger were standing by the fire, and there was a peculiar agitation about them. They were silent, but it seemed to Lucy that they had been speaking of her. Mrs. Crowley impulsively seized her hands and kissed her. Lucy's first thought was that something had happened to her brother. Lady Kelsey's generous allowance had made it possible for him to hunt, and the thought flashed through her that some terrible accident had happened.

' Is anything the matter with George? ' she asked, with a gasp of terror.

' No,' answered Boulger.

The colour came to Lucy's cheeks as she felt a sudden glow of relief.

' Thank God,' she murmured. ' I was so frightened.'

She gave him, now, a smile of welcome as she shook hands with him. It could be nothing so very dreadful after all.

Lucy's uncle, Sir George Boulger, had been for many years senior partner in the great firm of Boulger & Kelsey. After sitting in Parliament for the quarter of a century and voting assiduously for his party, he had been given a baronetcy on the celebration of Queen Victoria's second Jubilee, and had finished a prosperous life by dying of apoplexy at the opening of a park, which he was presenting to the nation. He had been a fine type of the wealthy merchant, far-sighted in business affairs and proud to serve his native city in every way open to him. His son, Robert, now reigned in his stead, but the firm had been made into a company, and the responsibility that he undertook, notwithstanding that the greater number of shares were in his hands, was much less. The partner who had been taken into the house on Sir Alfred Kelsey's death now managed the more important part of the business in Manchester, while Robert, brought up by his father to be a man of affairs, had taken charge of the London branch. Commerce was in his blood, and he settled down to work with praiseworthy energy. He had considerable shrewdness, and it was plain that he would eventually become as good a merchant as his father. He was little older than Lucy, but his fair hair and his clean-shaven face gave him a more youthful look. With his spruce air and well-made clothes, his conversation about hunting and golf, few would have imagined that he arrived regularly at his office at ten in the morning, and was as keen to make a good bargain as any of the men he came in contact with.

Lucy, though very fond of him, was mildly scornful of his Philistine outlook. He cared nothing for books, and the only form of art that appealed to him was the musical comedy. She treated him as a rule with pleasant banter and refused to take him seriously. It required a good deal of energy to keep their friendship on a light footing, for she knew that he had been in love with her since he was eighteen. She could not help feeling flattered, though on her side there was no more than the cousinly affection due to their having been thrown together all their lives, and she was aware that they were little suited to one another. He had proposed to her a dozen times, and she was obliged to use many devices to protect herself from his assiduity. It availed nothing to tell him that she did not love him. He was only too willing to marry her on whatever conditions she chose to make. Her friends and her relations were anxious that she should accept him. Lady Kelsey had reasoned with her. Here was a man whom she had known always and could trust utterly; he had ten thousand a year, an honest heart, and a kindly disposition. Her father, seeing in the match a resource in his constant difficulties, was eager that she should take the boy, and George, who was devoted to him, had put in his word, too. Bobbie had asked her to marry him when he was twenty-one, and again when she was twenty-one, when George went to Oxford, when her father went into bankruptcy, and when Hamlyn's Purlieu was sold. He had urged his own father to buy it, when it was known that a sale was inevitable, hoping that the possession of it would incline Lucy's heart towards him; but the first baronet was too keen a man of business to make an u⋅·profitable investment for sentimental reasons. Bobbie had proposed for the last time when he succeeded to the baronetcy and a large fortune. Lucy recognised his goodness and the advantages of the match, but she did not care for him. She felt, too, that she needed a free hand to watch over her father and George. Even Mrs. Crowley's suggestion that with her guidance Robert Boulger might become a man of consequence, did not move her. Bobbie, on the other hand, had set all his heart on marrying his cousin. It was the supreme interest of his life, and he hoped that his patience would eventually triumph over every obstacle. He was willing to wait.

When Lucy's first alarm was stayed, it occurred to her that Bobbie had come once more to ask her the eternal question, but the anxious look in his eyes drove the idea away. His pleasant, boyish expression was overcast with gravity; Mrs. Crowley flung herself in a chair and turned her face away.

' I have something to tell you which is very terrible, Lucy,' he said.

The effort he made to speak was noticeable. His voice was strained by the force with which he kept it steady.

' Would you like me to leave you? ' asked Alec, who had accompanied Lucy into the drawing-room.

She gave him a glance. It seemed to her that whatever it was, his presence would help her to bear it.

' Do you wish to see me alone, Bobbie? '

' I've already told Dick and Mrs. Crowley.'

' What is it? ' she asked.

Bobbie gave Dick an appealing look. It seemed too hard that he should have to break the awful news to her. He had not the heart to give her so much pain. And yet he had hurried down to the country so that he might soften the blow by his words: he would not trust to the callous cruelty of a telegram. Dick saw the agitation which made his good-humoured mouth twitch with pain, and stepped forward.

' Your father has been arrested for fraud,' he said gravely.

For a moment no one spoke. The silence was intolerable to Mrs. Crowley, and she inveighed inwardly against the British stolidity. She could not look at Lucy, but the others, full of sympathy, kept their eyes upon her. Mrs. Crowley wondered why she did not faint. It seemed to Lucy that an icy hand clutched her heart so that the blood was squeezed out of it. She made a determined effort to keep her clearness of mind.

'It's impossible,' she said at last, quietly.

'He was arrested last night, and brought up at Bow Street Police Court this morning. He was remanded for a week.'

Lucy felt the tears well up to her eyes, but with all her strength she forced them back. She collected her thoughts.

'It was very good of you to come down and tell me,' she said to Boulger gently.

'The magistrate agreed to accept bail in five thousand pounds. Aunt Alice and I have managed it between us.'

'Is he staying with Aunt Alice now?'

'No, he wouldn't do that. He's gone to his flat in Shaftesbury Avenue.'

Lucy's thoughts went to the lad who was dearest to her in the world, and her heart sank.

'Does George know?'

'Not yet.'

Dick saw the relief that came into her face, and thought he divined what was in her mind.

'But he must be told at once,' he said. 'He's sure to see something about it in the papers. We had better wire to him to come to London immediately.'

'Surely father could have shown in two minutes that the whole thing was a mistake.'

Bobbie made a hopeless gesture. He saw the sternness of her eyes, and he had not the heart to tell her the truth. Mrs. Crowley began to cry.

'You don't understand, Lucy,' said Dick. 'I'm afraid it's a very serious charge. Your father will be committed for trial.'

'You know just as well as I do that father can't have done anything illegal. He's weak and rash, but he's no more than that. He would as soon think of doing anything wrong as of flying to the moon. If in his ignorance of business he's committed some technical offence, he can easily show that it was unintentional.'

'Whatever it is, he'll have to stand his trial at the Old Bailey,' answered Dick gravely.

He saw that Lucy did not for a moment appreciate the gravity of her father's position. After the first shock of dismay she was disposed to think that there could be nothing in it. Robert Boulger saw there was nothing for it but to tell her everything.

'Your father and a man called Saunders have been running a bucketshop under the name of Vernon and Lawford. They were obliged to trade under different names, because Uncle Fred is an undischarged bankrupt, and Saunders is the sort of man who only uses his own name on the charge sheet of a police court.'

'Do you know what a bucketshop is, Lucy?' asked Dick.

He did not wait for a reply, but explained that it was a term used to describe a firm of outside brokers whose dealings were more or less dishonest.

'The action is brought against the pair of them by a Mrs. Sabidon, who accuses them of putting to their own uses various sums amounting altogether to more than eight thousand pounds, which she intrusted to them to invest.'

Now that the truth was out, Lucy quailed before it.

The intense seriousness on the faces of Alec and Dick Lomas, the piteous anxiety of her cousin, terrified her.

'You don't think there's anything in it?' she asked quickly.

Robert did not know what to answer. Dick interrupted with wise advice.

'We'll hope for the best. The only thing to do is to go up to London at once and get the best legal advice.'

But Lucy would not allow herself, even for a moment, to doubt her father. Now that she thought of the matter, she saw that it was absurd. She forced herself to give a laugh.

'I'm quite reassured. You don't think for a moment that father would deliberately steal somebody else's money. And it's nothing short of theft.'

'At all events it's something that we've been able to get him released on bail. It will make it so much easier to arrange the defence.'

A couple of hours later Lucy, accompanied by Dick Lomas and Bobbie, was on her way to London. Alec, thinking his presence would be a nuisance to them, arranged with Mrs. Crowley to leave by a later train; and, when the time came for him to start, his hostess suddenly announced that she would go with him. With her party thus broken up and her house empty, she could not bear to remain at Court Leys. She was anxious about Lucy and eager to be at hand if her help were needed.

A telegram had been sent to George, and it was supposed that he would arrive at Lady Kelsey's during the evening. Lucy wanted to tell him herself what had happened. But she could not wait till then to see her father, and persuaded Dick to drive with her from the station to Shaftesbury Avenue. Fred Allerton was not in. Lucy wanted to go into the flat and stay there till he came, but the porter had no key and did not know when he would return. Dick was much relieved. He was afraid that the excitement and the anxiety from which Fred Allerton had suffered, would have caused him to drink heavily; and he could not let Lucy see him the worse for liquor. He induced her, after leaving a note to say that she would call early next morning, to go quietly home. When they arrived at Charles Street, where was Lady Kelsey's house, they found a wire from George to say he could not get up to town till the following day.

To Lucy this had, at least, the advantage that she could see her father alone, and at the appointed hour she made her way once more to his flat. He took her in his arms and kissed her warmly. She succumbed at once to the cheeriness of his manner.

' I can only give you two minutes, darling,' he said. ' I'm full of business, and I have an appointment with my solicitor at eleven.'

Lucy could not speak. She clung to her father, looking at him with anxious, sombre eyes; but he laughed and patted her hand.

' You mustn't make too much of all this, my love,' he said brightly. ' These little things are always liable to happen to a man of business; they are the perils of the profession, and we have to put up with them, just as kings and queens have to put up with bomb-shells.'

' There's no truth in it, father? '

She did not want to ask that wounding question, but the words slipped from her lips against her will. He broke away from her.

'Truth? My dear child, what do you mean? You don't suppose I'm the man to rob the widow and the orphan? Of course, there's no truth in it.'

'Oh, I'm so glad to hear that,' she exclaimed, with a deep sigh of relief.

'Have they been frightening you?'

Lucy flushed under his frank look of amusement. She felt that there was a barrier between herself and him, the barrier that had existed for years, and there was something in his manner which filled her with unaccountable anxiety. She would not analyse that vague emotion. It was a dread to see what was so carefully hidden by that breezy reserve. She forced herself to go on.

'I know that you're often carried away by your fancies, and I thought you might have got into an ambiguous position.'

'I can honestly say that no one can bring anything up against me,' he answered. 'But I do blame myself for getting mixed up with that man Saunders. I'm afraid there's no doubt that he's a wrong 'un—and heaven only knows what he's been up to—but for my own part I give you my solemn word of honour that I've done nothing, absolutely nothing, that I have the least reason to be ashamed of.'

Lucy took his hand, and a charming smile lit up her face.

'Oh, father, you've made me so happy by saying that. Now I shall be able to tell George that there's nothing to worry about.'

Their conversation was interrupted by the arrival of Dick. Fred Allerton greeted him heartily.

' You've just come in time to take Lucy home. I've got to go out. But look here, George is coming up, isn't he? Let us all lunch at the *Carlton* at two, and get Alice to come. We'll have a jolly little meal together."

Dick was astounded to see the lightness with which Allerton took the affair. He seemed unconscious of the gravity of his position and unmindful of the charge which was hanging over him. Dick was not anxious to accept the invitation, but Allerton would hear of no excuses. He wanted to have his friends gathered around him, and he needed relaxation after the boredom of spending a morning in his lawyer's office.

' Come on,' he said. ' I can't wait another minute.'

He opened the door, and Lucy walked out. It seemed to Dick that Allerton was avoiding any chance of conversation with him. But no man likes to meet his creditor within four walls, and this disinclination might be due merely to the fact that Allerton owed him a couple of hundred pounds. But he meant to get in one or two words.

' Are you fixed up with a solicitor? ' he asked.

' Do you think I'm a child, Dick? ' answered the other. ' Why, I've got the smartest man in the whole profession, Teddie Blakeley—you know him, don't you? '

' Only by reputation,' answered Dick drily. ' I should think that was enough for most people.'

Fred Allerton gave that peculiarly honest laugh of his, which was so attractive. Dick knew that the so-

licitor he mentioned was a man of evil odour, who had
made a specialty of dealing with the most doubtful
sort of commercial work, and his name had been prominent in every scandal for the last fifteen years. It
was surprising that he had never followed any of his
clients to the jail he richly deserved.

' I thought it no good going to one of the old
crusted family solicitors. I wanted a man who knew
the tricks of the trade.'

They were walking down the stairs, while Lucy waited
at the bottom. Dick stopped and turned round. He
looked at Allerton keenly.

' You're not going to do a bolt, are you? '

Allerton's face lit up with amusement. He put his
hands on Dick's shoulders.

' My dear old Dick, don't be such an ass. I don't
know about Saunders—he's a fishy sort of customer—
but I shall come out of all this with flying colours.
The prosecution hasn't a leg to stand on.'

Allerton, reminding them that they were to lunch
together, jumped into a cab. Lucy and Dick walked
slowly back to Charles Street. Dick was very silent.
He had not seen Fred Allerton for some time and
was surprised to see that he had regained his old
smartness. The flat had pretty things in it which tes-
tified to the lessee's taste and to his means, and the
clothes he wore were new and well-cut. The invitation
to the *Carlton* showed that he was in no want of ready
money, and there was a general air of prosperity about
him which gave Dick much to think of.

Lucy did not ask him to come in, since George, by
now, must have arrived, and she wished to see him
alone. They agreed to meet again at two. As she

shook hands with Dick, Lucy told him what her father
had said.

'I had a sleepless night,' she said. 'It was so stupid
of me; I couldn't get it out of my head that father,
unintentionally, had done something rash or foolish;
but I've got his word of honour that nothing is the
matter, and I feel as if a whole world of anxiety were
suddenly lifted from my shoulders.'

The party at the *Carlton* was very gay. Fred Allerton seemed in the best of spirits, and his good-humour
was infectious. He was full of merry quips. Lucy
had made as little of the affair as possible to George.
Her eyes rested on him, as he sat opposite to her, and
she felt happy and proud. Now and then he looked at
her, and an affectionate smile came to his lips. She
was delighted with his slim handsomeness. There was
a guileless look in his blue eyes which was infinitely
attractive. His mouth was beautifully modelled. She
took an immense pride in the candour of soul which
shone with so clear a light on his face, and she was
affected as a stranger might have been by the exquisite
charm of manner which he had inherited from his
father. She wanted to have him to herself that evening and suggested that they should go to a play together. He accepted the idea eagerly, for he admired
his sister with all his heart; he felt in himself a need
for protection, and she was able to minister to this.
He was never so happy as when he was by her side. He
liked to tell her all he did, and, when she fired him
with noble ambitions, he felt capable of anything.

They were absurdly light-hearted, as they started on
their little jaunt. Lady Kelsey had slipped a couple of

banknotes into George's hand and told them to have a good time. They dined at the *Carlton,* went to a musical comedy, which amused Lucy because her brother laughed so heartily—she was fascinated by his keen power of enjoyment—and finished by going to the *Savoy* for supper. For the moment all her anxieties seemed to fall from her, and the years of trouble were forgotten. She was as merry and as irresponsible as George. He was enchanted. He had never seen Lucy so tender and so gay; there was a new brilliancy in her eyes; and, without quite knowing what it was that differed, he found a soft mellowness in her laughter which filled him with an uncomprehended delight. Neither did Lucy know why the world on a sudden seemed fuller than it had ever done before, nor why the future smiled so kindly: it never occurred to her that she was in love.

When Lucy, exhausted but content, found herself at length in her room, she thanked God for the happiness of the evening. It was the last time she could do that for many weary years.

A few days later Allerton appeared again at the police court, and the magistrate, committing him for trial, declined to renew his bail. The prisoner was removed in custody.

# VI

DURING the fortnight that followed, Alec spent much time with Lucy. Together, in order to cheat the hours that hung so heavily on her hands, they took long walks in Hyde Park, and, when Alec's business permitted, they went to the National Gallery. Then he took her to the Natural History Museum, and his conversation, in face of the furred and feathered things from Africa, made the whole country vivid to her. Lucy was very grateful to him because he drew her mind away from the topic that constantly absorbed it. Though he never expressed his sympathy in so many words, she felt it in every inflection of his voice. His patience was admirable.

At last came the day fixed for the trial.

Fred Allerton insisted that neither Lucy nor George should come to the Old Bailey, and they were to await the verdict at Lady Kelsey's. Dick and Robert Boulger were subpœnaed as witnesses. In order that she might be put out of her suspense quickly, Lucy asked Alec MacKenzie to go into court and bring her the result as soon as it was known.

The morning passed with leaden feet.

After luncheon Mrs. Crowley came to sit with Lady Kelsey, and together they watched the minute hand go round the clock. Now the verdict might be expected at any moment. After some time Canon Spratte, the vicar of the church which Lady Kelsey attended, sent up to ask if he might see her; and Mrs. Crowley, thinking to distract her, asked him to come in. The Canon's breezy courtliness as a rule soothed Lady Kelsey's gravest troubles, but now she would not be comforted.

'I shall never get over it,' she said, with a handkerchief to her eyes. 'I shall never cease blaming myself. Nothing of all this would have happened, if it hadn't been for me.'

Canon Spratte and Mrs. Crowley watched her without answering. She was a stout, amiable woman, who had clothed herself in black because the occasion was tragic. Grief had made her garrulous.

'Poor Fred came to me one day and said he must have eight thousand pounds at once. He told me his partner had cheated him, and it was a matter of life and death. But it was such a large sum, and I've given him so much already. After all, I've got to think of Lucy and George. They only have me to depend on, and I refused to give it. Oh, I'd have given every penny I own rather than have this horrible shame.'

'You mustn't take it too much to heart, Lady Kelsey,' said Mrs. Crowley. 'It will soon be all over.'

'Our ways have parted for some time now,' said Canon Spratte, 'but at one period I used to see a good deal of Fred Allerton. I can't tell you how distressed I was to hear of this terrible misfortune.'

'He's always been unlucky,' returned Lady Kelsey. 'I only hope this will be a lesson to him. He's like a child in business matters. Oh, it's awful to think of my poor sister's husband standing in the felon's dock!'

'You must try not to think of it. I'm sure everything will turn out quite well. In another hour you'll have him with you again.'

The Canon got up and shook hands with Lady Kelsey.

'It was so good of you to come,' she said.

He turned to Mrs. Crowley, whom he liked because she was American, rich, and a widow.

'I'm grateful, too,' she murmured, as she bade him farewell. 'A clergyman always helps one so much to bear other people's misfortunes.'

Canon Spratte smiled and made a mental note of the remark, which he thought would do very well from his own lips.

'Where is Lucy?' asked Mrs. Crowley, when he had gone.

Lady Kelsey threw up her hands with the feeling, half of amazement, half of annoyance, which a very emotional person has always for one who is self-restrained.

'She's sitting in her room, reading. She's been reading all day. Heaven only knows how she can do it. I tried, and all the letters swam before my eyes. It drives me mad to see how calm she is.'

They began to talk of the immediate future. Lady Kelsey had put a large sum at Lucy's disposal, and it was arranged that the two children should take their father to some place in the south of France where he could rest after the terrible ordeal.

'I don't know what they would all have done without you,' said Mrs. Crowley. 'You have been a perfect angel.'

'Nonsense,' smiled Lady Kelsey. 'They're my only relations in the world, except Bobbie, who's very much too rich as it is, and I love Lucy and George as if they were my own children. What is the good of my money except to make them happy and comfortable?'

Mrs. Crowley remembered Dick's surmise that Lady Kelsey had loved Fred Allerton, and she wondered how much of the old feeling still remained. She felt a great pity for the kind, unselfish creature. Lady Kelsey started as she heard the street door slam. But it was only George who entered.

' Oh, George, where have you been? Why didn't you come in to luncheon?'

He looked pale and haggard. The strain of the last fortnight had told on him enormously, and it was plain that his excitement was almost unbearable.

' I couldn't eat anything. I've been walking about, waiting for the damned hours to pass. I wish I hadn't promised father not to go into court. Anything would have been better than this awful suspense. I saw the man who's defending him when they adjourned for luncheon, and he told me it was all right.'

' Of course it's all right. You didn't imagine that your father would be found guilty.'

' Oh, I knew he wouldn't have done a thing like that,' said George impatiently. ' But I can't help being frightfully anxious. The papers are awful. They've got huge placards out: *County gentleman at the Old Bailey. Society in a Bucket Shop.*'

George shivered with horror.

' Oh, it's awful!' he cried.

Lady Kelsey began to cry again, and Mrs. Crowley sat in silence, not knowing what to say. George walked about in agitation.

' But I know he's not guilty,' moaned Lady Kelsey.

' If he's guilty or not he's ruined me,' said George.

' I can't go up to Oxford again after this.  I don't know
what the devil's to become of me.  We're all utterly
disgraced.  Oh, how could he!  How could he!'

' Oh, George, don't,' said Lady Kelsey.

But George, with a weak man's petulance, could not
keep back the bitter words that he had turned over in
his heart so often since the brutal truth was told him.

' Wasn't it enough that he fooled away every penny
he had, so that we're simply beggars, both of us, and
we have to live on your charity?  I should have thought
that would have satisfied him, without getting locked
up for being connected in a beastly bucketshop swindle.'

' George, how can you talk of your father like that!'

He gave a sort of sob and looked at her with wild
eyes.  But at that moment a cab drove up, and he
sprang on to the balcony.

' It's Dick Lomas and Bobbie.  They've come to tell
us.'

He ran to the door and opened it.  They walked
up the stairs.

' Well?' he cried.  ' Well?'

' It's not over yet.  We left just as the judge was
summing up.'

' Damn you!' cried George, with an explosion of
sudden fury.

' Steady, old man,' said Dick.

' Why didn't you stay?' moaned Lady Kelsey.

' I couldn't,' said Dick.  ' It was too awful.'

' How was it going?'

' I couldn't make head or tail of it.  My mind was
in a whirl.  I'm an hysterical old fool.'

Mrs. Crowley went up to Lady Kelsey and kissed
her.

'Why don't you go and lie down for a little while, dear,' she said. 'You look positively exhausted.'

'I have a racking headache,' groaned Lady Kelsey.

'Alec MacKenzie has promised to come here as soon as it's over. But you mustn't expect him for another hour.'

'Yes, I'll go and lie down,' said Lady Kelsey.

George, unable to master his impatience, flung open the window and stood on the balcony, watching for the cab that would bring the news.

'Go and talk to him, there's a good fellow,' said Dick to Robert Boulger. 'Cheer him up a bit.'

'Yes, of course I will. It's rot to make a fuss now that it's nearly over. Uncle Fred will be here himself in an hour.'

Dick looked at him without answering. When Robert had gone on to the balcony, he flung himself wearily in a chair.

'I couldn't stand it any longer,' he said. 'You can't imagine how awful it was to see that wretched man in the dock. He looked like a hunted beast, his face was all grey with fright, and once I caught his eyes. I shall never forget the look that was in them.'

'But I thought he was bearing it so well,' said Mrs. Crowley.

'You know, he's a man who's never looked the truth in the face. He never seemed to realise the gravity of the charges that were brought against him, and even when the magistrate refused to renew his bail, his confidence never deserted him. It was only to-day, when the whole thing was unrolled before him, that he appeared to understand. Oh, if you'd heard the evidence that was given! And then the pitiful spectacle of those two men trying to throw the blame on one another!'

A look of terror came into Mrs. Crowley's face.

'You don't think he's guilty?' she gasped.

Dick looked at her steadily, but did not answer.

'But Lucy's convinced that he'll be acquitted.'

'I wonder.'

'What on earth do you mean?'

Dick shrugged his shoulders.

'But he can't be guilty,' cried Mrs. Crowley. 'It's impossible.'

Dick made an effort to drive away from his mind the dreadful fears that filled it.

'Yes, that's what I feel, too,' he said. 'With all his faults Fred Allerton can't have committed such a despicable crime. You've never met him, you don't know him; but I've known him intimately for twenty years. He couldn't have swindled that wretched woman out of every penny she had, knowing that it meant starvation to her. He couldn't have been so brutally cruel.'

'Oh, I'm so glad to hear you say that.'

Silence fell upon them for a while, and they waited. From the balcony they heard George talking rapidly, but they could not distinguish his words.

'I felt ashamed to stay in court and watch the torture of that unhappy man. I've dined with him times out of number; I've stayed at his house; I've ridden his horses. Oh, it was too awful.'

He got up impatiently and walked up and down the room.

'It must be over by now. Why doesn't Alec come?

He swore he'd bolt round the very moment the verdict was given.'

'The suspense is dreadful,' said Mrs. Crowley.

Dick stood still. He looked at the little American, but his eyes did not see her.

'There are some people who are born without a moral sense. They are as unable to distinguish between right and wrong as a man who is colour blind, between red and green.'

'Why do you say that?' asked Mrs. Crowley.

He did not answer. She went up to him anxiously.

'Mr. Lomas, I can't bear it. You must tell me. Do *you* think he's guilty?'

He passed his hands over his eyes.

'The evidence was damnable.'

At that moment George sprang into the room.

'There's Alec. He's just driving along in a cab.'

'Thank God, thank God!' cried Mrs. Crowley. 'If it had lasted longer I should have gone mad.'

George went to the door.

'I must tell Miller. He has orders to let no one up.'

He leaned over the banisters, as the bell of the front door was rung.

'Miller, Miller, let Mr. MacKenzie in.'

'Very good, sir,' answered the butler.

Lucy had heard the cab drive up, and she came into the drawing-room with Lady Kelsey. The elder woman had broken down altogether and was sobbing distractedly. Lucy was very white, but otherwise quite composed. She shook hands with Dick and Mrs. Crowley.

'It was kind of you to come,' she said.

'Oh, my poor Lucy,' said Mrs. Crowley, with a sob in her voice.

Lucy smiled bravely.

'It's all over now.'

Alec came in, and she walked eagerly towards him.

'Well? I was hoping you'd bring father with you. When is he coming?'

She stopped. She gave a gasp as she saw Alec's face. Though her cheeks were pale before, now their pallor was deathly.

'What is the matter?'

'Isn't it all right?' cried George.

Lucy put her hand on his arm to quieten him. It seemed that Alec could not find words. There was a horrible silence, but they all knew what he had to tell them.

'I'm afraid you must prepare yourself for a great unhappiness,' he said.

'Where's father?' cried Lucy. 'Where's father? Why didn't you bring him with you?'

With the horrible truth dawning upon her, she was losing her self-control. She made an effort. Alec would not speak, and she was obliged to question him. When the words came, her voice was hoarse and low.

'You've not told us what the verdict was.'

'Guilty,' he answered.

Then the colour flew back to her cheeks, and her eyes flashed with anger.

'But it's impossible. He was innocent. He swore that he hadn't done it. There must be some horrible mistake.'

'I wish to God there were,' said Alec.

'You don't think he's guilty?' she cried.

"SHE GAVE A GASP AS SHE SAW ALEC'S FACE"

He did not answer, and for a moment they looked at one another steadily.

'What was the sentence?' she asked.

'The judge was dead against him. He made some very violent remarks as he passed it.'

'Tell me what he said.'

'Why should you wish to torture yourself?'

'I want to know.'

'He seemed to think the fact that your father was a gentleman made the crime more odious, and the way in which he had induced that woman to part with her money made no punishment too severe. He sentenced him to seven years penal servitude.'

George gave a cry and sinking into a chair, burst into tears. Lucy put her hand on his shoulder.

'Don't, George,' she said. 'You must bear up. Now we want all our courage, now more than ever.'

'Oh, I can't bear it,' he moaned.

She bent down and kissed him tenderly.

'Be brave, my dearest, be brave for my sake.'

But he sobbed uncontrollably. It was a horribly painful sight. Dick took him by the arm and led him away. Lucy turned to Alec, who was standing where first he had stopped.

'I want to ask you a question. Will you answer me quite truthfully, whatever the pain you think it will cause me?'

'I will.'

'You followed the trial from the beginning, you know all the details of it. Do *you* think my father is guilty?'

'What can it matter what I think?'

'I beg you to tell me.'

Alec hesitated for a moment.  His voice was very low.

'If I had been on the jury I'm afraid I should have had no alternative but to decide as they did.'

Lucy bent her head, and heavy tears rolled down her cheeks.

## VII

NEXT morning Lucy received a note from Alec Mac-
Kenzie, asking if he might see her that day; he suggested calling upon her early in the afternoon and
expressed the hope that he might find her alone. She
sat in the library at Lady Kelsey's and waited for him.
She held a book in her hands, but she could not read.
And presently she began to weep. Ever since the dreadful news had reached her, Lucy had done her utmost to
preserve her self-control, and all night she had lain
with clenched hands to prevent herself from giving
way. For George's sake and for her father's, she felt
that she must keep her strength. But now the strain
was too great for her; she was alone; the tears began
to flow helplessly, and she made no effort to restrain
them.

She had been allowed to see her father. Lucy and
George had gone to the prison, and she recalled now the
details of the brief interview. The whole thing was
horrible. She felt that her heart would break.

In the night indignation had seized Lucy. After
reading accounts of the case in half a dozen papers
she could not doubt that her father was justly con-
demned, and she was horrified at the baseness of the
crime. His letters to the poor woman he had robbed,
were read in court, and Lucy flushed as she thought
of them. They were a tissue of lies, hypocritical and
shameless. Lucy remembered the question she had put
to Alec and his answer.

But neither the newspapers nor Alec's words were needed to convince her of her father's guilt; in the very depths of her being, notwithstanding the passion with which she reproached herself, she had been convinced of it. She would not acknowledge even to herself that she doubted him; and all her words, all her thoughts even, expressed a firm belief in his innocence; but a ghastly terror had lurked in some hidden recess of her consciousness. It haunted her soul like a mysterious shadow which there was no bodily shape to explain. The fear had caught her, as though with material hands, when first the news of his arrest was brought to Court Leys by Robert Boulger, and again at her father's flat in Shaftesbury Avenue, when she saw a secret shame cowering behind the good-humoured flippancy of his smile. Notwithstanding his charm of manner and the tenderness of his affection for his children, she had known that he was a liar and a rascal. She hated him.

But when Lucy saw him, still with the hunted look that Dick had noticed at the trial, so changed from when last they had met, her anger melted away, and she felt only pity. She reproached herself bitterly. How could she be so heartless when he was suffering? At first he could not speak. He looked from one to the other of his children silently, with appealing eyes; and he saw the utter wretchedness which was on George's face. George was ashamed to look at him and kept his eyes averted. Fred Allerton was suddenly grown old and bent; his poor face was sunken, and the skin had an ashy look like that of a dying man. He had already a cringing air, as if he must shrink away from his fellows. It was horrible to Lucy that she was not allowed to take him in her arms. He broke down utterly and sobbed.

'Oh, Lucy, you don't hate me?' he whispered.

'No, I've never loved you more than I love you now,' she said.

And she said it truthfully. Her conscience smote her, and she wondered bitterly what she had left undone that might have averted this calamity.

'I didn't mean to do it,' he said, brokenly.

Lucy looked at his poor, wearied eyes. It seemed very cruel that she might not kiss them.

'I'd have paid her everything if she'd only have given me time. Luck was against me all through. I've been a bad father to both of you.'

Lucy was able to tell him that Lady Kelsey would pay the eight thousand pounds the woman had lost. The good creature had thought of it even before Lucy made the suggestion. At all events none of them need have on his conscience the beggary of that unfortunate person.

'Alice was always a good soul,' said Allerton. He clung to Lucy as though she were his only hope. 'You won't forget me while I'm away, Lucy?'

'I'll come and see you whenever I'm allowed to.'

'It won't be very long. I hope I shall die quickly.'

'You mustn't do that. You must keep well and strong for my sake and George's. We shall never cease to love you, father.'

'What's going to happen to George now?' he asked.

'We shall find something for him. You need not worry about him.'

George flushed. He could find nothing to say. He was ashamed and angry. He wanted to get away

quickly from that place of horror, and he was relieved
when the warder told them it was time to go.

' Good-bye, George,' said Fred Allerton.

' Good-bye.'

He kept his eyes sullenly fixed on the ground. The
look of despair in Allerton's face grew more intense.
He saw that his son hated him. And it had been on
him that all his light affection was placed. He had
been very proud of the handsome boy. And now his
son merely wanted to be rid of him. Bitter words rose
to his lips, but his heart was too heavy to utter them,
and they expressed themselves only in a sob.

' Forgive me for all I've done against you, Lucy.'

' Have courage, father, we will never love you less.'

He forced a sad smile to his lips. She included
George in what she said, but he knew that she spoke
only for herself. They went. And he turned away
into the darkness.

Lucy's tears relieved her a little. They exhausted
her, and so made her agony more easy to bear. It was
necessary now to think of the future. Alec MacKenzie
must be there soon. She wondered why he had written,
and what he could have to say that mattered. She
could only think of her father, and above all of George.
She dried her eyes, and with a deep sigh set herself
methodically to consider the difficult problem.

When Alec came she rose gravely to receive him.
For a moment he was overcome by her loveliness, and
he gazed at her in silence. Lucy was a woman who
was at her best in the tragic situations of life; her
beauty was heightened by the travail of her soul, and

the heaviness of her eyes gave a pathetic grandeur to
her wan face. She advanced to meet sorrow with an
unquailing glance, and Alec, who knew something of
heroism, recognised the greatness of her heart. Of
late he had been more than once to see that portrait of
*Diana of the Uplands,* in which he, too, found the gra-
cious healthiness of Lucy Allerton; but now she seemed
like some sad queen, English to the very bones, who
bore with a royal dignity an intolerable grief, and yet
by the magnificence of her spirit turned into something
wholly beautiful.

' You must forgive me for forcing myself upon you
to-day,' he said slowly. ' But my time is very short,
and I wanted to speak to you at once.'

' It is very good of you to come.' She was embarrassed, and did not know what exactly to say. ' I am
always very glad to see you.'

He looked at her steadily, as though he were turning
over in his mind her commonplace words. She smiled.

' I wanted to thank you for your great kindness to
me during these two or three weeks. You've been very
good to me, and you've helped me to bear all that—I've
had to bear.'

' I would do far more for you than that,' he answered.
Suddenly it flashed through her mind why he had
come. Her heart gave a great beat against her chest.
The thought had never entered her head. She sat down
and waited for him to speak. He did not move. There
was a singular immobility about him when something
absorbed his mind.

' I wrote and asked if I might see you alone, because I had something that I wanted to say to you.
I've wanted to say it ever since we were at Court Leys

together, but I was going away—heaven only knows when I shall come back, and perhaps something may happen to me—and I thought it was unfair to you to speak.

He paused. His eyes were fixed upon hers. She waited for him to go on.

' I wanted to ask you if you would marry me.'

She drew a long breath. Her face kept its expression of intense gravity.

' It's very kind and chivalrous of you to suggest it. You mustn't think me ungrateful if I tell you I can't.'

' Why not? ' he asked quietly.

' I must look after my father. If it is any use I shall go and live near the prison.'

' There is no reason why you should not do that if you married me.'

She shook her head.

' No, I must be free. As soon as my father is released I must be ready to live with him. And I can't take an honest man's name. It looks as if I were running away from my own and taking shelter elsewhere.'

She hesitated for a while, since it made her very shy to say what she had in mind. When she spoke it was in a low and trembling voice.

' You don't know how proud I was of my name and my family. For centuries they've been honest, decent people, and I felt that we'd had a part in the making of England. And now I feel utterly ashamed. Dick Lomas laughed at me because I was so proud of my family. I daresay I was stupid. I never paid much attention to rank and that kind of thing, but it did seem to

me that family was different. I've seen my father, and
he simply doesn't realise for a moment that he's done
something horribly mean and shameful. There must
be some taint in our nature. I couldn't marry you; I
should be afraid that my children would inherit the rot-
tenness of my blood.'

He listened to what she said. Then he went up to
her and put his hands on her shoulders. His calmness,
and the steadiness of his voice seemed to quieten her.

'I think you will be able to help your father and
George better if you are my wife. I'm afraid your position will be very difficult. Won't you give me the great
happiness of helping you?'

'We must stand on our own feet. I'm very grateful,
but you can do nothing for us.'

'I'm very awkward and stupid, I don't know how to
say what I want to. I think I loved you from that
first day at Court Leys. I did not understand then
what had happened; I suddenly felt that something new
and strange had come into my life. And day by day
I loved you more, and then it took up my whole soul.
I've never loved anyone but you. I never can love
anyone but you. I've been looking for you all my
life.'

She could not stand the look of his eyes, and she cast
hers down. He saw the exquisite shadow of her eyelashes on her cheek.

'But I didn't dare say anything to you then. Even
if you had cared for me, it seemed unfair to bind you to
me when I was starting on this expedition. But now
I must speak. I go in a week. It would give me
so much strength and courage if I knew that I had your
love. I love you with all my heart.'

She looked up at him now, and her eyes were shining with tears, but they were not the tears of a hopeless pain.

'I can't marry you now. It would be unfair to you. I owe myself entirely to my father.'

He dropped his hands from her shoulders and stepped back.

'It must be as you will.'

'But don't think I'm ungrateful,' she said. 'I'm so proud that I have your love. It seems to lift me up from the depths. You don't know how much good you have done me.'

'I wanted to help you, and you will let me do nothing for you.'

On a sudden a thought flashed through her. She gave a little cry of amazement, for here was the solution of her greatest difficulty.

'Yes, you can do something for me. Will you take George with you?'

'George?'

He remained silent for a moment, while he considered the proposition.

'I can trust him in your hands. You will make a good and a strong man of him. Oh, won't you give him this chance of washing out the stain that is on our name?'

'Do you know that he will have to undergo hunger and thirst and every kind of hardship? It's not a picnic that I'm going on.'

'I'm willing that he should undergo everything. The cause is splendid. His self-respect is wavering in the balance. If he gets to noble work he will feel himself a man.'

'There will be a good deal of fighting.  It has seemed foolish to dwell on the dangers that await me, but I do realise that they are greater than I have ever faced before.  This time it is win or die.'

'The dangers can be no greater than those his ancestors have taken cheerfully.'

'He may be wounded or killed.'

Lucy hesitated for an instant.  The words she uttered came from unmoving lips.

'If he dies a brave man's death I can ask for nothing more.'

Alec smiled at her infinite courage.  He was immensely proud of her.

'Then tell him that I shall be glad to take him.'

'May I call him now?'

Alec nodded.  She rang the bell and told the servant who came that she wished to see her brother.  George came in.  The strain of the last fortnight, the horrible shock of his father's conviction, had told on him far more than on Lucy.  He looked worn and ill.  He was broken down with shame.  The corners of his mouth drooped querulously, and his handsome face bore an expression of utter misery.  Alec looked at him steadily.  He felt infinite pity for his youth, and there was a charm of manner about him, a way of appealing for sympathy, which touched the strong man.  He wondered what character the boy had.  His heart went out to him, and he loved him already because he was Lucy's brother.

'George, Mr. MacKenzie has offered to take you with him to Africa,' she said eagerly.  'Will you go?'

'I'll go anywhere so long as I can get out of this beastly country,' he answered wearily.  'I feel people are looking at me in the street when I go out, and they're saying to one another: there's the son of that swindling rotter who was sentenced to seven years.'

He wiped the palms of his hands with his handkerchief.

' I don't mind what I do. I can't go back to Oxford; no one would speak to me. There's nothing I can do in England at all. I wish to God I were dead.'

' George, don't say that.'

' It's all very well for you. You're a girl, and it doesn't matter. Do you suppose anyone would trust me with sixpence now? Oh, how could he? How could he?'

' You must try and forget it, George,' said Lucy, gently.

The boy pulled himself together and gave Alec a charming smile.

' It's awfully ripping of you to take pity on me.'

' I want you to know before you decide that you'll have to rough it all the time. It'll be hard and dangerous work.'

' Well, as far as I'm concerned it's Hobson's choice, isn't it?' he answered, bitterly.

Alec held out his hand, with one of his rare, quiet smiles.

' I hope we shall pull well together and be good friends.'

' And when you come back, George, everything will be over. I wish I were a man so that I might go with you. I wish I had your chance. You've got everything before you, George. I think no man has ever had such an opportunity. All our hope is in you. I want to be proud of you. All my self-respect depends on you. I want you to distinguish yourself, so that I may feel once more honest and strong and clean.'

Her voice was trembling with a deep emotion, and George, quick to respond, flushed.

'I am a selfish beast,' he cried. 'I've been thinking of myself all the time. I've never given a thought to you.'

'I don't want you to: I only want you to be brave and honest and steadfast.'

The tears came to his eyes, and he put his arms around her neck. He nestled against her heart as a child might have done.

'It'll be awfully hard to leave you, Lucy.'

'It'll be harder for me, dear, because you will be doing great and heroic things, while I shall be able only to wait and watch. But I want you to go.' Her voice broke, and she spoke almost in a whisper. 'And don't forget that you're going for my sake as well as for your own. If you did anything wrong or disgraceful it would break my heart.'

'I swear to you that you'll never be ashamed of me, Lucy,' he said.

She kissed him and smiled. Alec had watched them silently. His heart was very full.

'But we mustn't be silly and sentimental, or Mr. MacKenzie will think us a pair of fools.' She looked at him gaily. 'We're both very grateful to you.'

'I'm afraid I'm starting almost at once,' he said. 'George must be ready in a week.'

'George can be ready in twenty-four hours if need be,' she answered.

The boy walked towards the window and lit a cigarette. He wanted to steady his nerves.

'I'm afraid I shall be able to see little of you during the next few days,' said Alec. 'I have a great deal to do, and I must run up to Lancashire for the week-end.'

'I'm sorry.'

'Won't you change your mind?'

She shook her head.

'No, I can't do that. I must have complete freedom.'

'And when I come back?'

She smiled delightfully.

'When you come back, if you still care, ask me again.'

'And the answer?'

'The answer perhaps will be different.'

# VIII

A week later Alec MacKenzie and George Allerton started from Charing Cross. They were to go by P. & O. from Marseilles to Aden, and there catch a German boat which would take them to Mombassa. Lady Kelsey was far too distressed to see her nephew off; and Lucy was glad, since it gave her the chance of driving to the station alone with George. She found Dick Lomas and Mrs. Crowley already there. When the train steamed away, Lucy was standing a little apart from the others. She was quite still. She did not even wave her hand, and there was little expression on her face. Mrs. Crowley was crying cheerfully, and she dried her eyes with a tiny handkerchief. Lucy turned to her and thanked her for coming.

' Shall I drive you back in the carriage? ' sobbed Mrs. Crowley.

' I think I'll take a cab, if you don't mind,' Lucy answered quietly. ' Perhaps you'll take Dick.'

She did not bid them good-bye, but walked slowly away.

' How exasperating you people are! ' cried Mrs. Crowley. ' I wanted to throw myself in her arms and have a good cry on the platform. You have no heart.'

Dick walked along by her side, and they got into Mrs. Crowley's carriage. She soliloquised.

' I thank God that I have emotions, and I don't mind if I do show them. I was the only person who cried. I knew I should cry, and I brought three handkerchiefs on purpose. Look at them.' She pulled them out of her bag and thrust them into Dick's hand. 'They're soaking.'

'You say it with triumph,' he smiled.

'I think you're all perfectly heartless. Those two boys were going away for heaven knows how long on a dangerous journey, and they may never come back, and you and Lucy said good-bye to them just as if they were going off for a day's golf. I was the only one who said I was sorry, and that we should miss them dreadfully. I hate this English coldness. When I go to America, it's ten to one nobody comes to see me off, and if anyone does he just nods and says " Good-bye, I hope you'll have a jolly time." '

'Next time you go I will come and hurl myself on the ground, and gnash my teeth and shriek at the top of my voice.'

'Oh, yes, do. And then I'll cry all the way to Liverpool, and I shall have a racking headache and feel quite miserable and happy.'

Dick meditated for a moment.

'You see, we have an instinctive horror of exhibiting our emotion. I don't know why it is, I suppose training or the inheritance of our sturdy fathers, but we're ashamed to let people see what we feel. But I don't know whether on that account our feelings are any the less keen. Don't you think there's a certain beauty in a grief that forbids itself all expression? You know, I admire Lucy tremendously, and as she came towards us on the platform I thought there was something very fine in her calmness.'

'Fiddlesticks!' said Mrs. Crowley, sharply. 'I should have liked her much better if she had clung to her brother and sobbed and had to be torn away.'

'Did you notice that she left us without even shaking hands? It was a very small omission, but it meant that she was quite absorbed in her grief.'

They reached Mrs. Crowley's tiny house in Norfolk Street, and she asked Dick to come in.

'Sit down and read the paper,' she said, 'while I go and powder my nose.'

Dick made himself comfortable. He blessed the charming woman when a butler of imposing dimensions brought in all that was necessary to make a cocktail. Mrs. Crowley cultivated England like a museum specimen. She had furnished her drawing-room with Chippendale furniture of an exquisite pattern. No chintzes were so smartly calendered as hers, and on the walls were mezzotints of the ladies whom Sir Joshua had painted. The chimney-piece was adorned with Lowestoft china, and on the silver table was a collection of old English spoons. She had chosen her butler because he went so well with the house. His respectability was portentous, his gravity was never disturbed by the shadow of a smile; and Mrs. Crowley treated him as though he were a piece of decoration, with an impertinence that fascinated him. He looked upon her as an outlandish freak, but his heavy British heart was surrendered to her entirely, and he watched over her with a solicitude that amused and touched her.

Dick thought that the little drawing-room was very comfortable, and when Mrs. Crowley returned, after an unconscionable time at the toilet-table, he was in the happiest mood. She gave a rapid glance at the glasses.

'You're a perfect hero,' she said. 'You've waited till I came down to have your cocktail.'

'Richard Lomas, madam, is the soul of courtesy,' he replied, with a flourish. 'Besides, base is the soul that drinks in the morning by himself. At night, in your slippers and without a collar, with a pipe in your mouth and a good book in your hand, a solitary glass of whisky and soda is eminently desirable; but the anteprandial cocktail needs the sparkle of conversation.'

'You seem to be in excellent health,' said Mrs. Crowley.

'I am. Why?'

'I saw in yesterday's paper that your doctor had ordered you to go abroad for the rest of the winter.'

'My doctor received the two guineas, and I wrote the prescription,' returned Dick. 'Do you remember that I explained to you the other day at length my intention of retiring into private life?'

'I do. I strongly disapprove of it.'

'Well, I was convinced that if I relinquished my duties without any excuse people would say I was mad and shut me up in a lunatic asylum. I invented a breakdown in my health, and everything is plain sailing. I've got a pair for the rest of the session, and at the general election the excellent Robert Boulger will step into my unworthy shoes.'

'And supposing you regret the step you've taken?'

'In my youth I imagined, with the romantic fervour of my age, that in life everything was irreparable. That is a delusion. One of the greatest advantages of life is that hardly anything is. One can make ever so many fresh starts. The average man lives long enough for a good many experiments, and it's they that give life its savour.'

'I don't approve of this flippant way you talk of life,' said Mrs. Crowley severely. 'It seems to me something infinitely serious and complicated.'

' That is an illusion of moralists. As a matter of fact, it's merely what you make it. Mine is quite light and simple.'

Mrs. Crowley looked at Dick reflectively.

' I wonder why you never married,' she said.

' I can tell you easily. Because I have a considerable gift for repartee. I discovered in my early youth that men propose not because they want to marry, but because on certain occasions they are entirely at a loss for topics of conversation.'

' It was a momentous discovery,' she smiled.

' No sooner had I made it than I began to cultivate my powers of small talk. I felt that my only chance was to be ready with appropriate subjects at the smallest notice, and I spent a considerable part of my last year at Oxford in studying the best masters.'

' I never noticed that you were particularly brilliant,' murmured Mrs. Crowley, raising her eyebrows.

' I never played for brilliancy, I played for safety. I flatter myself that when prattle was needed, I have never been found wanting. I have met the ingenuousness of sweet seventeen with a few observations on Free Trade, while the haggard efforts of thirty have struggled in vain against a brief exposition of the higher philosophy.'

' When people talk higher philosophy to me I make it a definite rule to blush,' said Mrs. Crowley.

' The skittish widow of uncertain age has retired in disorder before a complete acquaintance with the Restoration dramatists, and I have frequently routed the serious spinster with religious leanings by my remarkable knowledge of the results of missionary endeavour in Central Africa. Once a dowager sought to ask me my intentions, but I flung at her astonished head an article from the Encyclopedia Brittanica. An American *divorcée* swooned when I poured into her shell-like ear a few facts about the McKinley Tariff. These are only my serious efforts. I need not tell you how often I have evaded a flash of the eyes by an epigram, or ignored a sigh by an apt quotation from the poets.'

' I don't believe a word you say,' retorted Mrs. Crowley. ' I believe you never married for the simple reason that nobody would have you.'

' Do me the justice to acknowledge that I'm the only man who's known you for ten days without being tempted by those coal-mines of yours in Pennsylvania to offer you his hand and heart.'

' I don't believe the coal has anything to do with it,' answered Mrs. Crowley. ' I put it down entirely to my very considerable personal attractions.'

Dick looked at the time and found that the cocktail had given him an appetite. He asked Mrs. Crowley if she would lunch with him, and gaily they set out for a fashionable restaurant. Neither of them gave a thought to Alec and George speeding towards the unknown, nor to Lucy shut up in her room, given over to utter misery.

For Lucy it was the first of many dreary days. Dick went to Naples, and enjoying his new-won idleness, did not even write to her. Mrs. Crowley, after deciding on a trip to Egypt, was called to America by the illness of a sister; and Lady Kelsey, unable to stand the rigour of a Northern winter, set out for Nice. Lucy refused to accompany her. Though she knew it would be impossible to see her father, she could not bear to leave England; she could not face the gay people who thronged the Riviera, while he was bound to degrading tasks. The luxury of her own life horrified her when she compared it with his hard fare; and she could not look upon the comfortable rooms she lived in, with their delicate refinements, without thinking of the bare cell to which he was confined. Lucy was glad to be alone.

She went nowhere, but passed her days in solitude, striving to acquire peace of mind; she took long walks in the parks with her dogs, and spent much time in the picture galleries. Without realising the effect they had upon her, she felt vaguely the calming influence of beautiful things; often she would sit in the National Gallery before some royal picture, and the joy of it would fill her soul with quiet relief. Sometimes she would go to those majestic statues that decorated the pediment of the Parthenon, and the tears welled up in her clear eyes as she thanked the gods for the graciousness of their peace. She did not often listen to music, for then she could remain no longer mistress of her emotions; the tumultuous sounds of a symphony, the final anguish of *Tristan,* made vain all her efforts at self-control; and when she got home, she could only throw herself on her bed and weep passionately.

In reading she found her greatest solace. Many things that Alec had said returned dimly to her memory; and she began to read the Greek writers who had so profoundly affected him. She found a translation of Euripides which gave her some impression of the original, and her constant mood was answered by those old, exquisite tragedies. The complexity of that great poet, his doubt, despair, and his love of beauty, spoke to her heart as no modern writer could; and in the study of those sad deeds, in which men seemed always playthings of the fates, she found a relief to her own keen sorrow. She did not reason it out with herself, but almost unconsciously the thought came to her that the slings and arrows of the gods could be transformed into beauty by resignation and courage. Nothing was irreparable but a man's own weakness, and even in shame, disaster, and poverty, it was possible to lead a life that was not without grandeur. The man who was beaten to the ground by an outrageous fortune might be a finer thing than the unseeing, cruel powers that conquered him.

It was in this wise that Lucy battled with the intolerable shame that oppressed her. In that quiet corner of Hampshire in which her early years had been spent, among the memories of her dead kindred, the pride of her race had grown to unreasonable proportions; and now in the reaction she was terrified lest its decadence was in her, too, and in George. She could do nothing but suffer whatever pain it pleased the gods to send; but George was a man. In him were placed all her hopes. But now and again wild panic seized her. Then the agony was too great to bear, and she pressed her hands to her eyes in order to drive away the hateful thought: what if George failed her? She knew well enough that he had his father's engaging ways and his father's handsome face; but his father had had a smile as frank and a charm as great. What if with the son, too, they betokened only insincerity and weakness? A malicious devil whispered in her ear that now and again she had averted her eyes in order not to see George do things she hated. But it was youth that drove him. She had taken care to keep from him knowledge of the sordid struggles that occupied her, and how could she wonder if he was reckless and uncaring? She would not doubt him, she could not doubt him, for if anything went wrong with him there was no hope left. She could only cease to believe in herself.

When Lucy was allowed to write to her father, she set herself to cheer him. The thought that over five years must elapse before she would have him by her side once more, paralysed her pen; but she would not allow herself to be discouraged. And she sought to give courage to him. She wanted him to see that her love was undiminished, and that he could count on it. Presently she received a letter from him. After a few weeks, the unaccustomed food, the change of life, had told upon him; and a general breakdown in his health had driven him into the infirmary. Lucy was thankful for the respite which his illness afforded. It must be a little less dreary in a prison hospital than in a prison cell.

A letter came from George, and another from Alec. Alec's was brief, telling of their journey down the Red Sea and their arrival at Mombassa; it was abrupt and awkward, making no reference to his love, or to the engagement which she had almost promised to make when he returned. He began and ended quite formally. George, apparently in the best of spirits, wrote as he always did, in a boyish, inconsequent fashion. His letter was filled with slang and gave no news. There was little to show that it was written from Mombassa, on the verge of a dangerous expedition into the interior, rather than from Oxford on the eve of a football match. But she read them over and over again. They were very matter of fact, and she smiled as she thought of Julia Crowley's indignation if she had seen them.

From her recollection of Alec's words, Lucy tried to make out the scene that first met her brother's eyes. She seemed to stand by his side, leaning over the rail, as the ship approached the harbour. The sea was blue with a blue she had never seen, and the sky was like an inverted bowl of copper. The low shore, covered with bush, stretched away in the distance; a line of waves was breaking on the reef. They came in sight of the island of Mombassa, with the overgrown ruins of a battery that had once commanded the entrance; and there were white-roofed houses, with deep verandas, which stood in little clearings with coral cliffs below them. On the opposite shore thick groves of palm-trees rose with their singular, melancholy beauty. Then as the channel narrowed, they passed an old Portuguese fort which carried the mind back to the bold adventurers who had first sailed those distant seas, and directly afterwards a mass of white buildings that reached to the edge of the lapping waves. They saw the huts of the native town, wattled and thatched, nestling close together; and below them was a fleet of native craft. On the jetty was the African crowd, shouting and jostling, some half-naked, and some strangely clad, Arabs from across the sea, Swahilis, and here and there a native from the interior.

In course of time other letters came from George, but Alec wrote no more. The days passed slowly. Lady Kelsey returned from the Riviera. Dick came back from Naples to enjoy the pleasures of the London season. He appeared thoroughly to enjoy his idleness, signally falsifying the predictions of those who had told him that it was impossible to be happy without regular work. Mrs. Crowley settled down once more in her house in Norfolk Street. During her absence she had written reams by every post to Lucy, and Lucy had looked forward very much to seeing her again. The little American was almost the only one of her friends with whom she did not feel shy. The apartness which her nationality gave her, made Mrs. Crowley more easy to talk to. She was too fond of Lucy to pity her. The general election came before it was expected, and Robert Boulger succeeded to the seat which Dick Lomas was only too glad to vacate. Bobbie was very charming. He surrounded Lucy with a protecting care, and she could not fail to be touched by his entire devotion. When he thought she had recovered somewhat from the first blow of her father's sentence, he sent her a letter in which once more he besought her to marry him. She was grateful to him for having chosen that method of expressing himself, for it seemed possible in writing to tell him with greater tenderness that if she could not accept his love she deeply valued his affection.

It seemed to Lucy that the life she led in London, or at Lady Kelsey's house on the river, was no more than a dream. She was but a figure in the procession of shadow pictures cast on a sheet in a fair, and nothing that she did signified. Her spirit was away in the heart of Africa, and by a vehement effort of her fancy she sought to see what each day her friend and her brother were doing.

Now they had long left the railway and such civilisation as was to be found in the lands where white men had already made their mark. She knew the exultation which Alec felt, and the thrill of independence, when he left behind him all traces of it. He held himself more proudly because he knew that thenceforward he must rely on his own resources, and success or failure depended only on himself.

Often as she lay awake and saw the ghostly dawn steal across the sky, she seemed borne to the African camp, where the break of day, like a gust of wind in a field of ripe corn, brought a sudden stir among the sleepers. Alec had described to her so minutely the changing scene that she was able to bring it vividly before her eyes. She saw him come out of his tent, in heavy boots, buckling on his belt. He wore knee-breeches and a pith helmet, and he was more bronzed than when she had bidden him farewell. He gave the order to the headman of the caravan to take up the loads. At the word there was a rush from all parts of the camp; each porter seized his load, carrying it off to lash on his mat and his cooking-pot, and then, sitting upon it, ate a few grains of roasted maize or the remains of last night's game. And as the sun appeared above the horizon, Alec, as was his custom, led the way, followed by a few *askari*. A band of natives struck up a strange and musical chant, and the camp, but now a scene of busy life, was deserted. The smouldering fires died out with the rising sun, and the silent life of the forest replaced the chatter and the hum of human kind. Giant beetles came from every quarter and carried away pieces of offal; small shy beasts stole out to gnaw the white bones upon which savage teeth had left but little; a gaunt hyena, with suspicious looks, snatched at a bone and dashed back into the jungle. Vultures settled down heavily, and with deliberate air sought out the foulest refuse.

Then Lucy followed Alec upon his march, with his fighting men and his long string of porters. They went along a narrow track, pushing their way through bushes and thorns, or tall rank grass, sometimes with difficulty forcing through elephant reeds which closed over their heads and showered the cold dew down on their faces. Sometimes they passed through villages, with rich soil and extensive population; sometimes they plunged into heavy forests of gigantic trees, festooned with creepers, where the silence was unbroken even by the footfall of the traveller on the bottomless carpet of leaves; sometimes they traversed vast swamps, hurrying to avoid the deadly fever, and sometimes scrub jungles, in which as far as the eye could reach was a forest of cactus and thorn bush. Sometimes they made their way through grassy uplands with trees as splendid as those of an English park, and sometimes they toiled painfully along a game-track that ran by the bank of a swift-rushing river.

At midday a halt was called. The caravan had opened out by then; men who were sick or had stopped to adjust a load, others who were weak or lazy, had lagged behind; but at last they were all there; and the rear guard, perhaps with George in charge of it, whose orders were on no account to allow a single man to remain behind them, reported that no one was missing. During the heat of noon they made fires and cooked food. Presently they set off once more and marched till sundown.

When they reached the place which had been fixed on for camping, a couple of shots were fired as signals;

and soon the natives, men and women, began to stream
in with little baskets of grain or flour, with potatoes
and chickens, and perhaps a pot or two of honey. Very
quickly the tents were pitched, the bed gear arranged,
the loads counted and stacked. The party whose duty it
was to construct the *zeriba* cut down boughs and dragged
them in to form a fence. Each little band of men se-
lected the site for their bivouac; one went off to collect
materials to build the huts, another to draw water, a
third for firewood and stones, on which to place the
cooking-pot. At sunset the headman blew his whistle
and asked if all were present. A lusty chorus replied.
He reported to his chief and received the orders for the
next day's march.

Alec had told Lucy that from the cry that goes up in
answer to the headman's whistle, you could always gauge
the spirit of the men. If game had been shot, or from
scarcity the caravan had come to a land of plenty, there
was a perfect babel of voices. But if the march had
been long and hard, or if food had been issued for a
number of days, of which this was the last, isolated
voices replied; and perhaps one, bolder than the rest,
cried out: I am hungry.

Then Alec and George, and the others sat down to
their evening meal, while the porters, in little parties,
were grouped around their huge pots of porridge. A
little chat, a smoke, an exchange of sporting anecdotes,
and the white men turned in. And Alec, gazing on
the embers of his camp fire was alone with his thoughts:
the silence of the night was upon him, and he looked
up at the stars that shone in their countless myriads in
the blue African sky. Lucy got up and stood at her
open window. She, too, looked up at the sky, and she

thought that she saw the same stars as he did. Now
in that last half hour, free from the burden of the day,
with everyone at rest, he could give himself over to
his thoughts, and his thoughts surely were of her.

During the months that had passed since Alec left
England, Lucy's love had grown. In her solitude there
was nothing else to give brightness to her life, and little
by little it filled her heart. Her nature was so strong
that she could do nothing by half measures, and it was
with a feeling of extreme relief that she surrendered
herself to this overwhelming passion. It seemed to her
that she was growing in a different direction. The
yearning of her soul for someone on whom to lean was
satisfied at last. Hitherto the only instincts that had
been fostered in her were those that had been useful to
her father and George; they had needed her courage
and her self-reliance. It was very comfortable to depend entirely upon Alec's love. Here she could be weak,
here she could find a greater strength which made her
own seem puny. Lucy's thoughts were absorbed in the
man whom really she knew so little. She exulted in
his unselfish striving and in his firmness of purpose,
and when she compared herself with him she felt unworthy. She treasured every recollection she had of
him. She went over in her mind all that she had heard
him say, and reconstructed the conversations they had
had together. She walked where they had walked, re-
membering how the sky had looked on those days and
what flowers then bloomed in the parks; she visited
the galleries they had seen in one another's company,
and stood before the pictures which he had lingered at.
And notwithstanding all there was to torment and

humiliate her, she was happy.  Something had come into her life which made all else tolerable.  It was easy to bear the extremity of grief when he loved her.

After a long time Dick received a letter from Alec. MacKenzie was not a good letter-writer.  He had no gift of self-expression, and when he had a pen in his hand seemed to be seized with an invincible shyness. The letter was dry and wooden.  It was dated from the last trading-station before he set out into the wild country which was to be the scene of his operations. It said that hitherto everything had gone well with him, and the white men, but for fever occasionally, were bearing the climate well.  One, named Macinnery, had made a nuisance of himself, and had been sent back to the coast.  Alec gave no reasons for this step.  He had been busy making the final arrangements.  A company had been formed, the North East Africa Trading Company, to exploit the commercial possibilities of these unworked districts, and a charter had been given them; but the unsettled state of the land had so hampered them that the directors had gladly accepted Alec's offer to join their forces with his, and the traders at their stations had been instructed to take service under him.  This increased the white men under his command to sixteen.  He had drilled the Swahilis whom he had brought from the coast, and given them guns, so that he had now an armed force of four hundred men.  He was collecting levies from the native tribes, and he gave the outlandish names of the chiefs, armed with spears, who were to accompany him.  The power of Mohammed the Lame was on the wane; for, during the three months which Alec had spent in England, an illness had seized him, which the natives asserted was a magic spell cast on him by one of his wives; and a son of his, taking advantage of this, had revolted and fortified himself in a stockade. The dying Sultan had taken the field against him, and this division of forces made Alec's position immeasurably stronger.

Dick handed Lucy the letter, and watched her while she read it.

' He says nothing about George,' he said.

' He's evidently quite well.'

Though it seemed strange that Alec made no mention of the boy, Dick said no more. Lucy appeared to be satisfied, and that was the chief thing. But he could not rid his mind of a certain uneasiness. He had received with misgiving Lucy's plan that George should accompany Alec. He could not help wondering whether those frank blue eyes and that facile smile did not conceal a nature as shallow as Fred Allerton's. But, after all, it was the boy's only chance, and he must take it.

Then an immense silence followed. Alec disappeared into those unknown countries as a man disappears into the night, and no more was heard of him. None knew how he fared. Not even a rumour reached the coast of success or failure. When he had crossed the mountains that divided the British protectorate from the lands that were to all intents independent, he vanished with his followers from human ken. The months passed, and there was nothing. It was a year now since he had arrived at Mombassa, then it was a year since the last letter had come from him. It was only possible to guess that behind those gaunt rocks fierce battles were fought, new lands explored, and the slavers beaten back foot by foot. Dick sought to persuade himself that the silence was encouraging, for it seemed to him that if the expedition had been cut to pieces the rejoicing of the Arabs would have spread itself abroad, and some news of a disaster would have travelled through Somaliland to the coast, or been carried by traders to Zanzibar. He made frequent inquiries at the Foreign Office, but there, too, nothing was known. The darkness had fallen upon them.

But Lucy suffered neither from anxiety nor fear. She had an immense confidence in Alec, and she believed in his strength, his courage, and his star. He had told her that he would not return till he had accomplished his task, and she expected to hear nothing till he had brought it to a triumphant conclusion. She did her little to help him. For at length the directors of the North East Africa Trading Company, growing anxious, proposed to get a question asked in Parliament, or to start an outcry in the newspapers which should oblige the government to send out a force to relieve Alec if he were in difficulties, or avenge him if he were dead. But Lucy knew that there was nothing Alec dreaded more than official interference. He was convinced that if this work could be done at all, he alone could do it; and she influenced Robert Boulger and Dick Lomas to use such means as they could to prevent anything from being done. She was certain that all Alec needed was time and a free hand.

# IX

BUT the monotonous round of Lucy's life, with its
dreams and its fond imaginings, was interrupted by
news of a different character.  An official letter came
to her from Parkhurst to say that the grave state of her
father's health had decided the authorities to remit the
rest of his sentence, and he would be set free the next
day but one at eight o'clock in the morning.  She knew
not whether to feel relief or sorrow; for if she was
thankful that the wretched man's long torture was
ended, she could not but realise that his liberty was
given him only because he was dying.  Mercy had been
shown him, and Fred Allerton, in sight of a freedom
from which no human laws could bar him, was given
up to die among those who loved him.

Lucy went down immediately to the Isle of Wight,
and there engaged rooms in the house of a woman who
had formerly served her at Hamlyn's Purlieu.

It was midwinter, and a cold drizzle was falling
when she waited for him at the prison gates.  Three
years had passed since they had parted.  She took him
in her arms and kissed him silently.  Her heart was
too full for words.  A carriage was waiting for them,
and she drove to the lodging-house; breakfast was ready,
and Lucy had seen that good things which he liked
should be ready for him to eat.  Fred Allerton looked
wistfully at the clean table-cloth, and at the flowers
and the dainty scones; but he shook his head.  He did

not speak, and the tears ran slowly down his cheeks. He sank wearily into a chair. Lucy tried to induce him to eat; she brought him a cup of tea, but he put it away. He looked at her with haggard, bloodshot eyes.

'Give me the flowers,' he muttered.

They were his first words. There was a large bowl of daffodils in the middle of the table, and she took them out of the water, deftly dried their stalks, and gave them to him. He took them with trembling hands and pressed them to his heart, then he buried his face in them, and the tears ran afresh, bedewing the yellow flowers.

Lucy put her arm around her father's neck and placed her cheek against his.

'Don't, father,' she whispered. 'You must try and forget.'

He leaned back, exhausted, and the pretty flowers fell at his feet.

'You know why they've let me out?' he said.

She kissed him, but did not answer.

'I'm so glad that we're together again,' she murmured.

'It's because I'm going to die.'

'No, you mustn't die. In a little while you'll get strong again. You have many years before you, and you'll be very happy.'

He gave her a long, searching look; and when he spoke, his voice had a hollowness in it that was strangely terrifying.

'Do you think I want to live?'

The pain seemed almost greater than Lucy could bear, and for a moment she had to remain silent so that her voice might grow steady.

' You must live for my sake.'

' Don't you hate me? ' he asked.

' No, I love you more than I ever did. I shall never cease to love you.'

' I suppose no one would marry you while I was in prison.'

His remark was so inconsequent that Lucy found nothing to say. He gave a bitter, short laugh.

' I ought to have shot myself. Then people would have forgotten all about it, and you might have had a chance. Why didn't you marry Bobbie? '

' I haven't wanted to marry.'

He was so tired that he could only speak a little at a time, and now he closed his eyes. Lucy thought that he was dozing, and began to pick up the fallen flowers. But he noticed what she was doing.

' Let me hold them,' he moaned, with the pleading quaver of a sick child.

As she gave them to him once more, he took her hands and began to caress them.

' The only thing for me is to hurry up and finish with life. I'm in the way. Nobody wants me, and I shall only be a burden. I didn't want them to let me go. I wanted to die there quietly.'

Lucy sighed deeply. She hardly recognised her father in the bent, broken man who was sitting beside her. He had aged very much and seemed now to be an old man, but it was a premature aging, and there was a horror in it as of a process contrary to nature. He was very thin, and his hands trembled constantly. Most of his teeth had gone; his cheeks were sunken, and he mumbled his words so that it was difficult to distinguish them. There was no light in his eyes, and his short

hair was quite white. Now and again he was shaken
with a racking cough, and this was followed by an attack of such pain in his heart that it was anguish even
to watch it. The room was warm, but he shivered with
cold and cowered over the roaring fire.

When the doctor whom Lucy had sent for, saw him,
he could only shrug his shoulders.

'I'm afraid nothing can be done,' he said. 'His
heart is all wrong, and he's thoroughly broken up.'

'Is there no chance of recovery?'

'I'm afraid all we can do is to alleviate the pain.'

'And how long can he live?'

'It's impossible to say. He may die to-morrow, he
may last six months.'

The doctor was an old man, and his heart was
touched by the sight of Lucy's grief. He had seen more
cases than one of this kind.

'He doesn't want to live. It will be a mercy when
death releases him.'

Lucy did not answer. When she returned to her
father, she could not speak. He was apathetic and did
not ask what the doctor had said. Lady Kelsey, hating the thought of Lucy and her father living amid
the discomfort of furnished lodgings, had written to
offer the use of her house in Charles Street; and Mrs.
Crowley, in case they wanted complete solitude, had put
Court Leys at their disposal. Lucy waited a few days
to see whether her father grew stronger, but no change
was apparent in him, and it seemed necessary at last
to make some decision. She put before him the alternative plans, but he would have none of them.

'Then would you rather stay here?' she said.

He looked at the fire and did not answer. Lucy

thought the sense of her question had escaped him, for often it appeared to her that his mind wandered. She was on the point of repeating it when he spoke.

'I want to go back to the Purlieu.'

Lucy stifled a gasp of dismay. She stared at the wretched man. Had he forgotten? He thought that the house of his fathers was his still; and all that had parted him from it was gone from his memory. How could she tell him?

'I want to die in my own home,' he faltered.

Lucy was in a turmoil of anxiety. She must make some reply. What he asked was impossible, and yet it was cruel to tell him the whole truth.

'There are people living there,' she answered.

'Are there?' he said, indifferently.

He looked at the fire still. The silence was dreadful.

'When can we go?' he said at last. 'I want to get there quickly.'

Lucy hesitated.

'We shall have to go into rooms.'

'I don't mind.'

He seemed to take everything as a matter of course. It was clear that he had forgotten the catastrophe that had parted him from Hamlyn's Purlieu, and yet, strangely, he asked no questions. Lucy was tortured by the thought of revisiting the place she loved so well. She had been able to deaden her passionate regret only by keeping her mind steadfastly averted from all thoughts of it, and now she must actually go there. The old wounds would be opened. But it was impossible to refuse, and she set about making the necessary arrangements. The rector, who had been given the living by Fred Allerton, was an old friend, and Lucy knew that she could trust in his affection. She wrote and told him that her father was dying and had set his heart on seeing once more his old home. She asked him to find rooms in one of the cottages. She did not mind how small nor how humble they were. The rector answered by telegram. He begged Lucy to bring her father to stay with him. She would be more comfortable than in lodgings, and, since he was a bachelor, there was plenty of room in the large rectory. Lucy, immensely touched by his kindness, gratefully accepted the invitation.

Next day they took the short journey across the Solent.

The rector had been a don, and Fred Allerton had offered him the living in accordance with the family tradition that required a man of attainments to live in the neighbouring rectory. He had been there now for many years, a spare, grey-haired, gentle creature, who lived the life of a recluse in that distant village, doing his duty exactly, but given over for the most part to his beloved books. He seldom went away. The monotony of his daily round was broken only by the occasional receipt of a parcel of musty volumes, which he had ordered to be bought for him at some sale. He was a man of varied learning, full of remote information, eccentric from his solitariness, but with a great sweetness of nature. His life was simple, and his wants were few.

In this house, in rooms lined from floor to ceiling with old books, Lucy and her father took up their abode. It seemed that Fred Allerton had been kept up only by the desire to get back to his native place, for he had no sooner arrived than he grew much worse.

Lucy was busily occupied with nursing him and could give no time to the regrets which she had imagined would assail her. She spent long hours in her father's room; and while he dozed, half-comatose, the kindly parson sat by the window and read to her in a low voice from queer, forgotten works.

One day Allerton appeared to be far better. For a week he had wandered much in his mind, and more than once Lucy had suspected that the end was near; but now he was singularly lucid. He wanted to get up, and Lucy felt it would be brutal to balk any wish he had. He asked if he might go out. The day was fine and warm. It was February, and there was a feeling in the air as if the spring were at hand. In sheltered places the snowdrops and the crocuses gave the garden the blitheness of an Italian picture; and you felt that on that multi-coloured floor might fitly trip the delicate angels of Messer Perugino. The rector had an old pony-chaise, in which he was used to visit his parishioners, and in this all three drove out.

' Let us go down to the marshes,' said Allerton.

They drove slowly along the winding road till they came to the broad salt marshes. Beyond glittered the placid sea. There was no wind. Near them a cow looked up from her grazing and lazily whisked her tail. Lucy's heart began to beat more quickly. She felt that her father, too, looked upon that scene as the most typical of his home. Other places had broad acres and fine trees, other places had forest land and purple heather, but there was something in those green flats that made them seem peculiarly their own. She took her father's hand, and silently their eyes looked onwards. A more peaceful look came into Fred Allerton's worn face, and the sigh that broke from him was not altogether of pain. Lucy prayed that it might still remain hidden from him that those fair, broad fields were his no longer.

That night. she had an intuition that death was at hand. Fred Allerton was very silent. Since his release from prison he had spoken barely a dozen sentences a day, and nothing served to wake him from his lethargy. But there was a curious restlessness about him now, and he would not go to bed. He sat in an armchair, and begged them to draw it near the window. The sky was cloudless, and the moon shone brightly. Fred Allerton could see the great old elms that surrounded Hamlyn's Purlieu; and his eyes were fixed steadily upon them. Lucy saw them, too, and she thought sadly of the garden which she had loved so well, and of the dear trees which old masters of the place had tended so lovingly. Her heart filled when she thought of the grey stone house and its happy, spacious rooms.

Suddenly there was a sound, and she looked up quickly. Her father's head had fallen back, and he was breathing with a strange noisiness. She called her friend.

'I think the end has come at last,' she said.

'Would you like me to fetch the doctor?'

'It will be useless.'

The rector looked at the man's wan face, lit dimly by the light of the shaded lamp, and falling on his knees, began to recite the prayers for the dying. A shiver passed through Lucy. In the farmyard a cock crew, and in the distance another cock answered cheerily. Lucy put her hand on the good rector's shoulder.

' It's all over,' she whispered.

She bent down and kissed her father's eyes.

A week later Lucy took a walk by the seashore. They had buried Fred Allerton three days before among the ancestors whom he had dishonoured. It was a lonely funeral, for Lucy had asked Robert Boulger, her only friend then in England, not to come; and she was the solitary mourner. The coffin was lowered into the grave, and the rector read the sad, beautiful words of the burial service. She could not grieve. Her father was at peace. She could only hope that his errors and his crimes would be soon forgotten; and perhaps those who had known him would remember then that he had been a charming friend, and a clever, sympathetic companion. It was little enough in all conscience that Lucy asked.

On the morrow she was leaving the roof of the hospitable parson. Surmising her wish to walk alone once more through the country which was so dear to her, he had not offered his company. Lucy's heart was full of sadness, but there was a certain peace in it, too; the peace of her father's death had entered into her, and she experienced a new feeling, the feeling of resignation.

Now her mind was set upon the future, and she was filled with hope. She stood by the water's edge, looking upon the sea as three years before, when she was staying at Court Leys, she had looked upon the sea that washed the shores of Kent. Many things had passed since then, and many griefs had fallen upon her; but for all that she was happier than then; since on that distant day—and it seemed ages ago—there had been scarcely a ray of brightness in her life, and now she had a great love which made every burden light.

Low clouds hung upon the sky, and on the horizon the greyness of the heavens mingled with the greyness of the sea. She looked into the distance with longing eyes. Now all her life was set upon that far-off corner of unknown Africa, where Alec and George were doing great deeds. She wondered what was the meaning of the silence which had covered them so long.

' Oh, if I could only see,' she murmured.

She sent her spirit upon that vast journey, trying to pierce the realms of space, but her spirit came back baffled. She could not know what they were at.

If Lucy's love had been able to bridge the abyss that parted them, if in some miraculous way she had been able to see what actions they did at that time, she would have witnessed a greater tragedy than any which she had yet seen.

# X

THE night was stormy and dark. The rain was falling, and the ground in Alec's camp was heavy with mud.
The faithful Swahilis whom he had brought from the
coast, chattered with cold around their fires; and the
sentries shivered at their posts. It was a night that
took the spirit out of a man and made all that he
longed for seem vain and trifling. In Alec's tent the
water was streaming. Great rats ran about boldly. The
stout canvas bellied before each gust of wind, and the
cordage creaked, so that one might have thought the
whole thing would be blown clean away. The tent was
unusually crowded, though there was in it nothing but
Alec's bed, covered with a mosquito-curtain, a fold-
ing table, with a couple of garden chairs, and the
cases which contained his more precious belongings.
A small tarpaulin on the floor squelched as one walked
on it.

On one of the chairs a man sat, asleep, with his face
resting on his arms. His gun was on the table in front
of him. It was Walker, a young man who had been
freshly sent out to take charge of the North East
Africa Company's most northerly station, and had
joined Alec's expedition a year before, taking the place
of an older man who had gone home on leave. He was
a funny, fat person with a round face and a comic
manner, the most unexpected sort of fellow to find in
the wildest of African districts; and he was eminently

unsuited for the life he led. He had come into a little money on attaining his majority, and this he had set himself resolutely to squander in every unprofitable way that occurred to him. When his last penny was spent he had been offered a post by a friend of his family's, who happened to be a director of the company, and had accepted it as his only refuge from starvation. Adversity had not been able to affect his happy nature. He was always cheerful no matter what difficulties he was in, and neither regretted the follies of his past nor repined over the hardships which had followed them. Alec had taken a great liking to him. A silent man himself, he found a certain relaxation in people like Dick Lomas and Walker who talked incessantly; and the young man's simplicity, his constant surprise at the difference between Africa and Mayfaïr, never ceased to divert him.

Presently Adamson came into the tent. He was the Scotch doctor who had already been Alec's companion on two of his expeditions; and there was a firm friendship between them. He was an Edinburgh man, with a slow drawl and a pawky humour, a great big fellow, far and away the largest of any of the whites; and his movements were no less deliberate than his conversation.

'Hulloa, there,' he called out, as he came in.

Walker started to his feet as if he were shot and instinctively seized his gun.

'All right!' laughed the doctor, putting up his hand. 'Don't shoot. It's only me.'

Walker put down the gun and looked at the doctor with a blank face.

'Nerves are a bit groggy, aren't they?'

The fat, cheerful man recovered his wits and gave a short laugh.

'Why the dickens did you wake me up? I was dreaming—dreaming of a high-heeled boot and a neat ankle and the swirl of a white lace petticoat.'

'Were you indeed?' said the doctor, with a slow smile. 'Then it's as well I woke ye up in the middle of it before ye made a fool of yourself. I thought I'd better have a look at your arm.'

'It's one of the most æsthetic sights I know.'

'Your arm?' asked the doctor, drily.

'No,' answered Walker. 'A pretty woman crossing Piccadilly at Swan & Edgar's. You are a savage, my good doctor, and a barbarian; you don't know the care and forethought, the hours of anxious meditation, it has needed to hold up that well-made skirt with the elegant grace that enchants you.'

'I'm afraid you're a very immoral man, Walker,' answered Adamson with his long drawl, smiling.

'Under the present circumstances I have to content myself with condemning the behaviour of the pampered and idle. Just now a camp-bed in a stuffy tent, with mosquitoes buzzing all around me, has allurements greater than those of youth and beauty. And I would not sacrifice my dinner to philander with Helen of Troy herself.'

'You remind me considerably of the fox who said the grapes were sour.'

Walker flung a tin plate at a rat that sat up on its hind legs and looked at him impudently.

'Nonsense. Give me a comfortable bed to sleep in, plenty to eat, tobacco to smoke; and Amaryllis may go hang.'

Dr. Adamson smiled quietly. He found a certain grim humour in the contrast between the difficulties of their situation and Walker's flippant talk.

'Well, let us look at this wound of yours,' he said, getting back to his business. 'Has it been throbbing?'

'Oh, it's not worth bothering about. It'll be as right as rain to-morrow.'

'I'd better dress it all the same.'

Walker took off his coat and rolled up his sleeve. The doctor removed the bandages and looked at the broad flesh wound. He put a fresh dressing on it.

'It looks as healthy as one can expect,' he murmured. 'It's odd what good recoveries men make here when you'd think that everything was against them.'

'You must be pretty well done up, aren't you?' asked Walker, as he watched the doctor neatly cut the lint.

'Just about dropping. But I've a devil of a lot more work to do before I turn in.'

'The thing that amuses me is to think that I came to Africa thinking I was going to have a rattling good time, plenty of shooting and practically nothing to do.'

'You couldn't exactly describe it as a picnic, could you?' answered the doctor. 'But I don't suppose any of us knew it would be such a tough job as it's turned out.'

Walker put his disengaged hand on the doctor's arm.

'My friend, if ever I return to my native land I will never be such a crass and blithering idiot as to give way again to a spirit of adventure. I shall look out for something safe and quiet, and end my days as a wine-merchant's tout or an insurance agent.'

'Ah, that's what we all say when we're out here. But when we're once home again, the recollection of the forest and the plains and the roasting sun and the mosquitoes themselves, come haunting us, and before we know what's up we've booked our passage back to this God-forsaken continent.'

The doctor's words were followed by a silence, which was broken by Walker inconsequently.

'Do you ever think of rumpsteaks?' he asked.

The doctor stared at him blankly, and Walker went on, smiling.

'Sometimes, when we're marching under a sun that just about takes the roof of your head off, and we've had the scantiest and most uncomfortable breakfast possible, I have a vision.'

'I would be able to bandage you better if you only gesticulated with one arm,' said Adamson.

'I see the dining-room of my club, and myself seated at a little table by the window looking out on Piccadilly. And there's a spotless tablecloth, and all the accessories are spick and span. An obsequious menial brings me a rumpsteak, grilled to perfection, and so tender that it melts in the mouth. And he puts by my side a plate of crisp fried potatoes. Can't you smell them? And then a liveried flunky brings me a pewter tankard, and into it he pours a bottle, a large bottle, mind you, of foaming ale.'

'You've certainly added considerably to our cheerfulness, my friend,' said Adamson.

Walker gaily shrugged his fat shoulders.

'I've often been driven to appease the pangs of

raging hunger with a careless epigram, and by the laborious composition of a limerick I have sought to deceive a most unholy thirst.'

He liked that sentence and made up his mind to remember it for future use. The doctor paused for a moment, and then he looked gravely at Walker.

'Last night I thought that you'd made your last joke, old man; and that I had given my last dose of quinine.'

'We were in rather a tight corner, weren't we?'

'This is the third expedition I've been with Mac-Kenzie, and I assure you I've never been so certain that all was over with us.'

Walker permitted himself a philosophical reflection.

'Funny thing death is, you know! When you think of it beforehand, it makes you squirm in your shoes, but when you've just got it face to face it seems so obvious that you forget to be afraid.'

Indeed it was only by a miracle that any of them was alive, and they had all a curious, light-headed feeling from the narrowness of the escape. They had been fighting, with their backs to the wall, and each one had shown what he was made of. A few hours before things had been so serious that now, in the first moment of relief, they sought refuge instinctively in banter. But Dr. Adamson was a solid man, and he wanted to talk the matter out.

'If the Arabs hadn't hesitated to attack us just those ten minutes, we would have been simply wiped out.'

'MacKenzie was all there, wasn't he?'

Walker had the shyness of his nationality in the exhibition of enthusiasm, and he could only express his admiration for the commander of the party in terms of slang.

'He was, my son,' answered Adamson, drily. 'My own impression is, he thought we were done for.'

'What makes you think that?'

'Well, you see, I know him pretty well. When things are going smoothly and everything's flourishing, he's apt to be a bit irritable. He keeps rather to himself, and he doesn't say much unless you do something he don't approve of.'

'And then, by Jove, he comes down on you like a thousand of bricks,' Walker agreed heartily. He remembered observations which Alec on more than one occasion had made to recall him to a sense of his great insignificance. 'It's not for nothing the natives call him *Thunder and Lightning.*'

'But when things look black, his spirits go up like one o'clock,' proceeded the doctor. 'And the worse they are the more cheerful he is.'

'I know. When you're starving with hunger, dead tired and soaked to the skin, and wish you could just lie down and die, MacKenzie simply bubbles over with good humour. It's a hateful characteristic. When I'm in a bad temper, I much prefer everyone else to be in a bad temper, too.'

'These last three days he's been positively hilarious. Yesterday he was cracking jokes with the natives.'

'Scotch jokes,' said Walker. 'I daresay they sound funny in an African dialect.'

'I've never seen him more cheerful,' continued the other, sturdily ignoring the gibe. 'By the Lord Harry, said I to myself, the chief thinks we're in a devil of a bad way.'

Walker stood up and stretched himself lazily.

'Thank heavens, it's all over now. We've none of us had any sleep for three days, and when I once get off I don't mean to wake up for a week.'

'I must go and see the rest of my patients. Perkins has got a bad dose of fever this time. He was quite delirious a little while ago.'

'By Jove, I'd almost forgotten.'

People changed in Africa. Walker was inclined to be surprised that he was fairly happy, inclined to make a little jest when it occurred to him; and it had nearly slipped his memory that one of the whites had been killed the day before, while another was lying unconscious with a bullet in his skull. A score of natives were dead, and the rest of them had escaped by the skin of their teeth.

'Poor Richardson,' he said.

'We couldn't spare him,' answered the doctor slowly. 'The fates never choose the right man.'

Walker looked at the brawny doctor, and his placid face was clouded. He knew to what the Scot referred and shrugged his shoulders. But the doctor went on.

'If we had to lose someone it would have been a damned sight better if that young cub Allerton had got the bullet which killed poor Richardson.'

'He wouldn't have been much loss, would he?' said Walker, after a silence.

'MacKenzie has been very patient with him. If I'd been in his shoes I'd have sent him back to the coast when he sacked Macinnery.'

Walker did not answer, and the doctor proceeded to moralise.

'It seems to me that some men have natures so

crooked that with every chance in the world to go
straight, they can't manage it. The only thing is to
let them go to the devil as best they may.'

At that moment Alec MacKenzie came in. He was
dripping with rain and threw off his macintosh. His
face lit up when he saw Walker and the doctor. Adamson was an old and trusted friend, and he knew
that on him he could rely always.

' I've been going the round of the outlying sentries,'
he said.

It was unlike him to volunteer even so trivial a piece
of information, and Adamson looked up at him.

' All serene? ' he asked.

' Yes.'

Alec's eyes rested on the doctor as though he were
considering something strange about him. The doctor
knew him well enough to suspect that something very
grave had happened, but also he knew him too well to
hazard an inquiry. Presently Alec spoke again.

' I've just seen a native messenger that Mindabi sent
me.'

' Anything important? '

' Yes.'

Alec's answer was so curt that it was impossible to
question him further. He turned to Walker.

' How's the arm? '

' Oh, that's nothing. It's only a scratch.'

' You'd better not make too light of it. The smallest wound has a way of being troublesome in this
country.'

' He'll be all right in a day or two,' said the doctor.

Alec sat down. For a minute he did not speak, but
seemed plunged in thought. He passed his fingers

through his beard, ragged now and longer than when
he was in England.

'How are the others?' he asked suddenly, looking
at Adamson.

'I don't think Thompson can last till the morning.'

'I've just been in to see him.'

Thompson was the man who had been shot through
the head and had lain unconscious since the day before.
He was an old gold-prospector, who had thrown in his
lot with the expedition against the slavers.

'Perkins of course will be down for several days
longer. And some of the natives are rather badly hurt.
Those devils have got explosive bullets.'

'Is there anyone in great danger?'

'No, I don't think so. There are two men who are
in a bad way, but I think they'll pull through with
rest.'

'I see,' said Alec, laconically.

He stared intently at the table, absently passing his
hand across the gun which Walker had left there.

'I say, have you had anything to eat lately?' asked
Walker, presently.

Alec shook himself out of his meditation and gave
the young man one of his rare, bright smiles. It was
plain that he made an effort to be gay.

'Good Lord, I quite forgot; I wonder when the
dickens I had some food last. These Arabs have been
keeping us so confoundedly busy.'

'I don't believe you've had anything to-day. You
must be devilish hungry.'

'Now you mention it, I think I am,' answered Alec,
cheerfully. 'And thirsty, by Jove! I wouldn't give
my thirst for an elephant tusk.'

'And to think there's nothing but tepid water to drink!' Walker exclaimed with a laugh.

'I'll go and tell the boy to bring you some food,' said the doctor. 'It's a rotten game to play tricks with your digestion like that.'

'Stern man, the doctor, isn't he?' said Alec, with twinkling eyes. 'It won't hurt me once in a way, and I shall enjoy it all the more now.'

But when Adamson went to call the boy, Alec stopped him.

'Don't trouble. The poor devil's half dead with exhaustion. I told him he might sleep till I called him. I don't want much, and I can easily get it myself.'

Alec looked about and presently found a tin of meat and some ship biscuits. During the fighting it had been impossible to go out on the search for game, and there was neither variety nor plenty about their larder. Alec placed the food before him, sat down, and began to eat. Walker looked at him.

'Appetising, isn't it?' he said ironically.

'Splendid!'

'No wonder you get on so well with the natives. You have all the instincts of the primeval savage. You take food for the gross and bestial purpose of appeasing your hunger, and I don't believe you have the least appreciation for the delicacies of eating as a fine art.'

'The meat's getting rather mouldy,' answered Alec.

He ate notwithstanding with a good appetite. His thoughts went suddenly to Dick who at the hour which corresponded with that which now passed in Africa, was getting ready for one of the pleasant little dinners at the *Carlton* upon which he prided himself. And then he thought of the noisy bustle of Piccadilly at night, the carriages and 'buses that streamed to and fro, the crowded pavements, the gaiety of the lights.

'I don't know how we're going to feed everyone to-morrow,' said Walker. 'Things will be going pretty bad if we can't get some grain in from somewhere.'

Alec pushed back his plate.

'I wouldn't worry about to-morrow's dinner if I were you,' he said, with a low laugh.

'Why?' asked Walker.

'Because I think it's ten to one that we shall be as dead as doornails before sunrise.'

The two men stared at him silently. Outside, the wind howled grimly, and the rain swept against the side of the tent.

'Is this one of your little jokes, MacKenzie?' said Walker at last.

'You have often observed that I joke with difficulty.'

'But what's wrong now?' asked the doctor quickly.

Alec looked at him and chuckled quietly.

'You'll neither of you sleep in your beds to-night. Another sell for the mosquitoes, isn't it? I propose to break up the camp and start marching in an hour.'

'I say, it's a bit thick after a day like this,' said Walker. 'We're all so done up that we shan't be able to go a mile.'

'You will have had two hours rest.'

Adamson rose heavily to his feet. He meditated for an appreciable time.

'Some of those fellows who are wounded can't possibly be moved,' he said.

'They must.'

'I won't answer for their lives.'

'We must take the risk. Our only chance is to make a bold dash for it, and we can't leave the wounded here.'

'I suppose there's going to be a deuce of a row,' said Walker.

'There is.'

'Your companions seldom have a chance to complain of the monotony of their existence,' said Walker, grimly. 'What are you going to do now?'

'At this moment I'm going to fill my pipe.'

With a whimsical smile, Alec took his pipe from his pocket, knocked it out on his heel, filled and lit it. The doctor and Walker digested the information he had given them. It was Walker who spoke first.

'I gather from the general amiability of your demeanour that we're in rather a tight place.'

'Tighter than any of your patent-leather boots, my friend.'

Walker moved uncomfortably in his chair. He no longer felt sleepy. A cold shiver ran down his spine.

'Have we any chance of getting through?' he asked gravely.

It seemed to him that Alec paused an unconscionable time before he answered.

'There's always a chance,' he said.

'I suppose we're going to do a bit more fighting?'

'We are.'

Walker yawned loudly.

'Well, at all events there's some comfort in that. If I am going to be done out of my night's rest, I should like to take it out of someone.'

Alec looked at him with approval. That was the frame of mind that pleased him. When he spoke again there was in his voice a peculiar charm that perhaps in part accounted for the power he had over his fellows. It inspired an extraordinary belief in him, so that anyone would have followed him cheerfully to certain death. And though his words were few and bald, he was so unaccustomed to take others into his confidence, that when he did so, ever so little, and in that tone, it seemed that he was putting his hearers under a singular obligation.

' If things turn out all right, we shall come near finishing the job, and there won't be much more slave-trading in this part of Africa.'

' And if things don't turn out all right? '

' Why then, I'm afraid the tea tables of Mayfair will be deprived of your scintillating repartee for ever.'

Walker looked down at the ground. Strange thoughts ran through his head, and when he looked up again, with a shrug of the shoulders, there was a queer look in his eyes.

' Well, I've not had a bad time in my life,' he said slowly. ' I've loved a little, and I've worked and played. I've heard some decent music, I've looked at nice pictures, and I've read some thundering fine books. If I can only account for a few more of those damned scoundrels before I die, I shouldn't think I had much to complain of.'

Alec smiled, but did not answer. A silence fell upon them. Walker's words brought to Alec the recollection of what had caused the trouble which now threatened them, and his lips tightened. A dark frown settled between his eyes.

' Well, I suppose I'd better go and get things straight.' said the doctor. ' I'll do what I can with those fellows and trust to Providence that they'll stand the jolting.'

' What about Perkins? ' asked Alec.

' Lord knows! I'll try and keep him quiet with choral.'

' You needn't say anything about our striking camp. I don't propose that anyone should know till a quarter of an hour before we start.'

' But that won't give them time.'

' I've trained them often enough to get on the march quickly,' answered Alec, with a curtness that allowed no rejoinder.

The doctor turned to go, and at the same moment George Allerton appeared.

# XI

GEORGE ALLERTON had changed since he left England. The flesh had fallen away from his bones, and his face was sallow. He had not stood the climate well. His expression had changed too, for there was a singular querulousness about his mouth, and his eyes were shifty and cunning. He had lost his good looks.

'Can I come in?' he said.

'Yes,' answered Alec, and then turning to the doctor: 'You might stay a moment, will you?'

'Certainly.'

Adamson stood where he was, with his back to the flap that closed the tent. Alec looked up quickly.

'Didn't Selim tell you I wanted to speak to you?'

'That's why I've come,' answered George.

'You've taken your time about it.'

'I say, could you give me a drink of brandy? I'm awfully done up.'

'There's no brandy left,' answered Alec.

'Hasn't the doctor got some?'

'No.'

There was a long pause. Adamson and Walker did not know what was the matter, but they saw that there was something serious. They had never seen Alec so cold, and the doctor, who knew him well, saw that he was very angry. Alec lifted his eyes again and looked at George slowly.

'Do you know anything about the death of that Turkana woman?' he asked abruptly.

George did not answer immediately.

' No. How should I?' he said presently.

' Come now, you must know something about it. Last Tuesday you came into camp and said the Turkana were very much excited.'

' Oh, yes, I remember,' answered George, unwillingly.

' Well?'

' I'm not very clear about it. The woman had been shot, hadn't she? One of the station boys had been playing the fool with her, and he seems to have shot her.'

' Have you made no attempt to find out which of the station boys it was?'

' I haven't had time,' said George, in a surly way. ' We've all been worked off our legs during the last three days.'

' Do you suspect no one?'

' I don't think so.'

' Think a moment.'

' The only man who might have done it is that big scoundrel we got on the coast, the Swahili beggar with one ear.'

' What makes you think that?'

' He's been making an awful nuisance of himself, and I know he's been running after the women.'

Alec did not take his eyes off George. Walker saw what was coming and looked down at the ground.

' You'll be surprised to hear that when the woman was found she wasn't dead.'

George did not move, but his cheeks became if possible more haggard. He was horribly frightened.

' She didn't die for nearly an hour.'

There was a very short silence. It seemed to George that they must hear the furious beating of his heart.

'Was she able to say anything?'

'She said you'd shot her.'

'What a damned lie!'

'It appears that *you* were—playing the fool with her. I don't know why you quarrelled. You took out your revolver and fired point blank.'

George laughed.

'It's just like these beastly niggers to tell a stupid lie like that. You wouldn't believe them rather than me, would you? After all, my word's worth more than theirs.'

Alec quietly took from his pocket the case of an exploded cartridge. It could only have fitted a revolver.

'This was found about two yards from the body and was brought to me this evening.'

'I don't know what that proves.'

'You know just as well as I do that none of the natives has a revolver. Beside ourselves only one or two of the servants have them.'

George took his handkerchief from his pocket and wiped his face. His throat was horribly dry, and he could hardly breathe.

'Will you give me your revolver,' said Alec, quietly.

'I haven't got it. I lost it this afternoon when we made that sortie. I didn't tell you as I thought you'd get in a wax about it.'

'I saw you cleaning it less than an hour ago,' said Alec, gravely.

George shrugged his shoulders pettishly.

'Perhaps it's in my tent. I'll go and see.'

'Stop here,' said Alec sharply.

'Look here, I'm not going to be ordered about like a dog. You've got no right to talk to me like that. I came out here of my own free will, and I won't let you treat me like a damned nigger.'

'If you put your hand to your hip-pocket I think you'll find your revolver there.'

'I'm not going to give it you,' said George, his lips white with fear.

'Do you want me to come and take it from you myself?'

The two men stared at one another for a moment. Then George slowly put his hand to his pocket and took out the revolver. But a sudden impulse seized him. He raised it, quickly aimed at Alec, and fired. Walker was standing near him, and seeing the movement, instinctively beat up the boy's hand as pulled the trigger. In a moment the doctor had sprung forward and seizing him round the waist, thrown him backwards. The revolver fell from his hand. Alec had not moved.

'Let me go, damn you!' cried George, his voice shrill with rage.

'You need not hold him,' said Alec.

It was second nature with them all to perform Alec's commands, and without thinking twice they dropped their hands. George sank cowering into a chair. Walker, bending down, picked up the revolver and gave it to Alec, who silently fitted into an empty chamber the cartridge that had been brought to him.

'You see that it fits,' he said. 'Hadn't you better make a clean breast of it?'

George was utterly cowed. A sob broke from him.

'Yes, I shot her,' he said brokenly. 'She made a

row and the devil got into me. I didn't know what
I'd done till she screamed and I saw the blood.'

He cursed himself for being such a fool as to throw
the cartridge away. His first thought had been to have
all the chambers filled.

' Do you remember that two months ago I hanged a
man to the nearest tree because he'd murdered one of
the natives? '

George sprang up in terror, and he began to tremble.

' You wouldn't do that to me.'

A wild prayer went up in his heart that mercy might
be shown him, and then bitter anger seized him because
he had ever come out to that country.

' You need not be afraid,' answered Alec coldly. ' In
any case I must preserve the native respect for the
white man.'

' I was half drunk when I saw the woman. I wasn't
responsible for my actions.'

' In any case the result is that the whole tribe has
turned against us.'

The chief was Alec's friend, and it was he who had
sent him the exploded cartridge. The news came to
Alec like a thunderclap, for the Turkana were the
best part of his fighting force, and he had always placed the utmost reliance on their fidelity.
The chief said that he could not hold in his young
men, and not only must Alec cease to count upon them,
but they would probably insist on attacking him openly.
They had stirred up the neighbouring tribes against
him and entered into communication with the Arabs.
He had been just at the turning point and on the verge
of a great success, but now all that had been done during three years was frustrated. The Arabs had seized

the opportunity and suddenly assumed the offensive. The unexpectedness of their attack had nearly proved fatal to Alec's party, and since then they had all had to fight for bare life.

George watched Alec as he stared at the ground.

'I suppose the whole damned thing's my fault,' he muttered.

Alec did not answer directly.

'I think we may take it for certain that the natives will go over to the slavers to-morrow, and then we shall be attacked on all sides. We can't hold out against God knows how many thousands. I've sent Rogers and Deacon to bring in all the Latukas, but heaven knows if they can arrive in time.'

'And if they don't?'

Alec shrugged his shoulders, but did not speak. George's breathing came hurriedly, and a sob rose to his throat.

'What are you going to do to me, Alec?'

MacKenzie walked up and down, thinking of the gravity of their position. In a moment he stopped and looked at Walker.

'I daresay you have some preparations to make,' he said.

Walker got up.

'I'll be off,' he answered, with a slight smile.

He was glad to go, for it made him ashamed to watch the boy's humiliation. His own nature was so honest, his loyalty so unbending, that the sight of viciousness affected him with a physical repulsion, and he turned away from it as he would have done from the sight of some hideous ulcer. The doctor surmised that his presence too was undesired. Murmur-

ing that he had no time to lose if he wanted to get
his patients ready for a night march, he followed Walker
out of the tent.  George breathed more freely when he
was alone with Alec.

'I'm sorry I did that silly thing just now,' he said.
'I'm glad I didn't hit you.'

'It doesn't matter at all,' smiled Alec.  'I'd forgotten all about it.'

'I lost my head.  I didn't know what I was doing.'

'You need not trouble about that.  In Africa even
the strongest of us are apt to lose our balance.'

Alec filled his pipe again, and lighting it, blew heavy
clouds of smoke into the damp air.  His voice was
softer when he spoke.

'Did you ever know that before we came away I
asked Lucy to marry me?'

George did not answer.  He stifled a sob, for the recollection of Lucy, the centre of his love and the
mainspring of all that was decent in him, transfixed
his heart with pain.

'She asked me to bring you here in the hope
that you'd,'—Alec had some difficulty in expressing
himself—'do something that would make people forget what happened to your father.  She's very proud
of her family.  She feels that your good name is—
besmirched, and she wanted you to give it a new lustre.
I think that is the object she has most at heart in
the world.  It is as great as her love for you.  The
plan hasn't been much of a success, has it?'

'She ought to have known that I wasn't suited for
this sort of life,' answered George, bitterly.

'I saw very soon that you were weak and irresolute,
but I thought I could put some backbone into you.

I hoped for her sake to make something of you after
all. Your intentions seemed good enough, but you
never had the strength to carry them out.' Alec had been
watching the smoke that rose from his pipe, but now
he looked at George. ' I'm sorry if I seem to be preach-
ing at you.'

' Oh, do you think I care what anyone says to me
now?'

Alec went on very gravely, but not unkindly.

' Then I found you were drinking. I told you that
no man could stand liquor in this country, and you
gave me your word of honour that you wouldn't touch
it again.'

' Yes, I broke it. I couldn't help myself. The temptation was too strong.'

' When we came to the station at Munias, and I was
laid up with fever, you and Macinnery took the opportunity to get into an ugly scrape with some native
women. You knew that that was the one thing I would
not stand. I have nothing to do with morality—everyone is free in these things to do as he chooses—but
I do know that nothing causes more trouble with the
natives, and I've made definite rules on the subject. If
the culprits are Swahilis I flog them, and if they're
whites I send them back to the coast. That's what I
ought to have done with you, but it would have broken
Lucy's heart.'

' It was Macinnery's fault.'

' It's because I thought Macinnery was chiefly to
blame that I sent him back alone. I determined to give
you another chance. It struck me that the feeling of
authority might have some influence on you, and so,
when I had to build a *boma* to guard the road down

to the coast, I put the chief part of the stores in your care and left you in command. I need not remind you what happened there.'

George looked down at the floor sulkily, and in default of excuses, kept silent. He felt a sullen resentment as he remembered Alec's anger. He had never seen him give way before or since to such a furious wrath, and he had seen Alec hold himself with all his strength so that he might not thrash him. Alec remembered too, and his voice once more grew hard and cold.

'I came to the conclusion that it was hopeless. You seemed to me rotten through and through.'

'Like my father before me,' sneered George, with a little laugh.

'I couldn't believe a word you said. You were idle and selfish. Above all you were loathsomely, wantonly cruel. I was aghast when I heard of the fiendish cruelty with which you'd used the wretched men whom I left with you. If I hadn't returned in the nick of time, they'd have killed you and looted all the stores.'

'It would have upset you to lose the stores, wouldn't it?'

'Is that all you've got to say?'

'You always believed their stories rather than mine.'

'It was difficult not to believe when a man showed me his back all torn and bleeding, and said you'd had him flogged because he didn't cook your food to your satisfaction.'

'I did it in a moment of temper. A man's not responsible for what he does when he's got fever.'

'It was too late to send you to the coast then, and I was obliged to take you on. And now the end has

come. Your murder of that woman has put us all in
deadly peril. Already to your charge lie the deaths of
Richardson and Thompson and about twenty natives.
We're as near destruction as we can possibly be; and
if we're killed, to-morrow the one tribe that has remained friendly will be attacked and their villages
burnt. Men, women and children, will be put to the
sword or sold into slavery.'

George seemed at last to see the abyss into which
he was plunged, and his resentment gave way to despair.

'What are you going to do?'

'We're far away from the coast, and I must take the
law into my own hands.'

'You're not going to kill me?' gasped George.

'No,' said Alec scornfully.

Alec sat on the little camp table so that he might
be quite near George.

'Are you fond of Lucy?' he asked gently.

George broke into a sob.

'O God, you know I am,' he cried piteously. 'Why
do you remind me of her? I've made a rotten mess
of everything, and I'm better out of the way. But
think of the disgrace of it. It'll kill Lucy. And she
was hoping I'd do so much.'

He hid his face in his hands and sobbed broken-
heartedly. Alec, strangely touched, put his hand on
his shoulder.

'Listen to me,' he said. 'I've sent Deacon and
Rogers to bring up as many Latukas as they can. If
we can tide over to-morrow we may be able to inflict
a crushing blow on the Arabs; but we must seize the
ford over the river. The Arabs are holding it and our

only chance is to make a sudden attack on them to-
night before the natives join them. We shall be
enormously outnumbered, but we may do some damage
if we take them by surprise, and if we can capture the
ford, Rogers and Deacon will be able to get across to
us. We've lost Richardson and Thompson. Perkins is
down with fever. That reduces the whites to Walker,
and the doctor, Condamine, Mason, you and myself.
I can trust the Swahilis, but they're the only natives
I can trust. Now, I'm going to start marching straight
for the ford. The Arabs will come out of their stockade
in order to cut us off. In the darkness I mean to slip
away with the rest of the white men and the Swahilis,
I've found a short cut by which I can take them in
the rear. They'll attack just as the ford is reached,
and I shall fall upon them. Do you see? '

George nodded, but he did not understand at what
Alec was driving. The words reached his ears vaguely,
as though they came from a long way off.

' I want one white man to lead the Turkana, and
that man will run the greatest possible danger. I'd
go myself only the Swahilis won't fight unless I lead
them. . . . Will you take that post? '

The blood rushed to George's head, and he felt his
ears singing.

' I? '

' I could order you to go, but the job's too dangerous
for me to force it on anyone. If you refuse I shall
call the others together and ask someone to volunteer.'

George did not answer.

' I won't hide from you that it means almost certain
death. But there's no other way of saving ourselves.
On the other hand, if you show perfect courage at the

moment the Arabs attack and the Turkana find we've given them the slip, you may escape. If you do, I promise you that nothing shall be said of all that has happened here.'

George sprang to his feet, and once more on his lips flashed the old, frank smile.

' All right! I'll do that. And I thank you with all my heart for giving me the chance.'

Alec held out his hand, and he gave a sigh of relief.

' I'm glad you've accepted. Whatever happens you'll have done one brave action in your life.'

George flushed. He wanted to speak, but hesitated.

' I should like to ask you a great favour,' he said at last.

Alec waited for him to go on.

' You won't let Lucy know the mess I've made of things, will you? Let her think I've done all she wanted me to do.'

' Very well,' answered Alec gently.

' Will you give me your word of honour that if I'm killed you won't say anything that will lead anyone to suspect how I came by my death.'

Alec looked at him silently. It flashed across his mind that it might be necessary under certain circumstances to tell the whole truth. George was greatly moved. He seemed to divine the reason of Alec's hesitation.

' I have no right to ask anything of you. Already you've done far more for me than I deserved. But it's for Lucy's sake that I implore you not to give me away.'

Alec, standing entirely still, uttered the words slowly.

' I give you my word of honour that whatever hap-

pens and in whatever circumstances I find myself
placed, not a word shall escape me that could lead
Lucy to suppose that you hadn't been always and in
every way upright, brave, and honourable. I will take
all the responsibility of your present action.'

' I'm awfully grateful to you.'

Alec moved at last. The strain of their conversation was become almost intolerable. Alec's voice became cheerful and brisk.

' I think there's nothing more to be said. You
must be ready to start in half an hour. Here's your
revolver.' There was a twinkle in his eyes as he continued: ' Remember that you've discharged one chamber. You'd better put in another cartridge.'

' Yes, I'll do that.'

George nodded and went out. Alec's face at once
lost the lightness which it had assumed a moment before. He knew that he had just done something which
might separate him from Lucy for ever. His love for
her was now the only thing in the world to him, and
he had jeopardised it for that worthless boy. He saw
that all sorts of interpretations might be put upon his
action, and he should have been free to speak the
truth. But even if George had not exacted from him
the promise of silence, he could never have spoken a
word. He loved Lucy far too deeply to cause her
such bitter pain. Whatever happened, she must think
that George was a brave man, and had died in the
performance of his duty. He knew her well enough to
be sure that if death were dreadful, it was more tolerable
than dishonour. He knew how keenly she had felt
her disgrace, how it affected her like a personal un-
cleanness, and he knew that she had placed all

her hopes in George. Her brother was rotten to the core, as rotten as her father. How could he tell her that? He was willing to make any sacrifice rather than allow her to have such knowledge. But if ever she knew that he had sent George to his death she would hate him. And if he lost her love he lost everything. He had thought of that before he answered: Lucy could do without love better than without self-respect.

But he had told George that if he had pluck he might get through. Would he show that last virtue of a blackguard—courage?

# XII

It was not till six months later that news of Alec Mac-
Kenzie's expedition reached the outer world, and at
the same time Lucy received a letter from him in
which he told her that her brother was dead. That
stormy night had been fatal to the light-hearted Walker
and to George Allerton, but success had rewarded
Alec's desperate boldness, and a blow had been inflicted
on the slavers which subsequent events proved to be
crushing. Alec's letter was grave and tender. He
knew the extreme grief he must inflict upon Lucy,
and he knew that words could not assuage it. It seemed
to him that the only consolation he could offer was that
the life which was so precious to her had been given
for a worthy cause. Now that George had made up
in the only way possible for the misfortune his crim-
inal folly had brought upon them, Alec was determined
to put out of his mind all that had gone before. It
was right that the weakness which had ruined him
should be forgotten, and Alec could dwell honestly on
the boy's charm of manner, and on his passionate love
for his sister.

The months followed one another, the dry season
gave place to the wet, and at length Alec was able to
say that the result he had striven for was achieved.
Success rewarded his long efforts, and it was worth the
time, the money, and the lives that it had cost. The
slavers were driven out of a territory larger than
the United Kingdom, treaties were signed with chiefs

ALEC

who had hitherto been independent, by which they accepted the suzerainty of Great Britain; and only one step remained, that the government should take over the rights of the company which had been given powers to open up the country, and annex the conquered district to the empire. It was to this that MacKenzie now set himself; and he entered into communication with the directors of the company and with the commissioner at Nairobi.

But it seemed as if the fates would snatch from him all enjoyment of the laurels he had won, for on their way towards Nairobi, Alec and Dr. Adamson were attacked by blackwater fever. For weeks Alec lay at the point of death. His fine constitution seemed to break at last, and he himself thought that the end was come. Condamine, one of the company's agents, took command of the party and received Alec's final instructions. Alec lay in his camp bed, with his faithful Swahili boy by his side to brush away the flies, waiting for the end. He would have given much to live till all his designs were accomplished, but that apparently was not to be. There was only one thing that troubled him. Would the government let the splendid gift he offered slip through their fingers? Now was the time to take formal possession of the territories which he had pacified: the prestige of the whites was at its height, and there were no difficulties to be surmounted. He impressed upon Condamine, whom he wished to be appointed sub-commissioner under a chief at Nairobi, the importance of making all this clear to the authorities. The post he suggested would have been pressed upon himself, but he had no taste for official restrictions, and his part of the work was done. So far as this went, his death was of little consequence.

And then he thought of Lucy. He wondered if she would understand what he had done. He could acknowledge now that she had cause to be proud of him. She would be sorry for his death. He did not think that she loved him, he did not expect it; but he was glad to have loved her, and he wished he could have told her how much the thought of her had been to him during these years of difficulty. It was very hard that he might not see her once more in order to thank her for all she had been to him. She had given his life a beauty it could never have had, and for this he was very grateful. But the secret of George's death would die with him; for Walker was dead, and Adamson, the only man left who could throw light upon it, might be relied on to hold his tongue. And Alec, losing strength each day, thought that perhaps it were well if he died.

But Condamine could not bear to see his chief thus perish. For four years that man had led them, and only his companions knew his worth. To his acquaintance he might seem hard and unsympathetic, he might repel by his taciturnity and anger by his sternness; but his comrades knew how eminent were his qualities. It was impossible for anyone to live with him continually without being conquered by his greatness. If his power with the natives was unparalleled, it was because they had taken his measure and found him sterling. And he had bound the whites to him by ties from which they could not escape. He asked no one to do anything which he was not willing to do himself. If any plan of his failed he took the failure upon himself; if it succeeded he attributed the success to those who had carried out his orders. If he demanded courage and endurance from others it was easy, since he showed them the way by his own example to be strong and brave. His honesty, justice, and forbearance made all who came in contact with him ashamed of their own weakness. They knew the unselfishness which considered the comfort of the meanest porter before his own; and his tenderness to those who were ill knew no bounds.

The Swahilis assumed an unaccustomed silence, and the busy, noisy camp was like a death chamber. When Alec's boy told them that his master grew each day weaker, they went about with tears running down their cheeks, and they would have wailed aloud, but that they knew he must not be disturbed. It seemed to Condamine that there was but one chance, and that was to hurry down, with forced marches, to the nearest station. There they would find a medical missionary to look after him and the comforts of civilisation which in the forest they so wofully lacked.

Alec was delirious when they moved him. It was fortunate that he could not be told of Adamson's death, which had taken place three days before. The good, strong Scotchman had succumbed at last to the African climate; and on this, his third journey, having surmounted all the perils that had surrounded him for so long, almost on the threshold of home, he had sunk and died. He was buried at the foot of a great tree, far down so that the jackals might not find him, and Condamine with a shaking voice read over him the burial service from an English prayerbook.

It seemed a miracle that Alec survived the exhaustion of the long tramp. He was jolted along elephant paths that led through dense bush, up stony hills and down again to the beds of dried-up rivers. Each time Condamine looked at the pale, wan man who lay in the litter, it was with a horrible fear that he would be dead. They began marching before sunrise, swiftly, to cover as much distance as was possible before the sun grew hot; they marched again towards sunset when a grateful coolness refreshed the weary patient. They passed through interminable forests, where the majestic trees sheltered under their foliage a wealth of graceful, tender plants: from trunk and branch swung all manner of creepers, which bound the forest giants in fantastic bonds. They forded broad streams, with exquisite care lest the sick man should come to hurt; they tramped through desolate marshes where the ground sunk under their feet. And at last they reached the station. Alec was still alive.

For weeks the tender skill of the medical missionary and the loving kindness of his wife wrestled with death, and at length Alec was out of danger. His convalescence was very slow, and it looked often as though he would never entirely get back his health. But as soon as his mind regained its old activity, he resumed direction of the affairs which were so near his heart; and no sooner was his strength equal to it than he insisted on being moved to Nairobi, where he was in touch with civilisation, and, through the commissioner, could influence a supine government to accept the precious gift he offered. All this took many months, months of anxious waiting, months of bitter disappointment; but at length everything was done: the worthy Condamine was given the appointment that Alec had desired and set out once more for the interior; Great Britain took possession of the broad lands which Alec, by his skill, tact, perseverance and strength, had wrested from barbarism. His work was finished, and he could return to England.

Public attention had been called at last to the greatness of his achievement, to the dangers he had run and the difficulties he had encountered; and before he sailed, he learned that the papers were ringing with his praise. A batch of cablegrams reached him, including one from Dick Lomas and one from Robert Boulger, congratulating him on his success. Two foreign potentates, through their consuls at Mombassa, bestowed decorations upon him; scientific bodies of all countries conferred on him the distinctions which were in their power to give; chambers of commerce passed resolutions expressing their appreciation of his services; publishers telegraphed offers for the book which they surmised he would write; newspaper correspondents came to him for a preliminary account of his travels. Alec smiled grimly when he read that an Under-Secretary for Foreign Affairs had referred to him in a debate with honeyed words. No such enthusiasm had been aroused in England since Stanley returned from the journey which he afterwards described in *Darkest Africa*. When he left Mombassa the residents gave a dinner in his honour, and everyone who had the chance jumped up on his legs and made a speech. In short, after many years during which Alec's endeavours had been coldly regarded, when the government had been inclined to look upon him as a busybody, the tide turned; and he was in process of being made a national hero.

Alec made up his mind to come home the whole way by sea, thinking that the rest of the voyage would give his constitution a chance to get the better of the ills which still troubled him; and at Gibraltar he received a letter from Dick. One had reached him at Suez; but that was mainly occupied with congratulations, and there was a tenderness due to the fear that Alec had hardly yet recovered from his dangerous illness, which made it, though touching to Alec, not so characteristic as the second.

> *My Dear Alec:*
>
> *I am delighted that you will return in the nick of time for the London season. You will put the noses of the Christian Scientists out of joint, and the New Theologians will argue no more in the columns of the halfpenny papers. For you are going to be the lion of the season. Comb your mane and have it neatly curled and scented, for we do not like our lions unkempt; and learn how to flap your tail; be sure you cultivate a proper roar because we expect to shiver delightfully in our shoes at the sight of you, and young ladies are already practising how to swoon with awe in your presence. We have come to the conclusion that you are a hero, and I, your humble servant, shine already with reflected glory because for twenty years I have had the privilege of your acquaintance. Duchesses, my dear boy, duchesses with strawberry leaves around their snowy brows, (like the French grocer I make a point of never believing a duchess is more than thirty,) ask me to tea so that they may hear me prattle of your childhood's happy days, and I have promised to bring you to lunch with them,*

*Tompkinson, whom you once kicked at Eton, has written an article in Blackwood on the beauty of your character; by which I take it that the hardness of your boot has been a lasting memory to him. All your friends are proud of you, and we go about giving the uninitiated to understand that nothing of all this would have happened except for our encouragement. You will be surprised to learn how many people are anxious to reward you for your services to the empire by asking you to dinner. So far as I am concerned, I am smiling in my sleeve; for I alone know what an exceedingly disagreeable person you are. You are not a hero in the least, but a pig-headed beast who conquers kingdoms to annoy quiet, self-respecting persons like myself who make a point of minding their own business.          Yours ever affectionately,*

*Richard Lomas.*

Alec smiled when he read the letter. It had struck him that there would be some attempt on his return to make a figure of him, and he much feared that his arrival in Southampton would be followed by an attack of interviewers. He was coming in a slow German ship, and at that moment a P. and O., homeward bound, put in at Gibraltar. By taking it he could reach England one day earlier and give everyone who came to meet him the slip. Leaving his heavy luggage, he got a steward to pack up the things he used on the journey, and in a couple of hours, after an excursion on shore to the offices of the company, found himself installed on the English boat.

But when the great ship entered the English Channel, Alec could scarcely bear his impatience. It would have astonished those who thought him unhuman if they had known the tumultuous emotions that rent his soul. His fellow-passengers never suspected that the bronzed, silent man who sought to make no acquaintance, was the explorer with whose name all Europe was ringing; and it never occurred to them that as he stood in the bow of the ship, straining his eyes for the first sight of England, his heart was so full that he would not have dared to speak. Each absence had intensified his love for that sea-girt land, and his eyes filled with tears of longing as he thought that soon now he would see it once more. He loved the murky waters of the English Channel because they bathed its shores, and he loved the strong west wind. The west wind seemed to him the English wind; it was the trusty wind of seafaring men, and he lifted his face to taste its salt buoyancy. He could not think of the white cliffs of England without a deep emotion; and when they passed the English ships, tramps outward bound or stout brigantines driving before the wind with their spreading sails, he saw the three-deckers of Trafalgar and the proud galleons of the Elizabethans. He felt a personal pride in those dead adventurers who were spiritual ancestors of his, and he was proud to be an Englishman because Frobisher and Effingham were English, and Drake and Raleigh and the glorious Nelson.

And then his pride in the great empire which had sprung from that small island, a greater Rome in a greater world, dissolved into love as his wandering thoughts took him to green meadows and rippling streams. Now at last he need no longer keep so tight a rein upon his fancy, but could allow it to wander at will; and he thought of the green hedgerows and the pompous elm trees; he thought of the lovely wayside cottages with their simple flowers and of the winding roads that were so good to walk on. He was breathing the English air now, and his spirit was uplifted. He loved the grey soft mists of low-lying country, and he loved the smell of the heather as he stalked across the moorland. There was no river he knew that equalled the kindly Thames, with the fair trees of its banks and its quiet backwaters, where white swans gently moved amid the waterlilies. His thoughts went to Oxford, with its spires, bathed in a violet haze, and in imagination he sat in the old garden of his college, so carefully tended, so great with memories of the past. And he thought of London. There was a subtle beauty in its hurrying crowds, and there was beauty in the thronged traffic of its river: the streets had that indefinable hue which is the colour of London, and the sky had the gold and the purple of an Italian brocade. Now in Piccadilly Circus, around the fountain sat the women who sold flowers; and the gaiety of their baskets, rich with roses and daffodils and tulips, yellow and red, mingled with the sombre tones of the houses, the dingy gaudiness of 'buses and the sunny greyness of the sky.

At last his thoughts went back to the outward voyage. George Allerton was with him then, and now he was alone. He had received no letter from Lucy since he wrote to tell her that George was dead. He understood her silence. But when he thought of George, his heart was bitter against fate because that young life had been so pitifully wasted. He remembered

so well the eagerness with which he had sought to
bind George to him, his desire to gain the boy's
affection; and he remembered the dismay with which
he learned that he was worthless. The frank smile,
the open countenance, the engaging eyes, meant nothing; the boy was truthless, crooked of nature, weak.
Alec remembered how, refusing to acknowledge the
faults that were so plain, he blamed the difficulty of his
own nature; and, when it was impossible to overlook
them, his earnest efforts to get the better of them.
But the effect of Africa was too strong. Alec had seen
many men lose their heads under the influence of that
climate. The feeling of an authority that seemed so
little limited, over a race that was manifestly inferior,
the subtle magic of the hot sunshine, the vastness,
the remoteness from civilisation, were very apt to throw
a man off his balance. The French had coined a name
for the distemper and called it *folie d'Afrique.* Men
seemed to go mad from a sense of power, to lose all the
restraints which had kept them in the way of righteousness. It needed a strong head or a strong morality
to avoid the danger, and George had neither. He succumbed. He lost all sense of shame, and there was
no power to hold him. And it was more hopeless because nothing could keep him from drinking. When
Macinnery had been dismissed for breaking Alec's most
stringent law, things, notwithstanding George's promise of amendment, had only gone from bad to worse.
Alec remembered how he had come back to the camp in
which he had left George, to find the men mutinous,
most of them on the point of deserting, and George
drunk. He had flown then into such a rage that he
could not control himself. He was ashamed to think

of it. He had seized George by the shoulders and shaken him, shaken him as though he were a rat; and it was with difficulty that he prevented himself from thrashing him with his own hands.

And at last had come the final madness and the brutal murder. Alec set his mind to consider once more those hazardous days during which by George's folly they had been on the brink of destruction. George had met his death on that desperate march to the ford, and lacking courage, had died miserably. Alec threw back his head with a curious movement.

'I was right in all I did,' he muttered.

George deserved to die, and he was unworthy to be lamented. And yet, at that moment, when he was approaching the shores which George, too, perhaps, had loved, Alec's heart was softened. He sighed deeply. It was fate. If George had inherited the wealth which he might have counted on, if his father had escaped that cruel end, he might have gone through life happily enough. He would have done no differently from his fellows. With the safeguards about him of a civilised state, his irresolution would have prevented him from going astray; and he would have been a decent country gentleman—selfish, weak, and insignificant perhaps, but not remarkably worse than his fellows—and when he died he might have been mourned by a loving wife and fond children.

Now he lay on the borders of an African swamp, unsepulchred, unwept; and Alec had to face Lucy, with the story in his heart that he had sworn on his honour not to tell.

# XIII

ALEC's first visit was to Lucy. No one knew that he had arrived, and after changing his clothes at the rooms in Pall Mall that he had taken for the summer, he walked to Charles Street. His heart leaped as he strolled up the hill of St. James Street, bright by a fortunate chance with the sunshine of a summer day; and he rejoiced in the gaiety of the well-dressed youths who sauntered down, bound for one or other of the clubs, taking off their hats with a rapid smile of recognition to charming women who sat in victorias or in electric cars. There was an air of opulence in the broad street, of a civilisation refined without brutality, which was very grateful to his eyes accustomed for so long to the wilderness of Africa.

The gods were favourable to his wishes that day, for Lucy was at home; she sat in the drawing-room, by the window, reading a novel. At her side were masses of flowers, and his first glimpse of her was against a great bowl of roses. The servant announced his name, and she sprang up with a cry. She flushed with excitement, and then the blood fled from her cheeks, and she became extraordinarily pale. Alec noticed that she was whiter and thinner than when last he had seen her; but she was more beautiful.

'I didn't expect you so soon,' she faltered.

And then unaccountably tears came to her eyes. Falling back into her chair, she hid her face. Her heart began to beat painfully.

'You must forgive me,' she said, trying to smile. 'I can't help being very silly.'

For days Lucy had lived in an agony of terror, fearing this meeting, and now it had come upon her unexpectedly. More than four years had passed since last they had seen one another, and they had been years of anxiety and distress. She was certain that she had changed, and looking with pitiful dread in the glass, she told herself that she was pale and dull. She was nearly thirty. There were lines about her eyes, and her mouth had a bitter droop. She had no mercy on herself. She would not minimise the ravages of time, and with a brutal frankness insisted on seeing herself as she might be in ten years, when an increasing leanness, emphasising the lines and increasing the prominence of her features, made her still more haggard. She was seized with utter dismay. He might have ceased to love her. His life had been so full, occupied with strenuous adventures, while hers had been used up in waiting, only in waiting. It was natural enough that the strength of her passion should only have increased, but it was natural too that his should have vanished before a more urgent preoccupation. And what had she to offer him now? She turned away from the glass because her tears blurred the image it presented; and if she looked forward to the first meeting with vehement eagerness, it was also with sickening dread.

And now she was so troubled that she could not adopt the attitude of civil friendliness which she had intended in order to show him that she made no claim upon him. She wanted to seem quite collected so that her behaviour should not lead him to think her heart at all affected, but she could only watch his eyes hungrily. She braced herself to restrain a wail of sorrow if she saw his disillusionment. He talked in order to give time for her to master her agitation.

'I was afraid there would be interviewers and boring people generally to meet me if I came by the boat by which I was expected, so I got into another, and I've arrived a day before my time.'

She was calmer now, and though she did not speak, she looked at him with strained attention, hanging on his words.

He was very bronzed, thin after his recent illness, but he looked well and strong. His manner had the noble self-confidence which had delighted her of old, and he spoke with the quiet deliberation she loved. Now and then a faint inflection betrayed his Scottish birth.

'I felt that I owed my first visit to you. Can you ever forgive me that I have not brought George home to you?'

Lucy gave a sudden gasp. And with bitter self-reproach she realised that in the cruel joy of seeing Alec once more she had forgotten her brother. She was ashamed. It was but eighteen months since he had died, but twelve since the cruel news had reached her, and now, at this moment of all others, she was so absorbed in her love that no other feeling could enter her heart.

She looked down at her dress. Its half-mourning still betokened that she had lost one who was very dear to her, but the black and white was a mockery. She remembered in a flash the stunning grief which Alec's letter had brought her. It seemed at first that there must be a mistake and that her tears were but part of a hateful dream. It was too monstrously unjust that the fates should have hit upon George. She had already suffered too much. And George was so young. It was very hard that a mere boy should be robbed of the precious jewel which is life. And when she realised that it was really true, her grief knew no bounds. All that she had hoped was come to nought, and now she could only despair. She bitterly regretted that she had ever allowed the boy to go on that fatal expedition, and she blamed herself because it was she who had arranged it. He must have died accusing her of his death. Her father was dead, and George was dead, and she was alone. Now she had only Alec; and then, like some poor stricken beast, her heart went out to him, crying for love, crying for protection. All her strength, the strength on which she had prided herself, was gone; and she felt utterly weak and utterly helpless. And her heart yearned for Alec, and the love which had hitherto been like a strong enduring light, now was a consuming fire.

But Alec's words brought the recollection of George back to her reproachful heart, and she saw the boy as she was always pleased to remember him, in his flannels, the open shirt displaying his fine white neck, with the Panama hat that suited him so well; and she saw again his pleasant blue eyes and his engaging smile. He was a picture of honest English manhood. There was a sob in her throat, and her voice trembled when she spoke.

' I told you that if he died a brave man's death I could ask no more.'

She spoke in so low a tone that Alec could scarcely

hear, but his pulse throbbed with pride at her courage.
She went on, almost in a whisper.

'I suppose it was predestined that our family should
come to an end in this way. I'm thankful that George
so died that his ancestors need have felt no shame for
him.'

'You are very brave.'

She shook her head slowly.

'No, it's not courage; it's despair. Sometimes, when
I think what his father was, I'm thankful that George
is dead. For at least his end was heroic. He died in
a noble cause, in the performance of his duty. Life
would have been too hard for him to allow me to regret
his end.'

Alec watched her. He foresaw the words that she
would say, and he waited for them.

'I want to thank you for all you did for him,' she
said, steadying her voice.

'You need not do that,' he answered, gravely.

She was silent for a moment. Then she raised her
eyes and looked at him steadily. Her voice now had
regained its usual calmness.

'I want you to tell me that he did all I could have
wished him to do.'

To Alec it seemed that she must notice the delay of
his answer. He had not expected that the question
would be put to him so abruptly. He had no moral
scruples about telling a deliberate lie, but it affected
him with a physical distaste. It sickened him like
nauseous water.

'Yes, I think he did.'

'It's my only consolation that in the short time there
was given to him, he did nothing that was small or

mean, and that in everything he was honourable, upright, and just dealing.'

'Yes, he was all that.'

'And in his death?'

It seemed to Alec that something caught at his throat. The ordeal was more terrible than he expected.

'In his death he was without fear.'

Lucy drew a deep breath of relief.

'Oh, thank God! Thank God! You don't know how much it means to me to hear all that from your own lips. I feel that in a manner his courage, above all his death, have redeemed my father's fault. It shows that we're not rotten to the core, and it gives me back my self-respect. I feel I can look the world in the face once more. I'm infinitely grateful to George. He's repaid me ten thousand times for all my love, and my care, and my anxiety.'

'I'm very glad that it is not only grief I have brought you. I was afraid you would hate me.'

Lucy blushed, and there was a new light in her eyes. It seemed that on a sudden she had cast away the load of her unhappiness.

'No, I could never do that.'

At that moment they heard the sound of a carriage stopping at the door.

'There's Aunt Alice,' said Lucy. 'She's been lunching out.'

'Then let me go,' said Alec. 'You must forgive me, but I feel that I want to see no one else to-day.'

He rose, and she gave him her hand. He held it firmly.

'You haven't changed?'

' Don't,' she cried.

She looked away, for once more the tears were coming to her eyes.  She tried to laugh.

' I'm frightfully weak and emotional now.  You'll utterly despise me.'

' I want to see you again very soon,' he said.

The words of Ruth came to her mind: *Why have I found grace in thine eyes, that thou shouldst take knowledge of me,* and her heart was very full.  She smiled in her old charming way.

When he was gone she drew a long breath.  It seemed that a new joy was come into her life, and on a sudden she felt a keen pleasure in all the beauty of the world.  She turned to the great bowl of flowers which stood on a table by the chair in which she had been sitting, and burying her face in them, voluptuously inhaled their fragrance.  She knew that he loved her still.

## XIV

THE fickle English weather for once belied its reputation, and the whole month of May was warm and fine. It seemed that the springtime brought back Lucy's youth to her; and, surrendering herself with all her heart to her new happiness, she took a girlish pleasure in the gaieties of the season. Alec had said nothing yet, but she was assured of his love, and she gave herself up to him with all the tender strength of her nature. She was a little overwhelmed at the importance which he seemed to have acquired, but she was very proud as well. The great ones of the earth were eager to do him honour. Papers were full of his praise. And it delighted her because he came to her for protection from lionising friends. She began to go out much more; and with Alec, Dick Lomas, and Mrs. Crowley, went much to the opera and often to the play. They had charming little dinner parties at the *Carlton* and amusing suppers at the *Savoy*. Alec did not speak much on these occasions. It pleased him to sit by and listen, with a placid face but smiling eyes, to the nonsense that Dick Lomas and the pretty American talked incessantly. And Lucy watched him. Every day she found something new to interest her in the strong, sunburned face; and sometimes their eyes met: then they smiled quietly. They were very happy.

One evening Dick asked the others to sup with him; and since Alec had a public dinner to attend, and Lucy was going to the play with Lady Kelsey, he took Julia Crowley to the opera. To make an even number he invited Robert Boulger to join them at the *Savoy*. After brushing his hair with the scrupulous thought his thinning locks compelled, Dick waited in the vestibule for Mrs. Crowley. Presently she came, looking very pretty in a gown of flowered brocade which made her vaguely resemble a shepherdess in an old French picture. With her diamond necklace and a tiara in her dark hair, she looked like a dainty princess playing fantastically at the simple life.

' I think people are too stupid,' she broke out, as she joined Dick. ' I've just met a woman who said to me: " Oh, I hear you're going to America. Do go and call on my sister. She'll be so glad to see you." " I shall be delighted," I said, " but where does your sister live? " " Jonesville, Ohio," " Good heavens," I said, " I live in New York, and what should I be doing in Jonesville, Ohio? " '

' Keep perfectly calm,' said Dick.

' I shall not keep calm,' she answered. ' I hate to be obviously thought next door to a red Indian by a woman who's slab-sided and round-shouldered. And I'm sure she has dirty petticoats.'

' Why? '

' English women do.'

' What a monstrous libel! ' cried Dick.

At that moment they saw Lady Kelsey come in with Lucy, and a moment later Alec and Robert Boulger joined them. They went in to supper and sat down.

' I hate Amelia,' said Mrs. Crowley emphatically, as she laid her long white gloves by the side of her.

' I deplore the prejudice with which you regard a very jolly sort of a girl,' answered Dick.

' Amelia has everything that I thoroughly object to in a woman. She has no figure, and her legs are much too long, and she doesn't wear corsets. In the daytime she has a weakness for picture hats, and she can't say boo to a goose.'

' Who is Amelia? ' asked Boulger.

' Amelia is Mr. Lomas' affianced wife,' answered the lady, with a provoking glance at him.

' I didn't know you were going to be married, Dick,' said Lady Kelsey, inclined to be a little hurt because nothing had been said to her of this.

' I'm not,' he answered. ' And I've never set eyes on Amelia yet. She is an imaginary character that Mrs. Crowley has invented as the sort of woman whom I would marry.'

' I know Amelia,' Mrs. Crowley went on. ' She wears quantities of false hair, and she'll adore you. She's so meek and so quiet, and she thinks you such a marvel. But don't ask me to be nice to Amelia.'

' My dear lady, Amelia wouldn't approve of you. She'd think you much too outspoken, and she wouldn't like your American accent. You must never forget that Amelia is the granddaughter of a baronet.'

' I shall hold her up to Fleming as an awful warning of the woman whom I won't let him marry at any price. " If you marry a woman like that, Fleming," I shall say to him, " I shan't leave you a penny. It shall all go the University of Pennsylvania." '

' If ever it is my good fortune to meet Fleming, I shall have great pleasure in kicking him hard,' said Dick. ' I think he's a most objectionable little beast.'

'How can you be so absurd? Why, my dear Mr. Lomas, Fleming could take you up in one hand and throw you over a ten-foot wall.'

'Fleming must be a sportsman,' said Bobbie, who did not in the least know whom they were talking about.

'He is,' answered Mrs. Crowley. 'He's been used to the saddle since he was three years old, and I've never seen the fence that would make him lift a hair. And he's the best swimmer at Harvard, and he's a wonderful shot—I wish you could see him shoot, Mr. MacKenzie—and he's a dear.'

'Fleming's a prig,' said Dick.

'I'm afraid you're too old for Fleming,' said Mrs. Crowley, looking at Lucy. 'If it weren't for that, I'd make him marry you.'

'Is Fleming your brother, Mrs. Crowley?' asked Lady Kelsey.

'No, Fleming's my son.'

'But you haven't got a son,' retorted the elder lady, much mystified.

'No, I know I haven't; but Fleming would have been my son if I'd had one.'

'You mustn't mind them, Aunt Alice,' smiled Lucy gaily. 'They argue by the hour about Amelia and Fleming, and neither of them exists; but sometimes they go into such details and grow so excited that I really begin to believe in them myself.'

But Mrs. Crowley, though she appeared a lighthearted and thoughtless little person, had much common sense; and when their party was ended and she was giving Dick a lift in her carriage, she showed that, notwithstanding her incessant chatter, her eyes throughout the evening had been well occupied.

' Did you owe Bobbie a grudge that you asked him to supper? ' she asked suddenly.

' Good heavens, no. Why? '

' I hope Fleming won't be such a donkey as you are when he's your age.'

' I'm sure Amelia will be much more polite than you to the amiable, middle-aged gentleman who has the good fortune to be her husband.'

' You might have noticed that the poor boy was eating his heart out with jealousy and mortification, and Lucy was too much absorbed in Alec to pay the very smallest attention to him.'

' What *are* you talking about? '

Mrs. Crowley gave him a glance of amused disdain.

' Haven't you noticed that Lucy is desperately in love with Mr. MacKenzie, and it doesn't move her in the least that poor Bobbie has fetched and carried for her for ten years, done everything she deigned to ask, and been generally nice and devoted and charming? '

' You amaze me,' said Dick. ' It never struck me that Lucy was the kind of girl to fall in love with anyone. Poor thing. I'm so sorry.'

' Why? '

' Because Alec wouldn't dream of marrying. He's not that sort of man.'

' Nonsense. Every man is a marrying man if a woman really makes up her mind to it.'

' Don't say that. You terrify me.'

' You need not be in the least alarmed,' answered Mrs. Crowley, coolly, ' because I shall refuse you.'

' It's very kind of you to reassure me,' he answered, smiling. ' But all the same I don't think I'll risk a proposal.'

' My dear friend, your only safety is in immediate flight.'

' Why? '

' It must be obvious to the meanest intelligence that you've been on the verge of proposing to me for the last four years.'

' Nothing will induce me to be false to Amelia.'

' I don't believe that Amelia really loves you.'

' I never said she did; but I'm sure she's quite willing to marry me.'

' I think that's detestably vain.'

' Not at all. However old, ugly, and generally undesirable a man is, he'll find a heap of charming girls who are willing to marry him. Marriage is still the only decent means of livelihood for a really nice woman.'

' Don't let's talk about Amelia; let's talk about me,' said Mrs. Crowley.

' I don't think you're half so interesting.'

' Then you'd better take Amelia to the play to-morrow night instead of me.'

' I'm afraid she's already engaged.'

' Nothing will induce me to play second fiddle to Amelia.'

' I've taken the seats and ordered an exquisite dinner at the *Carlton.*'

' What have you ordered? '

' *Potage bisque.*'

Mrs. Crowley made a little face.

' *Sole Normande.*'

She shrugged her shoulders.

' Wild duck.'

' With an orange salad? '

' Yes.'

' I don't positively dislike that.'

' And I've ordered a *souffle* with an ice in the middle of it.'

' I shan't come.'

' Why? '

' You're not being really nice to me.'

' I shouldn't have thought you kept very well abreast of dramatic art if you insist on marrying everyone who takes you to a theatre,' he said.

' I was very nicely brought up,' she answered demurely, as the carriage stopped at Dick's door.

She gave him a ravishing smile as he took leave of her. She knew that he was quite prepared to marry her, and she had come to the conclusion that she was willing to have him. Neither much wished to hurry the affair, and each was determined that he would only yield to save the other from a fancied desperation. Their love-making was pursued with a light heart.

At Whitsuntide the friends separated. Alec went up to Scotland to see his house and proposed afterwards to spend a week in Lancashire. He had always taken a keen interest in the colliery which brought him so large an income, and he wanted to examine into certain matters that required his attention. Mrs. Crowley went to Blackstable, where she still had Court Leys, and Dick, in order to satisfy himself that he was not really a day older, set out for Paris. But they all arranged to meet again on the day, immediately after the holidays, which Lady Kelsey, having persuaded Lucy definitely to renounce her life of comparative retirement, had fixed for a dance. It was the first

ball she had given for many years, and she meant it
to be brilliant. Lady Kelsey had an amiable weakness
for good society, and Alec's presence would add lustre
to the occasion. Meanwhile she went with Lucy to her
little place on the river, and did not return till two
days before the party. They were spent in a turmoil
of agitation. Lady Kelsey passed sleepless nights,
fearing at one moment that not a soul would appear,
and at another that people would come in such numbers that there would not be enough for them to eat.
The day arrived.

But then happened an event which none but Alec
could in the least have expected; and he, since his
return from Africa, had been so taken up with his
love for Lucy, that the possibility of it had slipped
his memory.

Fergus Macinnery, the man whom three years before
he had dismissed ignominiously from his service, found
a way to pay off an old score.

Of the people most nearly concerned in the matter,
it was Lady Kelsey who had first news of it. The
morning papers were brought into her *boudoir* with
her breakfast, and as she poured out her coffee, she ran
her eyes lazily down the paragraphs of the *Morning
Post* in which are announced the comings and goings
of society. Then she turned to the *Daily Mail*. Her
attention was suddenly arrested. Staring at her, in
the most prominent part of the page, was a column of
printed matter headed: *The Death of Mr. George
Allerton*. It was a letter, a column long, signed by
Fergus Macinnery. Lady Kelsey read it with amazement and dismay. At first she could not follow it, and
she read it again; now its sense was clear to her, and

she was overcome with horror. In set words, mincing
no terms, it accused Alec MacKenzie of sending George
Allerton to his death in order to save himself. The
words treachery and cowardice were used boldly. The
dates were given, and the testimony of natives was
adduced.

The letter adverted with scathing sarcasm to the
rewards and congratulations which had fallen to
MacKenzie as a result of his labours; and ended with
a challenge to him to bring an action for crim-
inal libel against the writer. At first the whole thing
seemed monstrous to Lady Kelsey, it was shameful,
shameful; but in a moment she found there was a
leading article on the subject, and then she did not
know what to believe. It referred to the letter in no
measured terms: the writer observed that *prima facie*
the case was very strong and called upon Alec to reply
without delay. Big words were used, and there was
much talk of a national scandal. An instant refuta-
tion was demanded. Lady Kelsey did not know what
on earth to do, and her thoughts flew to the dance,
the success of which would certainly be imperilled by
these revelations. She must have help at once. This
business, if it concerned the world in general, certainly
concerned Lucy more than anyone. Ringing for her
maid, she told her to get Dick Lomas on the telephone
and ask him to come at once. While she was waiting,
she heard Lucy come downstairs and knew that she
meant to wish her good-morning. She hid the paper
hurriedly.

When Lucy came in and kissed her, she said:

'What is the news this morning?'

'I don't think there is any,' said Lady Kelsey, uneasily. 'Only the *Post* has come; we shall really have to change our newsagent.'

She waited with beating heart for Lucy to pursue the subject, but naturally enough the younger woman did not trouble herself. She talked to her aunt of the preparations for the party that evening, and then, saying that she had much to do, left her. She had no sooner gone than Lady Kelsey's maid came back to say that Lomas was out of town and not expected back till the evening. Distractedly Lady Kelsey sent messages to her nephew and to Mrs. Crowley. She still looked upon Bobbie as Lucy's future husband, and the little American was Lucy's greatest friend. They were both found. Boulger had gone down as usual to the city, but in consideration of Lady Kelsey's urgent request, set out at once to see her.

He had changed little during the last four years, and had still a boyish look on his round, honest face. To Mrs. Crowley he seemed always an embodiment of British philistinism; and if she liked him for his devotion to Lucy, she laughed at him for his stolidity. When he arrived, Mrs. Crowley was already with Lady Kelsey. She had known nothing of the terrible letter, and Lady Kelsey, thinking that perhaps it had escaped him too, went up to him with the *Daily Mail* in her hand.

'Have you seen the paper, Bobbie?' she asked excitedly. 'What on earth are we to do?'

He nodded.

'What does Lucy say?' he asked.

'Oh, I've not let her see it. I told a horrid fib and said the newsagent had forgotten to leave it.'

'But she must know,' he answered gravely.

' Not to-day,' protested Lady Kelsey. ' Oh, it's too dreadful that this should happen to-day of all days. Why couldn't they wait till to-morrow? After all Lucy's troubles it seemed as if a little happiness was coming back into her life, and now this dreadful thing happens.'

' What are you going to do?' asked Bobbie.

' What can I do?' said Lady Kelsey desperately. ' I can't put the dance off. I wish I had the courage to write and ask Mr. MacKenzie not to come.'

Bobbie made a slight gesture of impatience. It irritated him that his aunt should harp continually on the subject of this wretched dance. But for all that he tried to reassure her.

' I don't think you need be afraid of MacKenzie. He'll never venture to show his face.'

' You don't mean to say you think there's any truth in the letter?' exclaimed Mrs. Crowley.

He turned and faced her.

' I've never read anything more convincing in my life.'

Mrs. Crowley looked at him, and he returned her glance steadily.

Of those three it was only Lady Kelsey who did not know that Lucy was deeply in love with Alec MacKenzie.

' Perhaps you're inclined to be unjust to him,' said Mrs. Crowley.

' We shall see if he has any answer to make,' he answered coldly. ' The evening papers are sure to get something out of him. The city is ringing with the story, and he must say something at once.'

' It's quite impossible that there should be anything

in it,' said Mrs. Crowley. ' We all know the circumstances under which George went out with him. It's inconceivable that he should have sacrificed him as callously as this man's letter makes out.'

' We shall see.'

' You never liked him, Bobbie,' said Lady Kelsey.

' I didn't,' he answered briefly.

' I wish I'd never thought of giving this horrid
dance,' she moaned.

Presently, however, they succeeded in calming Lady
Kelsey. Though both thought it unwise, they deferred
to her wish that everything should be hidden from
Lucy till the morrow. Dick Lomas was arriving from
Paris that evening, and it would be possible then to
take his advice. When at last Mrs. Crowley left the
elder woman to her own devices, her thoughts went to
Alec. She wondered where he was, and if he already
knew that his name was more prominently than ever
before the public.

MacKenzie was travelling down from Lancashire.
He was not a man who habitually read papers, and it
was in fact only by chance that he saw a copy of the
*Daily Mail.* A fellow traveller had with him a number
of papers, and offered one of them to Alec. He took
it out of mere politeness. His thoughts were otherwise occupied, and he scanned it carelessly. Suddenly
he saw the heading which had attracted Lady Kelsey's
attention. He read the letter, and he read the leading
article. No one who watched him could have guessed
that what he read concerned him so nearly. His face
remained impassive. Then, letting the paper fall to
the ground, he began to think. Presently he turned

to the amiable stranger who had given him the paper, and asked him if he had seen the letter.

'Awful thing, isn't it?' the man said.

Alec fixed upon him his dark, firm eyes. The man seemed an average sort of person, not without intelligence.

'What do you think of it?'

'Pity,' he said. 'I thought MacKenzie was a great man. I don't know what he can do now but shoot himself.'

'Do you think there's any truth in it?'

'The letter's perfectly damning.'

Alec did not answer. In order to break off the conversation he got up and walked into the corridor. He lit a cigar and watched the green fields that fled past them. For two hours he stood motionless. At last he took his seat again, with a shrug of the shoulders, and a scornful smile on his lips.

The stranger was asleep, with his head thrown back and his mouth slightly open. Alec wondered whether his opinion of the affair would be that of the majority. He thought Alec should shoot himself?

'I can see myself doing it,' Alec muttered.

# XV

A few hours later Lady Kelsey's dance was in full swing, and to all appearances it was a great success. Many people were there, and everyone seemed to enjoy himself. On the surface, at all events, there was nothing to show that anything had occurred to disturb the evening's pleasure, and for most of the party the letter in the *Daily Mail* was no more than a welcome topic of conversation.

Presently Canon Spratte went into the smoking-room. He had on his arm, as was his amiable habit, the prettiest girl at the dance, Grace Vizard, a niece of that Lady Vizard who was a pattern of all the proprieties and a devout member of the Church of Rome. He found that Mrs. Crowley and Robert Boulger were already sitting there, and he greeted them courteously.

' I really must have a cigarette,' he said, going up to the table on which were all the necessary things for refreshment.

' If you press me dreadfully I'll have one, too,' said Mrs. Crowley, with a flash of her beautiful teeth.

' Don't press her,' said Bobbie. ' She's had six already, and in a moment she'll be seriously unwell.'

' Well, I'll forego the pressing, but not the cagarette.'

Canon Spratte gallantly handed her the box, and gave her a light.

' It's against all my principles, you know,' he smiled.

' What is the use of principles except to give one an

agreeable sensation of wickedness when one doesn't act up to them?'

The words were hardly out of her mouth when Dick and Lady Kelsey appeared.

'Dear Mrs. Crowley, you're as epigrammatic as a dramatist,' he exclaimed. 'Do you say such things from choice or necessity?'

He had arrived late, and this was the first time she had seen him since they had all gone their ways before Whitsun. He mixed himself a whisky and soda.

'After all, is there anything you know so thoroughly insufferable as a ball?' he said, reflectively, as he sipped it with great content.

'Nothing, if you ask me pointblank,' said Lady Kelsey, smiling with relief because he took so flippantly the news she had lately poured into his ear. 'But it's excessively rude of you to say so.'

'I don't mind yours, Lady Kelsey, because I can smoke as much as I please, and keep away from the sex which is technically known as fair.'

Mrs. Crowley felt the remark was directed to her.

'I'm sure you think us a vastly overrated institution, Mr. Lomas,' she murmured.

'I venture to think the world was not created merely to give women an opportunity to wear Paris frocks.'

'I'm rather pleased to hear you say that.'

'Why?' asked Dick, on his guard.

'We're all so dreadfully tired of being goddesses. For centuries foolish men have set us up on a pedestal and vowed they were unworthy to touch the hem of our garments. And it *is* so dull.'

'What a clever woman you are, Mrs. Crowley. You always say what you don't mean.'

'You're really very rude.'

'Now that impropriety is out of fashion, rudeness is the only short cut to a reputation for wit.'

Canon Spratte did not like Dick. He thought he talked too much. It was fortunately easy to change the conversation.

'Unlike Mr. Lomas, I thoroughly enjoy a dance,' he said, turning to Lady Kelsey. 'My tastes are ingenuous, and I can only hope you've enjoyed your evening as much as your guests.'

'I?' cried Lady Kelsey. 'I've been suffering agonies.' They all knew to what she referred, and the remark gave Boulger an opportunity to speak to Dick Lomas.

'I suppose you saw the *Mail* this morning?' he asked.

'I never read the papers except in August,' answered Dick drily.

'When there's nothing in them?' asked Mrs. Crowley.

'Pardon me, I am an eager student of the sea-serpent and of the giant gooseberry.'

'I should like to kick that man,' said Bobbie, indignantly.

Dick smiled.

'My dear chap, Alec is a hardy Scot and bigger than you; I really shouldn't advise you to try.'

'Of course you've heard all about this business?' said Canon Spratte.

'I've only just arrived from Paris. I knew nothing of it till Lady Kelsey told me.'

'What do you think?'

' I don't think at all; I *know* there's not a word of truth in it. Since Alec arrived at Mombassa, he's been acclaimed by everyone, private and public, who had any right to an opinion. Of course it couldn't last. There was bound to be a reaction.'

' Do you know anything of this man Macinnery?' asked Boulger.

' It so happens that I do. Alec found him half starving at Mombassa, and took him solely out of charity. But he was a worthless rascal and had to be sent back.'

' He seems to me to give ample proof for every word he says,' retorted Bobbie.

Dick shrugged his shoulders scornfully.

' As I've already explained to Lady Kelsey, whenever an explorer comes home there's someone to tell nasty stories about him. People forget that kid gloves are not much use in a tropical forest, and they grow very indignant when they hear that a man has used a little brute force to make himself respected.'

' All that's beside the point,' said Boulger, impatiently. ' MacKenzie sent poor George into a confounded trap to save his own dirty skin.'

' Poor Lucy!' moaned Lady Kelsey. ' First her father died . . .'

' You're not going to count that as an overwhelming misfortune?' Dick interrupted. ' We were unanimous in describing that gentleman's demise as an uncommon happy release.'

' I was engaged to dine with him this evening,' said Bobbie, pursuing his own bitter reflections. ' I wired to say I had a headache and couldn't come.'

' What will he think if he sees you here? ' cried Lady Kelsey.

' He can think what he likes.'

Canon Spratte felt that it was needful now to put in the decisive word which he always expected from himself. He rubbed his hands blandly.

' In this matter I must say I agree entirely with our friend Bobbie. I read the letter with the utmost care, and I could see no loophole of escape. Until Mr. MacKenzie gives a definite answer I can hardly help looking upon him as nothing less than a murderer. In these things I feel that one should have the courage of one's opinions. I saw him in Piccadilly this evening, and I cut him dead. Nothing will induce me to shake hands with a man on whom rests so serious an accusation.'

' I hope to goodness he doesn't come,' said Lady Kelsey.

Canon Spratte looked at his watch and gave her a reassuring smile.

' I think you may feel quite safe. It's really growing very late.'

' You say that Lucy doesn't know anything about this? ' asked Dick.

' No,' said Lady Kelsey. ' I wanted to give her this evening's enjoyment unalloyed.'

Dick shrugged his shoulders again. He did not understand how Lady Kelsey expected no suggestion to reach Lucy of a matter which seemed a common topic of conversation. The pause which followed Lady Kelsey's words was not broken when Lucy herself appeared. She was accompanied by a spruce young man, to whom she turned with a smile.

' I thought we should find your partner here.'

He went to Grace Vizard, and claiming her for the dance that was about to begin, took her away. Lucy went up to Lady Kelsey and leaned over the chair in which she sat.

'Are you growing very tired, my aunt?' she asked kindly.

'I can rest myself till supper time. I don't think anyone else will come now.'

'Have you forgotten Mr. MacKenzie?'

Lady Kelsey looked up quickly, but did not reply. Lucy put her hand gently on her aunt's shoulder.

'My dear, it was charming of you to hide the paper from me this morning. But it wasn't very wise.'

'Did you see that letter?' cried Lady Kelsey. 'I so wanted you not to till to-morrow.'

'Mr. MacKenzie very rightly thought I should know at once what was said about him and my brother. He sent me the paper himself this evening.'

'Did he write to you?' asked Dick.

'No, he merely scribbled on a card: *I think you should read this.*'

No one answered. Lucy turned and faced them; her cheeks were pale, but she was very calm. She looked gravely at Robert Boulger, waiting for him to say what she knew was in his mind, so that she might express at once her utter disbelief in the charges that were brought against Alec. But he did not speak, and she was obliged to utter her defiant words without provocation.

'He thought it unnecessary to assure me that he hadn't betrayed the trust I put in him.'

'Do you mean to say the letter left any doubt in your mind?' said Boulger.

'Why on earth should I believe the unsupported

words of a subordinate who was dismissed for misbehaviour? '

' For my part, I can only say that I never read anything more convincing in my life.'

' I could hardly believe him guilty of such a crime if he confessed it with his own lips.'

Bobbie shrugged his shoulders. It was only with difficulty that he held back the cruel words that were on his lips. But as if Lucy read his thoughts, her cheeks flushed.

' I think it's infamous that you should all be ready to believe the worst,' she said hotly, in a low voice that trembled with indignant anger. ' You're all of you so petty, so mean, that you welcome the chance of spattering with mud a man who is so infinitely above you. You've not given him a chance to defend himself.'

Bobbie turned very pale. Lucy had never spoken to him in such a way before, and wrath flamed up in his heart, wrath mixed with hopeless love. He paused for a moment to command himself.

' You don't know apparently that interviewers went to him from the evening papers, and he refused to speak.'

' He has never consented to be interviewed. Why should you expect him now to break his rule? '

Bobbie was about to answer, when a sudden look of dismay on Lady Kelsey's face stopped him. He turned round and saw MacKenzie standing at the door. He came forward with a smile, holding out his hand, and addressed himself to Lady Kelsey.

' I thought I should find you here,' he said.

He was perfectly collected. He glanced around the

room with a smile of quiet amusement. A certain embarrassment seized the little party, and Lady Kelsey, as she shook hands with him, was at a loss for words.

'How do you do?' she faltered. 'We've just been talking of you.'

'Really?'

The twinkle in his eyes caused her to lose the remainder of her self-possession, and she turned scarlet.

'It's so late, we were afraid you wouldn't come. I should have been dreadfully disappointed.'

'It's very kind of you to say so. I've been at the *Travellers,* reading various appreciations of my character.'

A hurried look of alarm crossed Lady Kelsey's good-tempered face.

'Oh, I heard there was something about you in the papers,' she answered.

'There's a good deal. I really had no idea the world was so interested in me.'

'It's charming of you to come here to-night,' the good lady smiled, beginning to feel more at ease. 'I'm sure you hate dances.'

'Oh, no, they interest me enormously. I remember, an African king once gave a dance in my honour. Four thousand warriors in war-paint. I assure you it was a most impressive sight.'

'My dear fellow,' Dick chuckled, 'if paint is the attraction, you really need not go much further than Mayfair.'

The scene amused him. He was deeply interested in Alec's attitude, for he knew him well enough to be convinced that his discreet gaiety was entirely assumed. It was impossible to tell by it what course he meant to adopt; and at the same time there was about him a greater unapproachableness, which warned all and sundry that it would be wiser to attempt no advance. But for his own part he did not care; he meant to have a word with Alec at the first opportunity.

Alec's quiet eyes now rested on Robert Boulger.

" Ah, there's my little friend Bobbikins. I thought you had a headache? '

Lady Kelsey remembered her nephew's broken engagement and interposed quickly.

' I'm afraid Bobbie is dreadfully dissipated. He's not looking at all well.'

' You shouldn't keep such late hours,' said Alec, good-humouredly. ' At your age one needs one's beauty sleep.'

' It's very kind of you to take an interest in me,' said Boulger, flushing with annoyance. ' My headache has passed off.'

' I'm very glad. What do you use—phenacetin? '

' It went away of its own accord after dinner,' returned Bobbie frigidly, conscious that he was being laughed at, but unable to extricate himself.

' So you resolved to give the girls a treat by coming to Lady Kelsey's dance? How nice of you not to disappoint them ! '

Alec turned to Lucy, and they looked into one another's eyes.

' I sent you a paper this evening,' he said gravely.

' It was very good of you.'

There was a silence. All who were present felt that the moment was impressive, and it needed Canon Spratte's determination to allow none but himself to monopolise attention, to bring to an end a situation

which might have proved awkward.  He came forward
and offered his arm to Lucy.

'I think this is my dance.  May I take you in?'

He was trying to repeat the direct cut which he had
given Alec earlier in the day.  Alec looked at him.

'I saw you in Piccadilly this evening.  You were
dashing about like a young gazelle.'

'I didn't see you,' said the Canon, frigidly.

'I observed that you were deeply engrossed in the
shop windows as I passed.  How are you?'

He held out his hand.  For a moment the Canon hesitated to take it, but Alec's gaze compelled him.

'How do you do?' he said.

He felt, rather than heard, Dick's chuckle, and reddening, offered his arm to Lucy.

'Won't you come, Mr. MacKenzie?' said Lady Kelsey, making the best of her difficulty.

'If you don't mind, I'll stay and smoke a cigarette
with Dick Lomas.  You know, I'm not a dancing man.'

It seemed that Alec was giving Dick the opportunity
he sought, and as soon as they found themselves alone,
the sprightly little man attacked him.

'I suppose you know we were all beseeching Providence you'd have the grace to stay away to-night?' he
said.

'I confess that I suspected it,' smiled Alec.  'I
shouldn't have come, only I wanted to see Miss Allerton.'

'This fellow Macinnery proposes to make things
rather uncomfortable, I imagine.'

'I made a mistake, didn't I?' said Alec, with a thin
smile.  'I should have dropped him in the river when
I had no further use for him.'

' What are you going to do? '

' Nothing.'

Dick stared at him.

' Do you mean to say you're going to sit still and let them throw mud at you? '

' If they want to.'

' But look here, Alec, what the deuce is the meaning of the whole thing? '

Alec looked at him quietly.

' If I had intended to take the world in general into my confidence, I wouldn't have refused to see the interviewers who came to me this evening.'

' We've known one another for twenty years, Alec,' said Dick.

' Then you may be quite sure that if I refuse to discuss this matter with you, it must be for excellent reasons.'

Dick sprang up excitedly.

' But, good God! you must explain. You can't let a charge like this rest on you. After all, it's not Tom, Dick, or Harry that's concerned; it's Lucy's brother. You must speak.'

' I've never yet discovered that I must do anything that I don't choose,' answered Alec.

Dick flung himself into a chair. He knew that when Alec spoke in that fashion no power on earth could move him. The whole thing was entirely unexpected, and he was at a loss for words. He had not read the letter which was causing all the bother, and knew only what Lady Kelsey had told him. He had some hope that on a close examination various things would appear which must explain Alec's attitude; but at present it was incomprehensible.

' Has it occurred to you that Lucy is very much in love with you, Alec? ' he said at last.

Alec did not answer. He made no movement.

' What will you do if this loses you her love? '

' I have counted the cost,' said Alec, coldly.

He got up from his chair, and Dick saw that he did not wish to continue the discussion. There was a moment of silence, and then Lucy came in.

' I've given my partner away to a wall-flower,' she said, with a faint smile. ' I felt I must have a few words alone with you.'

' I will make myself scarce,' said Dick.

They waited till he was gone. Then Lucy turned feverishly to Alec.

' Oh, I'm so glad you've come. I wanted so much to see you.'

' I'm afraid people have been telling you horrible things about me.'

' They wanted to hide it from me.'

' It never occurred to me that people *could* say such shameful things,' he said gravely.

It tormented him a little because it had been so easy to care nothing for the world's adulation, and it was so hard to care as little for its censure. He felt very bitter.

He took Lucy's hand and made her sit on the sofa by his side.

' There's something I must tell you at once.'

She looked at him without answering.

' I've made up my mind to give no answer to the charges that are brought against me.'

Lucy looked up quickly, and their eyes met.

' I give you my word of honour that I've done nothing

which I regret. I swear to you that what I did was right with regard to George, and if it were all to come again I would do exactly as I did before.'

She did not answer for a long time.

'I never doubted you for a single moment,' she said at last.

'That is all I care about.' He looked down, and there was a certain shyness in his voice when he spoke again. 'To-day is the first time I've wanted to be assured that I was trusted; and yet I'm ashamed to want it.'

'Don't be too hard upon yourself,' she said gently. 'You're so afraid of letting your tenderness appear.'

He seemed to give earnest thought to what she said. Lucy had never seen him more grave.

'The only way to be strong is *never* to surrender to one's weakness. Strength is merely a habit. I want you to be strong, too. I want you never to doubt me whatever you hear said.'

'I gave my brother into your hands, and I said that if he died a brave man's death, I could ask for no more. You told me that such a death was his.'

'I thought of you always, and everything I did was for your sake. Every single act of mine during these four years in Africa has been done because I loved you.'

It was the first time since his return that he had spoken of love. Lucy bent her head still lower.

'Do you remember, I asked you a question before I went away? You refused to marry me then, but you told me that if I asked again when I came back, the answer might be different.'

'Yes.'

'The hope bore me up in every difficulty and in every danger. And when I came back I dared not ask you at once; I was so afraid that you would refuse once more. And I didn't wish you to think yourself bound by a vague promise. But each day I loved you more passionately."

' I knew, and I was very grateful for your love.'

' Yesterday I could have offered you a certain name. I only cared for the honours they gave me so that I might put them at your feet. But what can I offer you now?'

' You must love me always, Alec, for now I have only you.'

' Are you sure that you will never believe that I am guilty of this crime?'

' Why can you say nothing in self-defence?'

' That I can't tell you either.'

There was a silence between them. At last Alec spoke again.

' But perhaps it will be easier for you to believe in me than for others, because you know that I loved you, and I can't have done the odious thing of which that man accuses me.'

' I will never believe it. I do not know what your reasons are for keeping all this to yourself, but I trust you, and I know that they are good. If you cannot speak, it is because greater interests hold you back. I love you, Alec, with all my heart, and if you wish me to be your wife I shall be proud and honoured.'

He took her in his arms, and as he kissed her, she wept tears of happiness. She did not want to think. She wanted merely to surrender herself to his strength.

# XVI

LADY KELSEY'S devout hope that her party would finish
without unpleasantness was singularly frustrated. Robert Boulger was irritated beyond endurance by the
things Lucy had said to him; and Lucy besides, as if to
drive him to distraction, had committed a peculiar in-
discretion. In her determination to show the world
in general, represented then by the two hundred people
who were enjoying Lady Kelsey's hospitality, that she,
the person most interested, did not for an instant believe what was said about Alec, Lucy had insisted on
dancing with him. Alec thought it unwise thus to out-
rage conventional opinion, but he could not withstand
her fiery spirit. Dick and Mrs. Crowley were partners
at the time, and the disapproval which Lucy saw in
their eyes, made her more vehement in her defiance.
She had caught Bobbie's glance, too, and she flung
back her head a little as she saw his livid anger.

Little by little Lady Kelsey's guests bade her farewell, and at three o'clock few were left. Lucy had
asked Alec to remain till the end, and he and Dick had
taken refuge in the smoking-room. Presently Boulger
came in with two men, named Mallins and Carbery,
whom Alec knew slightly. He glanced at Alec, and went
up to the table on which were cigarettes and various
things to drink. His companions had no idea that he
was bent upon an explanation and had asked them of
set purpose to come into that room.

' May we smoke here, Bobbie? ' asked one of them, a little embarrassed at seeing Alec, but anxious to carry things off pleasantly.

' Certainly. Dick insisted that this room should be particularly reserved for that purpose.'

' Lady Kelsey is the most admirable of all hostesses,' said Dick lightly.

He took out his case and offered a cigarette to Alec. Alec took it.

' Give me a match, Bobbikins, there's a good boy,' he said carelessly.

Boulger, with his back turned to Alec, took no notice of the request. He poured himself out some whisky, and raising the glass, deliberately examined how much there was in it. Alec smiled faintly.

" Bobbie, throw me over the matches,' he repeated.

At that moment Lady Kelsey's butler came into the room with a salver, upon which he put the dirty glasses. Bobbie, his back still turned, looked up at the servant.

' Miller.'

' Yes, sir.'

' Mr. MacKenzie is asking for something.'

' Yes, sir.'

' You might give me a match, will you? ' said Alec.

' Yes, sir.'

The butler put the matches on his salver and took them over to Alec, who lit his cigarette.

' Thank you.'

No one spoke till the butler left the room. Alec occupied himself idly in making smoke rings, and he watched them rise into the air. When they were alone he turned slowly to Boulger.

'I perceive that during my absence you have not added good manners to your other accomplishments,' he said.

Boulger wheeled round and faced him.

'If you want things you can ask servants for them.'

'Don't be foolish,' smiled Alec, good-humouredly.

Alec's contemptuous manner robbed Boulger of his remaining self-control. He strode angrily to Alec.

'If you talk to me like that I'll knock you down.'

Alec was lying stretched out on the sofa, and did not stir. He seemed completely unconcerned.

'You could hardly do that when I'm already lying on my back,' he murmured.

Boulger clenched his fists. He gasped in the fury of his anger.

'Look here, MacKenzie, I'm not going to let you play the fool with me. I want to know what answer you have to make to Macinnery's accusation.'

'Might I suggest that only Miss Allerton has the least right to receive answers to her questions? And she hasn't questioned me.'

'I've given up trying to understand her attitude. If I were she, it would make me sick with horror to look at you. But after all I have the right to know something. George Allerton was my cousin.'

Alec rose slowly from the sofa. He faced Boulger with an indifference which was peculiarly irritating.

'That is a fact upon which he did not vastly pride himself.'

'Since this morning you've rested under a perfectly direct charge of causing his death in a dastardly manner. And you've said nothing in self-defence.'

' I haven't.'

' You've been given an opportunity of explaining yourself, and you haven't taken it.'

' Quite true.'

' What are you going to do? '

Alec had already been asked that question by Dick, and he returned the same answer.

' Nothing.'

Bobbie looked at him for an instant. Then he shrugged his shoulders.

' In that case I can draw only one conclusion. There appears to be no means of bringing you to justice, but at least I can tell you what an indescribable blackguard I think you.'

' All is over between us,' smiled Alec, faintly amused at the young man's violence. ' And shall I return your letters and your photographs? '

' I assure you that I'm not joking,' answered Bobbie grimly.

' I have observed that you joke with difficulty. It's singular that though I'm Scotch and you are English, *I* should be able to see how ridiculous you are, while you're quite blind to your own absurdity.'

' Come, Alec, remember he's only a boy,' remonstrated Dick, who till now had been unable to interpose.

Boulger turned upon him angrily.

' I'm perfectly able to look after myself, Dick, and I'll thank you not to interfere.' He looked again at Alec: ' If Lucy's so indifferent to her brother's death that she's willing to keep up with you, that's her own affair.'

Dick interrupted once more.

' For heaven's sake don't make a scene, Bobbie. How can you make such a fool of yourself? '

' Leave me alone, confound you! '

' Do you think this is quite the best place for an altercation? ' asked Alec quietly. ' Wouldn't you gain more notoriety if you attacked me in my club or at Church Parade on Sunday? '

' It's mere shameless impudence that you should come here to-night,' cried Bobbie, his voice hoarse with passion. ' You're using these wretched women as a shield, because you know that as long as Lucy sticks to you, there are people who won't believe the story.'

' I came for the same reason as yourself, dear boy. Because I was invited.'

' You acknowledge that you have no defence.'

' Pardon me, I acknowledge nothing and deny nothing.'

' That won't do for me,' said Boulger. ' I want the truth, and I'm going to get it. I've got a right to know.'

' Don't make such an ass of yourself,' cried Alec, shortly.

' By God, I'll make you answer.'

He went up to Alec furiously, as if he meant to seize him by the throat, but Alec, with a twist of the arm, hurled him backwards.

' I could break your back, you silly boy,' he cried, in a voice low with anger.

With a cry of rage Bobbie was about to spring at Alec when Dick got in his way.

' For God's sake, let us have no scenes here. And you'll only get the worst of it, Bobbie. Alec could just crumple you up.' He turned to the two men who stood

behind, startled by the unexpectedness of the quarrel.
' Take him away, Mallins, there's a good chap.'

' Let me alone, you fool!' cried Bobbie.

' Come along, old man,' said Mallins, recovering
himself.

When his two friends had got Bobbie out of the
room, Dick heaved a great sigh of relief.

' Poor Lady Kelsey!' he laughed, beginning to see
the humour of the situation. ' To-morrow half London will be saying that you and Bobbie had a stand-up
fight in her drawing-room.'

Alec looked at him angrily. He was not a man of
easy temper, and the effort he had put upon himself
was beginning to tell.

' You really needn't have gone out of your way to in-
furiate the boy,' said Dick.

Alec wheeled round wrathfully.

' The damned cubs,' he said. ' I should like to break
their silly necks.'

' You have an amiable character, Alec,' retorted
Dick.

Alec began to walk up and down excitedly. Dick had
never seen him before in such a state.

' The position is growing confoundedly awkward,' he
said drily.

Then Alec burst out.

' They lick my boots till I loathe them, and then
they turn against me like a pack of curs. Oh, I despise
them, these silly boys who stay at home wallowing in
their ease, while men work—work and conquer. Thank
God, I've done with them now. They think one can
fight one's way through Africa as easily as walk down
Piccadilly. They think one goes through hardship and

danger, illness and starvation, to be the lion of a dinner-party in Mayfair.'

'I think you're unfair to them,' answered Dick. 'Can't you see the other side of the picture? You're accused of a particularly low act of treachery. Your friends were hoping that you'd be able to prove at once that it was an abominable lie, and for some reason which no one can make out, you refuse even to notice it.'

'My whole life is proof that it's a lie.'

'Don't you think you'd better change your mind and make a statement that can be sent to the papers?'

'No, damn you!'

Dick's good nature was imperturbable, and he was not in the least annoyed by Alec's vivacity.

'My dear chap, do calm down,' he laughed.

Alec started at the sound of his mocking. He seemed again to become aware of himself. It was interesting to observe the quite visible effort he made to regain his self-control. In a moment he had mastered his excitement, and he turned to Dick with studied nonchalance.

'Do you think I look wildly excited?' he asked blandly.

Dick smiled.

'If you will permit me to say so, I think butter would have *no* difficulty in melting in your mouth,' he replied.

'I never felt cooler in my life.'

'Lucky man, with the thermometer at a hundred and two!'

Alec laughed and put his arm through Dick's.

'Perhaps we had better go home,' he said.

'Your common sense is no less remarkable than your personal appearance,' answered Dick gravely.

They had already bidden their hostess good-night, and getting their things, they set out to walk their different ways. When Dick got home he did not go to bed. He sat in an armchair, considering the events of the evening, and trying to find some way out of the complexity of his thoughts. He was surprised when the morning sun sent a bright ray of light into his room.

But Lady Kelsey was not yet at the end of her troubles. Bobbie, having got rid of his friends, went to her and asked if she would not come downstairs and drink a cup of soup. The poor lady, quite exhausted, thought him very considerate. One or two persons, with their coats on, were still in the room, waiting for their womenkind; and in the hall there was a little group of belated guests huddled around the door, while cabs and carriages were being brought up for them. There was about everyone the lassitude which follows the gaiety of a dance. The waiters behind the tables were heavy-eyed. Lucy was bidding good-bye to one or two more intimate friends.

Lady Kelsey drank the hot soup with relief.

' My poor legs are dropping,' she said. ' I'm sure I'm far too tired to go to sleep.'

' I want to talk to Lucy before I go,' said Bobbie, abruptly.

' To-night? ' she asked in dismay.

' Yes, I want you to send her a message that you wish to see her in your *boudoir.*'

' Why, what on earth's the matter? '

' She can't go on in this way. It's perfectly monstrous. Something must be done immediately.'

Lady Kelsey understood what he was driving at. She knew how great was his love, and she, too, had seen his anger when Lucy danced with Alec MacKenzie. But the whole affair perplexed her utterly. She put down her cup.

'Can't you wait till to-morrow?' she asked nervously.

'I feel it ought to be settled at once.'

'I think you're dreadfully foolish. You know how Lucy resents any interference with her actions.'

'I shall bear her resentment with fortitude,' he said, with great bitterness.

Lady Kelsey looked at him helplessly.

'What do you want me to do?' she asked.

'I want you to be present at our interview.'

He turned to a servant and told him to ask Miss Allerton from Lady Kelsey if she would kindly come to the *boudoir*. He gave his arm to Lady Kelsey, and they went upstairs. In a moment Lucy appeared.

'Did you send for me, my aunt? I'm told you want to speak to me here.'

'I asked Aunt Alice to beg you to come here,' said Boulger. 'I was afraid you wouldn't if *I* asked you.'

Lucy looked at him with raised eyebrows and answered lightly.

'What nonsense! I'm always delighted to enjoy your society.'

'I wanted to speak to you about something, and I thought Aunt Alice should be present.'

Lucy gave him a quick glance. He met it coolly.

'Is it so important that it can't wait till to-morrow?'

'I venture to think it's very important. And by now everybody has gone.'

'I'm all attention,' she smiled.

Boulger hesitated for a moment, then braced himself for the ordeal.

' I've told you often, Lucy, that I've been desperately in love with you for more years than I can remember,' he said, flushing with nervousness.

' Surely you've not snatched me from my last chance of a cup of soup in order to make me a proposal of marriage? '

' I'm perfectly serious, Lucy.'

' I assure you it doesn't suit you at all,' she smiled.

' The other day I asked you again to marry me, just before Alec MacKenzie came back.'

A softer light came into Lucy's eyes, and the bantering tones fell away from her voice.

' It was very charming of you,' she said gravely. ' You mustn't think that because I laugh at you a little, I'm not very grateful for your affection.'

' You know how long he's cared for you, Lucy,' said Lady Kelsey.

Lucy went up to him and very tenderly placed her hand on his arm.

' I'm immensely touched by your great devotion, Bobbie, and I know that I've done nothing to deserve it. I'm very sorry that I can't give you anything in return. One's not mistress of one's love. I can only hope—with all my heart—that you'll fall in love with some girl who cares for you. You don't know how much I want you to be happy.'

Boulger drew back coldly. He would not allow himself to be touched, though the sweetness of her voice tore his heart-strings.

' Just now it's not my happiness that's concerned,' he said. ' When Alec MacKenzie came back I thought I saw why nothing that I could do, had the power to change the utter indifference with which you looked at me.'

He paused a moment and coughed uneasily.

' I don't know why you think it necessary to say all this,' said Lucy, in a low voice.

' I tried to resign myself. You've always worshipped strength, and I understood that you must think Alec MacKenzie very wonderful. I had little enough to offer you when I compared myself with him. I hoped against hope that you weren't in love with him.'

' Well ? '

' Except for that letter in this morning's paper I should never have dared to say anything to you again. But that changes everything.'

He paused once more. Though he tried to seem so calm, his heart was beating furiously. He really loved Lucy with all his soul, and he was doing what seemed to him a plain duty.

' I ask you again if you'll be my wife.'

' I don't understand what you mean,' she said slowly.

' You can't marry Alec MacKenzie now.'

Lucy flung back her head. She grew very pale.

' You have no right to talk to me like this,' she said. ' You really presume too much upon my good nature.'

' I think I have some right. I'm the only man who's related to you at all, and I love you.'

They saw that Lady Kelsey wanted to speak, and Lucy turned round to her.

' I think you should listen to him, Lucy. I'm growing old, and soon you'll be quite alone in the world.'

The simple kindness of her words calmed the passions of the other two, and brought down the conversation to a gentler level.

'I'll try my best to make you a good husband, Lucy,' said Bobbie, very earnestly. 'I don't ask you to care for me; I only want to serve you.'

'I can only repeat that I'm very grateful to you. But I can't marry you, and I shall never marry you.'

Boulger's face grew darker, and he was silent.

'Are you going to continue to know Alec MacKenzie?' he asked at length.

'You have no right to ask me such a question.'

'If you'll take the advice of any unprejudiced person about that letter, you'll find that he'll say the same as I. There can be no shadow of a doubt that the man is guilty of a monstrous crime.'

'I don't care what the evidence is,' said Lucy. 'I know he can't have done a shameful thing.'

'But, good God, have you forgotten that it's your own brother whom he killed!' he cried hotly. 'The whole country is up in arms against him, and you are quite indifferent.'

'Oh, Bobbie, how can you say that?' she wailed, suddenly moved to the very depths of her being. 'How can you be so cruel?'

He went up to her, and they stood face to face. He spoke very quickly, flinging the words at her with indignant anger.

'If you cared for George at all, you must wish to punish the man who caused his death. At least you can't continue to be his'—he stopped as he saw the agony in her eyes, and changed his words—'his greatest friend. It was your doing that George went to Africa at all. The least thing you can do is to take some interest in his death.'

She put up her hands to her eyes, as though to drive away the sight of hateful things.

' Oh, why do you torment me? ' she cried pitifully. ' I tell you he isn't guilty.'

' He's refused to answer anyone. I tried to get something out of him, but I couldn't, and I lost my temper. He might give you the truth if you asked him pointblank.'

' I couldn't do that.'

' Why not? '

' It's very strange that he should insist on this silence,' said Lady Kelsey. ' One would have thought if he had nothing to be ashamed of, he'd have nothing to hide.'

' Do you believe that story, too? ' asked Lucy.

' I don't know what to believe. It's so extraordinary. Dick says he knows nothing about it. If the man's innocent, why on earth doesn't he speak? '

' He knows I trust him,' said Lucy. ' He knows I'm proud to trust him. Do you think I would cause him the great pain of asking him questions? '

' Are you afraid he couldn't answer them? ' asked Boulger.

' No, no, no.'

' Well, just try. After all you owe as much as that to the memory of George. Try.'

' But don't you see that if he won't say anything, it's because there are good reasons,' she cried distractedly. ' How do I know what interests are concerned in the matter, beside which the death of George is insignificant . . .'

' Do you look upon it so lightly as that? '

She turned away, bursting into tears. She was like a hunted beast. There seemed no escape from the taunting questions.

' I must show my faith in him,' she sobbed.

' I think you're a little nervous to go into the matter too closely.'

' I believe in him implicitly. I believe in him with all the strength I've got.'

' Then surely it can make no difference if you ask him. There can be no reason for him not to trust you.'

' Oh, why don't you leave me alone? ' she wailed.

' I do think it's very unreasonable, Lucy,' said Lady Kelsey. ' He knows you're his friend. He can surely count on your discretion.'

' If he refused to answer me it would mean nothing. You don't know him as I do. He's a man of extraordinary character. If he has made up his mind that for certain reasons which we don't know, he must preserve an entire silence, nothing whatever will move him. Why should he answer? I believe in him absolutely. I think he's the greatest and most honourable man I've ever known. I should feel happy and grateful to be allowed to wait on him.'

' Lucy, what *do* you mean? ' cried Lady Kelsey.

But now Lucy had cast off all reserve. She did not mind what she said.

' I mean that I care more for his little finger than for the whole world. I love him with all my heart. And that's why he can't be guilty of this horrible thing, because I've loved him for years, and he's known it. And he loves me, and he's loved me always.'

She sank exhausted into a chair, gasping for breath.

Boulger looked at her for a moment, and he turned sick with anguish. What he had only suspected before, he knew now from her own lips; and it was harder than ever to bear. Now everything seemed ended.

'Are you going to marry him?' he asked.

'Yes.'

'In spite of everything?'

'In spite of everything,' she answered defiantly.

Bobbie choked down the groan of despairing rage that forced its way to his throat. He watched her for a moment.

'Good God,' he said at last, 'what is there in the man that he should have made you forget love and honour and common decency!'

Lucy made no reply. But she buried her face in her hands and wept. She rocked to and fro with the violence of her tears.

Without another word Bobbie turned round and left them. Lady Kelsey heard the door slam as he went out into the silent street.

# XVII

NEXT day Alec was called up to Lancashire.

When he went out in the morning, he saw on the placards of the evening papers that there had been a colliery explosion, but, his mind absorbed in other things, he paid no attention to it; and it was with a shock that, on opening a telegram which waited for him at his club, he found that the accident had occurred in his own mine. Thirty miners were entombed, and it was feared that they could not be saved. Immediately all thought of his own concerns fled from him, and sending for a time-table, he looked out a train. He found one that he could just catch. He took a couple of telegram forms in the cab with him, and on one scribbled instructions to his servant to follow him at once with clothes; the other he wrote to Lucy.

He just caught the train and in the afternoon found himself at the mouth of the pit. There was a little crowd around it of weeping women. All efforts to save the wretched men appeared to be useless. Many had been injured, and the manager's house had been converted into a hospital. Alec found everyone stunned by the disaster, and the attempts at rescue had been carried on feebly. He set himself to work at once. He put heart into the despairing women. He brought up everyone who could be of the least use and inspired them with his own resourceful courage. The day was drawing to a close, but no time could be lost; and all night they toiled. Alec, in his shirt sleeves, laboured as heartily as the strongest miner; he seemed to want neither rest nor food. With clenched teeth, silently, he fought a battle with death, and the prize was thirty living men. In the morning he refreshed himself with a bath, paid a hurried visit to the injured, and returned to the pit mouth.

He had no time to think of other things. He did not know that on this very morning another letter appeared in the *Daily Mail,* filling in the details of the case against him, adding one damning piece of evidence to another; he did not know that the papers, amazed and indignant at his silence, now were unanimous in their condemnation. It was made a party matter, and the radical organs used the scandal as a stick to beat the dying donkey which was then in power. A question was put down to be asked in the House.

Alec waged his good fight and neither knew nor cared that the bubble of his glory was pricked. Still the miners lived in the tomb, and forty-eight hours passed. Hope was failing in the stout hearts of those who laboured by his side, but Alec urged them to greater endeavours. And now nothing was needed but a dogged perseverance. His tremendous strength stood him in good stead, and he was able to work twenty hours on end. He did not spare himself. And he seemed able to call prodigies of endurance out of those who helped him; with that example it seemed easier to endure. And still they toiled unrestingly. But their hope was growing faint. Behind that wall thirty men were lying, hopeless, starving; and some perhaps were dead already. And it was terrible to think of the horrors that assailed them, the horror of rising water, the horror of darkness, and the gnawing pangs of hunger. Among them was a boy of fourteen. Alec had spoken to him by chance on one of the days he had recently spent there, and had been amused by his cheeky brightness. He was a blue-eyed lad with a laughing mouth. It was pitiful to think that all that joy of life should have been crushed by a blind, stupid disaster. His father had been killed, and his body, charred and disfigured, lay in the mortuary. The boy was imprisoned with his brother, a man older than himself, married, and the father of children. With angry vehemence Alec set to again. He would not be beaten.

At last they heard sounds, faint and muffled, but unmistakable. At all events some of them were still alive. The rescuers increased their efforts. Now it was only a question of hours. They were so near that it renewed their strength; all fatigue fell from them; it needed but a little courage.

At last!

With a groan of relief which tried hard to be a cheer, the last barrier was broken, and the prisoners were saved. They were brought out one by one, haggard, with sunken eyes that blinked feebly in the sunlight; their faces were pale with the shadow of death, and they could not stand on their feet. The bright-eyed boy was carried out in Alec's strong arms, and he tried to make a jest of it; but the smile on his lips was changed into a sob, and hiding his face in Alec's breast, he cried from utter weakness. They carried out his brother, and he was dead. His wife was waiting for him at the pit's mouth, with her children by her side.

This commonplace incident, briefly referred to in the

corner of a morning paper, made his own affairs strangely unimportant to Alec. Face to face with the bitter tragedy of women left husbandless, of orphaned children, and the grim horror of men cut off in the prime of their manhood, the agitation which his own conduct was causing fell out of view. He was harassed and anxious. Much business had to be done which would allow of no delay. It was necessary to make every effort to get the mine once more into working order; it was necessary to provide for those who had lost the breadwinner. Alec found himself assailed on all sides with matters of urgent importance, and he had not a moment to devote to his own affairs. When at length it was possible for him to consider himself at all, he felt that the accident had raised him out of the narrow pettiness which threatened to submerge his soul; he was at close quarters with malignant fate, and he had waged a desperate battle with the cruel blindness of chance. He could only feel an utter scorn for the people who bespattered him with base charges. For, after all, his conscience was free.

When he wrote to Lucy, it never struck him that it was needful to refer to the events that had preceded his departure from London, and his letter was full of the strenuous agony of the past days. He told her how they had fought hand to hand with death and had snatched the prey from his grasp. In a second letter he told her what steps he was taking to repair the damage that had been caused, and what he was doing for those who were in immediate need. He would have given much to be able to write down the feelings of passionate devotion with which Lucy filled him, but with the peculiar shyness which was natural to him, he

could not bring himself to it. Of the accusation with
which the world was ringing, he said never a word.

Lucy read his letters over and over again. She
could not understand them, and they seemed strangely
indifferent. At that distance from the scene of the disaster she could not realise its absorbing anxiety, and she
was bitterly disappointed at Alec's absence. She wanted
his presence so badly, and she had to bear alone, on
her own shoulders, the full weight of her trouble. When
Macinnery's second letter appeared, Lady Kelsey gave
it to her without a word. It was awful. The whole
thing was preposterous, but it hung together in a way
that was maddening, and there was an air of truth about
it which terrified her. And why should Alec insist on
this impenetrable silence? She had offered herself the
suggestion that political exigencies with regard to the
states whose spheres of influence bordered upon the territory which Alec had conquered, demanded the strict-
est reserve; but this explanation soon appeared fantastic. She read all that was said in the papers and
found that opinion was dead against Alec. Now that
it was become a party matter, his own side defended
him; but in a half-hearted way, which showed how poor
the case was. And since all that could be urged in his
favour, Lucy had already repeated to herself a thousand
times, what was said against him seemed infinitely more
conclusive than what was said for him. And then her
conscience smote her. Those cruel words of Bobbie's
came back to her, and she was overwhelmed with self-
reproach when she considered that it was her own
brother of whom was all this to-do. She must be utterly heartless or utterly depraved. And then with a

despairing energy she cried out that she believed in
Alec; he was incapable of a treacherous act.

At last she could bear it no longer, and she wired to
him: *For God's sake come quickly.*

She felt that she could not endure another day of this
misery. She waited for him, given over to the wildest
fears; she was ashamed and humiliated. She counted
the hours which must pass before he could arrive; surely
he would not delay. All her self-possession had vanished, and she was like a child longing for the protecting
arms that should enfold it.

At last he came. Lucy was waiting in the same room
in which she had sat on their first meeting after his return to England. She sprang up, pale and eager, and
flung herself passionately into his arms.

'Thank God, you've come,' she said. 'I thought the
hours would never end.'

He did not know what so vehemently disturbed her,
but he kissed her tenderly, and on a sudden she felt
strangely comforted. There was an extraordinary
honesty about him which strengthened and consoled
her. For a while she could not speak, but clung to him,
sobbing.

'What is it?' he asked at length. 'Why did you
send for me?'

'I want your love. I want your love so badly.'

It was inconceivable, the exquisite tenderness with
which he caressed her. No one would have thought
that dour man capable of such gentleness.

'I felt I must see you,' she sobbed. 'You don't
know what tortures I've endured.'

'Poor child.'

He kissed her hair and her white, pained forehead.

'Why did you go away? You knew I wanted you.'

'I'm very sorry.'

'I've been horribly wretched. I didn't know I could suffer so much.'

'Come and sit down and tell me all about it.'

He led her to the sofa and made her sit beside him. His arms were around her, and she nestled close to him. For a moment she remained silent, enjoying the feeling of great relief after the long days of agony. She smiled lightly through her tears.

'The moment I'm with you I feel so confident and happy.'

'Only when you're with me?'

He asked the question caressingly, in a low passionate voice that she had never heard from his lips before. She did not answer, but clung more closely to him. Smiling, he repeated the question.

'Only when you're with me, darling?'

'I've told Bobbie and my aunt that we're going to be married. They made me suffer so dreadfully. I had to tell them. I couldn't keep it back, they said such horrible things about you.'

He did not answer for a moment.

'It's very natural.'

'It's nothing to you,' she cried desperately. 'But to me. . . . Oh, you don't know what agony I had to endure.'

'I'm glad you told them.'

'Bobby said I must be heartless and cruel. And it's true: George is nothing to me now when I think of you. My heart is so filled with my love for you that I haven't room for anything else.'

'I hope my love will make up for all that you have lost. I want you to be happy.'

She withdrew from his arms and leaned back, against the corner of the sofa. It was absolutely necessary to say what was gnawing at her heartstrings, but she felt ashamed and could not look at him.

'That wasn't the only reason I told them. I'm such a coward. I thought I was much braver.'

'Why?'

Lucy felt on a sudden sick at heart. She began to tremble a little, and it was only by great strength of will that she forced herself to go on. She was horribly frightened. Her mouth was dry, and when at last the words came, her voice sounded unnatural.

'I wanted to burn my ships behind me. I wanted to reassure myself.'

This time it was Alec who did not answer, for he understood now what was on her mind. His heart sank, since he saw already that he must lose her. But he had faced that possibility long ago in the heavy forests of Africa, and he had made up his mind that Lucy could do without love better than without self-respect.

He made a movement to get up, but quickly Lucy put out her hand. And then suddenly a fire seized him, and a vehement determination not to give way till the end.

'I don't understand you,' he said quietly.

'Forgive me, dear,' she said.

She held his hand in hers, and she spoke quickly.

'You don't know how terrible it is. I stand so dreadfully alone. Everyone is so bitter against you, and not a soul has a good word to say for you. It's all so extraordinary and so inexplicable. It seems as if I am the only person who isn't convinced that you caused poor George's death. Oh, how callous and utterly heartless people must think me!'

'Does it matter very much what people think?' he said gravely.

'I'm so ashamed of myself. I try to put the thoughts out of my head, but I can't. I simply can't. I've tried to be brave. I've refused to discuss the possibility of there being anything in those horrible charges. I wanted to talk to Dick—I knew he was fond of you—but I didn't dare. It seemed treacherous to you, and I wouldn't let anyone see that it meant anything to me. The first letter wasn't so bad, but the second—oh, it looks so dreadfully true.'

Alec gave her a rapid glance. This was the first he had heard of another communication to the paper. During the frenzied anxiety of those days at the colliery, he had had time to attend to nothing but the pressing work of rescue. But he made no reply.

'I've read it over and over again, and I *can't* understand. When Bobbie says it's conclusive, I tell him it means nothing—but—don't you see what I mean? The uncertainty is more than I can bear.'

She stopped suddenly, and now she looked at him. There was a pitiful appeal in her eyes.

'At the first moment I felt so absolutely sure of you.'

'And now you don't?' he asked quietly.

She cast down her eyes once more, and a sob caught her breath.

'I trust you just as much as ever. I know it's impossible that you should have done a shameful deed.

But there it stands in black and white, and you have nothing to say in answer.'

' I know it's very difficult. That's why I asked you to believe in me.'

' I do, Alec,' she cried vehemently. ' With all my soul. But have mercy on me. I'm not as strong as I thought. It's easy for you to stand alone. You're iron. You're a mountain of granite. But I'm a weak woman, pitifully weak.'

He shook his head.

' Oh, no, you're not like other women.'

' It was easy to be brave where my father was concerned, or George, but now it's so different. Love has changed me. I haven't the courage any more to withstand the opinion of all my fellows.'

Alec got up and walked once or twice across the room. He seemed to be thinking deeply. Lucy fancied that he must hear the beating of her heart. He stopped in front of her. Her heart was wrung by the great pain that was in his voice.

' Don't you remember that only a few days ago I told you that I'd done nothing which I wouldn't do again? I gave you my word of honour that I could reproach myself for nothing.'

' Oh, I know,' she cried. ' I'm so utterly ashamed of myself. But I can't bear the doubt.'

' *Doubt*. You've said the word at last.'

' I tell myself that I don't believe a word of these horrible charges. I repeat to myself: I'm certain, I'm certain that he's innocent.'

She gathered strength in the desperation of her love, and now at the crucial moment she had all the courage she needed.

'And yet at the bottom of my heart there's the doubt. And I *can't* crush it.'

She waited for him to answer, but he did not speak.

'I wanted to kill that bitter pain of suspicion. I thought if I stood up before them and cried out that my trust in you was so great, I was willing to marry you notwithstanding everything—I should at last have peace in my heart.'

Alec went to the window and looked out. The westering sun slanted across the street. Carriages and motors were waiting at the door of the house opposite, and a little crowd of footmen clustered about the steps. They were giving a party, and through the open windows Alec could see a throng of women. The sky was very blue. He turned back to Lucy.

'Will you show me the second letter of which you speak?'

'Haven't you seen it?' she asked in astonishment.

'I was so busy, I had no time to look at the papers. I suppose no one thought it his business to draw my attention to it.'

Lucy went into the second drawing-room, divided from that in which they sat by an archway, and brought him the copy of the *Daily Mail* for which he asked. She gave it, and he took it silently. He sat down and with attention read the letter through. He observed with bitter scorn the thoroughness with which Macinnery had set out the case against him. In this letter he filled up the gaps which had been left in the first, adding here and there details which gave a greater coherency to the whole; and his evidence had an air of truth, since he quoted the very words of porters and askari who had been on the expedition. It was

wonderful what power had that small admixture of
falsehood joined with what was admittedly true, to
change the whole aspect of the case. Alec was obliged
to confess that Lucy had good grounds for her suspicion. There was a specious look about the story,
which would have made him credit it himself if some
other man had been concerned. The facts were given
with sufficient exactness, and the untruth lay only
in the motives that were ascribed to him; but who
could tell what another's motives were? Alec put the
paper on the table, and leaning back, his face resting
in his hand, thought deeply. He saw again that scene
in his tent when the wind was howling outside and the
rain falling, falling; he recalled George's white face,
the madness that came over him when he fired at Alec,
the humility of his submission. The earth covered the
boy, his crime, and his weakness. It was not easy
to save one's self at a dead man's expense. And he
knew that George's strength and courage had meant
more than her life to Lucy. How could he cause her
the bitter pain? How could he tell her that her brother
died because he was a coward and a rogue? How could
he tell her the pitiful story of the boy's failure to
redeem the good name that was so dear to her? And
what proof could he offer of anything he said? Walker
had been killed on the same night as George, poor
Walker with his cheerfulness in difficulties and his
buoyant spirits: his death too must be laid to the
charge of George Allerton; Adamson had died of
fever. Those two alone had any inkling of the truth;
they could have told a story that would at least have
thrown grave doubts upon Macinnery's. But Alec set
his teeth; he did not want their testimony. Finally

there was the promise. He had given his solemn oath, and the place and the moment made it seem more binding, that he would utter no word that should lead Lucy to suspect even for an instant that her brother had been untrue to the trust she had laid upon him. Alec was a man of scrupulous truthfulness, not from deliberately moral motives but from mere taste, and he could not have broken his promise for the great discomfort it would have caused him. But it was the least of the motives which influenced him. Even if George had exacted nothing, he would have kept silence. And then, at the bottom of his heart, was a fierce pride. He was conscious of the honesty of his motives, and he expected that Lucy should share his consciousness. She must believe what he said to her because he said it. He could not suffer the humiliation of defending himself, and he felt that her love could not be very great if she could really doubt him. And because he was very proud perhaps he was unjust. He did not know that he was putting upon her a trial which he should have asked no one to bear.

He stood up and faced Lucy.

'What is it precisely you want me to do?' he asked.

'I want you to have mercy on me because I love you. Don't tell the world if you choose not to. But tell me the truth. I know you're incapable of lying. If I only have it from your own lips I shall believe. I want to be certain, certain.'

'Don't you realise that I would never have asked you to marry me if my conscience hadn't been quite clear?' he said slowly. 'Don't you see that the reasons I have for holding my tongue must be overwhelm-

ing, or I wouldn't stand by calmly while my good name
was torn from me shred by shred?'

'But I'm going to be your wife, and I love you, and
I know you love me.'

'I implore you not to insist, Lucy. Let us remember only that the past is gone and that we love one
another. It is impossible for me to tell you anything.'

'Oh, but you must now,' she implored. 'If anything has happened, if any part of the story is true,
you must give me a chance of judging for myself.'

'I'm very sorry. I can't.'

'But you'll kill my love for you.'

She sprang to her feet and pressed both hands to
her heart.

'The doubt that lurked at the bottom of my soul,
now fills me. How can you let me suffer such maddening torture?'

An expression of anguish passed across his calm eyes.
He made a gesture of despair.

'I thought you trusted me.'

'I'll be satisfied if you'll only tell me one thing.'
She put her hands to her head with a rapid, aimless
movement that showed the extremity of her agitation.
'Oh, what has love done with me?' she cried desperately. 'I was so proud of my brother and so utterly
devoted to him. But I loved you so much that there
wasn't any room in my heart for the past. I forgot all
my unhappiness and all my loss. And even now they
seem so little to me beside your love that it's you I
think of first. I want to know that I can love you
freely. I'll be satisfied if you'll only tell me that
when you sent George out that night, you didn't *know*
he'd be killed.'

Alec looked at her steadily. And once more he saw himself in the African tent amid the rain and the boisterous wind. At the time he sought to persuade himself that George had a chance of escape. He told him with his own lips that if he showed perfect self-confidence at the moment of danger he might save himself alive; but at the bottom of his heart he knew, he had known all along, that it was indeed death he was sending him to, for George had not the last virtue of a scoundrel, courage.

' Only say that, Alec,' she repeated. ' Say that's not true, and I'll believe you.'

There was a silence. Lucy's heart beat against her breast like a caged bird. She waited in horrible suspense.

' But it is true,' he said, very quietly.

Lucy did not answer. She stared at him with terrified eyes. Her brain reeled, and she feared that she was going to faint. She had to put forth all her strength to drive back the enveloping night that seemed to crowd upon her.

' It is true,' he repeated.

She gave a gasp of pain.

' I don't understand. Oh, my dearest, don't treat me as a child. Have mercy on me. You must be serious now. It's a matter of life and death to both of us.'

' I'm perfectly serious.'

A frightful coldness appeared to seize her, and the tips of her fingers were strangely numbed.

' You knew that you were sending George into a death-trap? You knew that he could not escape alive? '

' Except by a miracle.'

' And you don't believe in miracles? '

Alec made no answer. She looked at him with increasing horror. Her eyes were staring wildly. She repeated the question.

'And you don't believe in miracles?'

'No.'

She was seized with all manner of conflicting emotions. They seemed to wage a tumultuous battle in the depths of her heart. She was filled with horror and dismay, bitter anger, remorse for her callous indifference to George's death; and at the same time she felt an overwhelming love for Alec. And how could she love him now?

'Oh, it can't be true,' she cried. 'It's infamous. Oh, Alec, Alec, Alec . . . O God, what shall I do.'

Alec held himself upright. He set his teeth, and his heavy jaw seemed squarer than ever. There was a great sternness in his voice.

'I tell you that whatever I did was inevitable.'

Lucy flushed at the sound of his voice, and anger and sudden hatred took the place of all other feelings.

'Then if that's true, the rest must be true. Why don't you acknowledge as well that you sacrificed my brother's life in order to save your own?'

But the mood passed quickly, and in a moment she was seized with dismay.

'Oh, it's awful. I can't realise it.' She turned to him with a desperate appeal. 'Haven't you anything to say at all? You know how much I loved my brother. You know how much it meant to me that he should live to wipe out all memory of my father's crime. All the future was centred upon him. You can't have sacrificed him callously.'

Alec hesitated for an instant.

'I think I might tell you this,' he said. 'We were entrapped by the Arabs, and our only chance of escape entailed the death of one of us.'

'So you chose my brother because you loved me.'

Alec looked at her. There was an extraordinary sadness in his eyes, but she did not see it. He answered very gravely.

'You see, the fault was his. He had committed a grave error. It was not unjust that he should suffer for the catastrophe that he had brought about.'

'At those times one doesn't think of justice. He was so young, so frank and honest. Wouldn't it have been nobler to give your life for his?'

'Oh, my dear,' he answered, with all the gentleness that was in him, 'you don't know how easy it is to give one's life, how much more difficult it is to be just than generous. How little you know me! Do you think I should have hesitated if the difficulty had been one that my death could solve? It was necessary that I should live. I had my work to do. I was bound by solemn treaties to the surrounding tribes. Even if that had been all, it would have been cowardly for me to die.'

'It is easy to find excuses for not acting like a brave man.' She flung the words at him with indignant scorn.

'I was indispensable,' he answered. 'The whites I took with me I chose as instruments, not as leaders. If I had died the expedition would have broken in pieces. It was my influence that held together such of the native tribes as remained faithful to us. I had given my word that I would not desert them till I had exterminated the slave-raiders. Two days after my death my force would have melted away, and the whites would have been helpless. Not one of them would have escaped. And then the country would have been given up, defenceless, to those cursed Arabs. Fire and sword would have come instead of the peace I promised; and the whole country would have been rendered desolate. I tell you that it was my duty to live till I had carried out my work.'

Lucy drew herself up a little. She looked at him firmly, and said very quietly and steadily:

'You coward! You coward!'

'I knew at the time that what I did might cost me your love, and though you won't believe this, I did it for your sake.'

'I wish I had a whip in my hand that I might slash you across the face.'

For a moment he did not say anything. She was quivering with indignation and with contempt.

'You see, it has cost me your love,' he said. 'I suppose it was inevitable.'

'I am ashamed that I ever loved you.'

'Good-bye.'

He turned round and walked slowly to the door. He held his head erect, and there was no sign of emotion on his face. But as soon as he was gone Lucy could keep her self-control no longer. She sank into a chair, and hiding her face, began to sob as though her poor tortured heart would break.

## XVIII

ALEC went back to Lancashire next day. Much was still required before the colliery could be put once more in proper order, and he was overwhelmed with work. Lucy was not so fortunate. She had nothing to do but to turn over in her mind the conversation they had had. She passed one sleepless night after another. She felt ill and wretched. She told Lady Kelsey that her engagement with MacKenzie was broken off, but gave no reason; and Lady Kelsey, seeing her white, tortured face, had not the heart to question her. The good lady knew that her niece was desperately unhappy, but she did not know how to help her. Lucy never sought for the sympathy of others and chose rather to bear her troubles alone. The season was drawing to a close, and Lady Kelsey suggested that they should advance by a week or two the date of their departure for the country; but Lucy would do nothing to run away from her suffering.

'I don't know why you should alter your plans,' she said quietly.

Lady Kelsey looked at her compassionately, but did not insist. She felt somehow that Lucy was of different clay from herself, and for all her exquisite gentleness, her equanimity and pleasant temper, she had never been able to get entirely at close quarters with her. She would have given much to see Lucy give way openly to her grief; and her arms would have been open to receive her, if her niece had only flung herself

simply into them. But Lucy's spirit was broken. With
the extreme reserve that was part of her nature, she put
all her strength into the effort to behave in the world
with decency; and dreading any attempt at commiseration, she forced herself to be no less cheerful than
usual. The strain was hardly tolerable. She had set
all her hopes of happiness upon Alec, and he had failed
her. She thought more of her brother and her father
than she had done of late, and she mourned for them
both as though the loss she had sustained were quite recent. It seemed to her that the only thing now was to
prevent herself from thinking of Alec, and with angry
determination she changed her thoughts as soon as
he came into them.

Presently something else occurred to her. She felt
that she owed some reparation to Bobbie: he had seen
the truth at once, and because he had pointed it out
to her, as surely it was his duty to do, she had answered
him with bitter words. He had shown himself extraordinarily kind, and she had been harsh and cruel.
Perhaps he knew that she was no longer engaged to
marry Alec MacKenzie, and he must guess the reason;
but since the night of the dance he had not been near
them. She looked upon what Alec had told her as addressed to her only, and she could not repeat it to all
and sundry. When acquaintances had referred to the
affair, her manner had shown them quickly that she
did not intend to discuss it. But Robert Boulger was
different. It seemed necessary, in consideration of all
that had passed, that he should be told the little she
knew; and then she thought also, seized on a sudden
with a desire for self-sacrifice, that it was her duty
perhaps to reward him for his long devotion. She

might at least try to make him a good wife; and she could explain exactly how she felt towards him. There would be no deceit. Her life had no value now, and if it really meant so much to him to marry her, it was right that she should consent. And there was another thing: it would put an irrevocable barrier between herself and Alec.

Lady Kelsey was accustomed to ask a few people to luncheon every Tuesday, and Lucy suggested that they should invite Bobbie on one of these occasions. Lady Kelsey was much pleased, for she was fond of her nephew, and it had pained her that she had not seen him. She had sent a line to tell him that Lucy was no longer engaged, but he had not answered. Lucy wrote the invitation herself.

*My Dear Bobbie:*
*Aunt Alice will be very glad if you can lunch with us on Tuesday at two. We are asking Dick, Julia Crowley, and Canon Spratte. If you can come, and I hope you will, it would be very kind of you to arrive a good deal earlier than the others; I want to talk to you about something.*

*Yours affectionately,*

*Lucy.*

He answered at once.

*My Dear Lucy:*
*I will come with pleasure. I hope half-past one will suit you.* *Your affectionate cousin,*

*Robert Boulger.*

'Why haven't you been to see us?' she said, holding his hand, when at the appointed time he appeared.

'I thought you didn't much want to see me.'

'I'm afraid I was very cruel and unkind to you last time you were here,' she said.

'It doesn't matter at all,' he said gently.

'I think I should tell you that I did as you suggested to me. I asked Alec MacKenzie pointblank, and he confessed that he was guilty of George's death.'

'I'm very sorry,' said Bobbie.

'Why?' she asked, looking up at him with tear-laden eyes.

'Because I know that you were very much in love with him,' he answered.

Lucy flushed. But she had much more to say.

'I was very unjust to you on the night of that dance. You were right to speak to me as you did, and I was very foolish. I regret what I said, and I beg you to forgive me.'

'There's nothing to forgive, Lucy,' he said warmly. 'What does it matter what you said? You know I love you.'

'I don't know what I've done to deserve such love,' she said. 'You make me dreadfully ashamed of myself.'

He took her hand, and she did not attempt to withdraw it.

'Won't you change your mind, Lucy?' he said earnestly.

'Oh, my dear, I don't love you. I wish I did. But I don't and I'm afraid I never can.'

'Won't you marry me all the same?'

'Do you care for me so much as that?' she cried painfully.

'Perhaps you will learn to love me in time.'

LUCY

'Don't be so humble; you make me still more ashamed. Bobbie, I should like to make you happy if I thought I could. It seems very wonderful to me that you should want to have me. But I must be honest with you. I know that if I pretend I'm willing to marry you merely for your sake I'm deceiving myself. I want to marry you because I'm afraid. I want to crush my love for Alec. I want to make it impossible for me ever to weaken in my resolve. You see, I'm horrid and calculating, and it's very little I can offer you.'

'I don't care why you're marrying me,' he said. 'I want you so badly.'

'Oh, no, don't take me like that. Let me say first that if you really think me worth having, I will do my duty gladly. And if I have no love to give, I have a great deal of affection and a great deal of gratitude. I want you to be happy.'

He went down on his knees and kissed her hands passionately.

'I'm so thankful,' he murmured. 'I'm so thankful.'

Lucy bent down and gently kissed his hair. Two tears rolled heavily down her cheeks.

Five minutes later Lady Kelsey came in. She was delighted to see that her nephew and her niece were apparently once more on friendly terms; but she had no time to find out what had happened, for Canon Spratte was immediately announced. Lady Kelsey had heard that he was to be offered a vacant bishopric, and she mourned over his disappearance from London. He was a spiritual mentor who exactly suited her, handsome, urbane, attentive notwithstanding her mature age, and well-connected. He was just the man to be a bishop. Then Mrs. Crowley appeared. They waited a little, and presently Dick was announced. He sauntered in jauntily, unaware that he had kept the others waiting a full quarter of an hour; and the party was complete.

No gathering could be tedious when Canon Spratte was present, and the conversation proceeded merrily. Mrs. Crowley looked ravishing in a summer frock, and since she addressed herself exclusively to the handsome parson it was no wonder that he was in a good humour. She laughed appreciatively at his facile jests and gave him provoking glances of her bright eyes. He did not attempt to conceal from her that he thought American women the most delightful creatures in the world, and she made no secret of her opinion that ecclesiastical dignitaries were often fascinating. They paid one another outrageous compliments. It never struck the good man that these charms and graces were displayed only for the purpose of vexing a gentleman of forty, who was eating his luncheon irritably on the other side of her. She managed to avoid talking to Dick Lomas afterwards, but when she bade Lady Kelsey farewell, he rose also.

'Shall I drive you home?' he asked.

'I'm not going home, but if you like to drive me to Victoria Street, you may. I have an appointment there at four.'

They went out, stepped into a cab, and quite coolly Dick told the driver to go to Hammersmith. He sat himself down by her side, with a smile of self-satisfaction.

'What on earth are you doing?' she cried.

'I want to have a talk to you.'

'I'm sure that's charming of you,' she answered, 'but I shall miss my appointment.'

'That's a matter of complete indifference to me.'

'Don't bother about my feelings, will you?' she replied, satirically.

'I have no intention of doing so,' he smiled.

Mrs. Crowley was obliged to laugh at the neatness with which he had entrapped her. Or had he fallen into the trap which she had set for him? She really did not quite know.

'If your object in thus abducting me was to talk, hadn't you better do so?' she asked. 'I hope you will endeavour to be not only amusing but instructive.'

'I wanted to point out to you that it is not civil pointedly to ignore a man who is sitting next to you at luncheon.'

'Did I do that? I'm so sorry. But I know you're greedy, and I thought you'd be absorbed in the lobster mayonnaise.'

'I'm beginning to think I dislike you rather than otherwise,' he murmured reflectively.

'Ah, I suppose that is why you haven't been in to see me for so long.'

'May I venture to remind you that I've called upon you three times during the last week.'

'I've been out so much lately,' she answered, with a little wave of her hand.

'Nonsense. Once I heard you playing scales in the drawing-room, and once I positively saw you peeping at me through the curtains.'

'Why didn't you make a face at me?' she asked.

'You're not going to trouble to deny it?'

'It's perfectly true.'

Dick could not help giving a little laugh. He didn't quite know whether he wanted to kiss Julia Crowley or to shake her.

'And may I ask why you've treated me in this abominable fashion?' he asked blandly.

She looked at him sideways from beneath her long eyelashes. Dick was a man who appreciated the artifices of civilisation in the fair sex, and he was pleased with her pretty hat and with the flounces of her muslin frock.

'Because I chose,' she smiled.

He shrugged his shoulders and put on an air of resignation.

'Of course if you're going to make yourself systematically disagreeable unless I marry you, I suppose I must bow to the inevitable.'

'I don't know if you have the least idea what you're talking about,' she answered, raising her eybrows. 'I'm sure I haven't.'

'I was merely asking you in a rather well-turned phrase to name the day. The lamb shall be ready for the slaughter.'

'Is that a proposal of marriage?' she asked gaily.

'If not it must be its twin brother,' he returned.

'I'm so glad you've told me, because if I'd met it in the street I should never have recognised it, and I should simply have cut it dead.'

'You show as little inclination to answer a question as a cabinet minister in the House of Commons.'

'Couldn't you infuse a little romance into it? You see, I'm American, and I have a certain taste for sentiment in affairs of the heart.'

' I should be charmed, only you must remember that
I have no experience in these matters.'

' That is visible to the naked eye,' she retorted. ' But
I would suggest that it is only decent to go down on
your bended knees.'

' That sounds a perilous feat to perform in a hansom
cab, and it would certainly attract an amount of attention from passing 'bus-drivers which would be em-
barrassing.'

' You could never convince me of the sincerity of
your passion unless you did something of the kind,' she
replied.

' I assure you that it is quite out of fashion. Lovers
now-a-days are much too middle-aged, and their joints
are creaky. Besides it ruins the trousers.'

' I admit your last reason is overwhelming. No nice
woman should ask a man to make his trousers baggy
at the knees.'

' How could she love him if they were!' exclaimed
Dick.

' But at all events there can be no excuse for your
not saying that you know you are utterly unworthy
of me.'

' Wild horses wouldn't induce me to make a statement which is so remote from the truth,' he replied
coolly. ' I did it with my little hatchet.'

' And of course you must threaten to commit suicide
if I don't consent. That is only decent.'

' Women are such sticklers for routine,' he sighed.
' They have no originality. They have a passion for
commonplace, and in moments of emotion they fly
with unerring instinct into the flamboyance of melo-
drama.

'I like to hear you use long words. It makes me feel so grown up.'

'By the way, how old are you?' he asked suddenly.

'Twenty-nine,' she answered promptly.

'Nonsense. There is no such age.'

'Pardon me,' she protested gravely. 'Upper parlour maids are always twenty-nine. But I deplore your tendency to digress.'

'Am I digressing? I'm so sorry. What were we talking about?'

Julia giggled. She did not know where the cab was going, and she certainly did not care. She was thoroughly enjoying herself.

'You were taking advantage of my vast experience in such matters to learn how a man proposes to an eligible widow of great personal attractions.'

'Your advice can't be very valuable, since you always refused the others.'

'I didn't indeed,' she replied promptly. 'I made a point of accepting them all.'

'That at all events is encouraging.'

'Of course you may do it in your own way if you choose. But I must have a proposal in due form.'

'My intelligence may be limited, but it seems to me that only four words are needed.' He counted them out deliberately on his fingers. 'Will—you—marry —me?'

'That is both clear and simple.' She pressed back the thumb which he had left untouched. 'I reply in one: no.'

He looked at her with every sign of astonishment.

'I beg your pardon?' he said.

' You heard quite correctly,' she smiled. ' The reply is in the negative.'

She resisted a mad, but inconvenient, temptation to dance a breakdown on the floor of the hansom.

' You're joking,' said Dick calmly. ' You're certainly joking.'

' I will be a sister to you.'

Dick reflected for a moment, and he rubbed his chin.

' The chance will never recur, you know,' he remarked.

' I will bear the threat that is implied in that with fortitude.'

He turned round and taking her hand, raised it to his lips.

' I thank you from the bottom of my heart,' he said earnestly.

This puzzled her.

' The man's mad,' she murmured to a constable who stood on the curb as they passed. ' The man's nothing short of a raving lunatic.'

' It is one of my most cherished convictions that a really nice woman is never so cruel as to marry a man she cares for. You have given me proof of esteem which I promise I will never forget.'

Mrs. Crowley could not help laughing.

' You're much too flippant to marry anybody, and you're perfectly odious into the bargain.'

' I will be a brother to you, Mrs. Crowley.'

He opened the trap and told the cabman to drive back to Victoria Street, but at Hyde Park Corner he suggested that Mrs. Crowley might drop him so that he could take a stroll in the park. When he got out and closed the doors behind him, Julia leaned forward.

' Would you like some letters of introduction before you go? ' she said.

' What for? '

' It is evident that unless your soul is dead to all the finer feelings, you will seek to assuage your sorrow by shooting grizzlies in the Rocky Mountains. I thought a few letters to my friends in New York might be useful to you.'

' I'm sure that's very considerate of you, but I fancy it's scarcely the proper season. I was thinking of a week in Paris.'

' Then pray send me a dozen pairs of black suède gloves,' she retorted coolly. ' Sixes.'

' Is that your last word? ' he asked lightly.

' Yes, why? '

' I thought you might mean six and a half.'

He lifted his hat and was gone.

# XIX

A few days later, Lady Kelsey and Lucy having gone on the river, Julia Crowley went to Court Leys. When she came down to breakfast the day after her arrival, she found waiting for her six pairs of long suède gloves. She examined their size and their quality, smiled with amusement, and felt a little annoyed. She really had every intention of accepting Dick when he proposed to her, and she did not in the least know why she had refused him. The conversation had carried her away in her own despite. She loved a repartee and notwithstanding the consequences could never resist making any that occurred to her. It was very stupid of Dick to take her so seriously, and she was inclined to be cross with him. Of course he had only gone to Paris to tease, and in a week he would be back again. She knew that he was just as much in love with her as she was with him, and it was absurd of him to put on airs. She awaited the post each day impatiently, for she constantly expected a letter from him to say he was coming down to luncheon. She made up her mind about the *menu* of the pleasant little meal she would set before him, and in imagination rehearsed the scene in which she would at length succumb to his passionate entreaties. It was evidently discreet not to surrender with unbecoming eagerness. But no letter came. A week went by. She began to think that Dick had no sense of humour. A second week passed, and then a third. Perhaps it was because she had nothing to do that Master Dick absorbed a quite unmerited degree of her attention. It was very inconvenient and very absurd. She tormented herself with all sorts of reasons to explain his absence, and once or twice, like the spoiled child she was, she cried. But Mrs. Crowley was a sensible woman and soon made up her mind that if she could not live without the man—though heaven only knew why she wanted him—she had better take steps to secure his presence. It was the end of August now, and she was bored and lonely. She sent him a very untruthful telegram.

*I have to be in town on Friday to see my lawyer, May I come to tea at five?*                    *Julia.*

His answer did not arrive for twenty-four hours, and then it was addressed from Homburg.

*Regret immensely, but shall be away.*
                              *Richard Lomas.*

Julia stamped her tiny foot with indignation and laughed with amusement at her own anger. It was monstrous that while she was leading the dullest existence imaginable, he should be enjoying the gaieties of a fashionable watering-place. She telegraphed once more.

*Thanks very much. Shall expect to see you on Friday.*                              *Julia.*

She travelled up to town on the appointed day and went to her house in Norfolk Street to see that the journey had left no traces on her appearance. May-

fair seemed quite deserted, and half the windows were
covered with newspapers to keep out the dust. It was
very hot, and the sun beat down from a cloudless sky.
The pavements were white and dazzling. Julia realised
with pleasure that she was the only cool person in
London, and the lassitude she saw in the passers-by
added to her own self-satisfaction. The month at the
seaside had given an added freshness to her perfection,
and her charming gown had a breezy lightness that
must be very grateful to a gentleman of forty lately
returned from foreign parts. As she looked at herself in the glass, Mrs. Crowley reflected that she did
not know anyone who had a figure half so good as hers.

When she drove up to Dick's house, she noticed that
there were fresh flowers in the window boxes, and when
she was shown into his drawing-room, the first thing
that struck her was the scent of red roses which were
in masses everywhere. The blinds were down, and
after the baking street the dark coolness of the room
was very pleasant. The tea was on a little table, waiting to be poured out. Dick of course was there to
receive her. As she shook hands with him, she smoth-
ered a little titter of wild excitement.

' So you've come back,' she said.

' I was just passing through town,' he answered, with
an airy wave of the hand.

' From where to where? '

' From Homburg to the Italian Lakes.'

' Rather out of your way, isn't it? ' she smiled.

' Not at all,' he replied. ' If I were going from
Manchester to Liverpool, I should break the journey
in London. That's one of my hobbies.'

Julia laughed gaily, and as they both made a capital

tea, they talked of all manner of trivial things. They were absurdly glad to see one another again, and each was ready to be amused at everything the other said. But the conversation would have been unintelligible to a listener, since they mostly talked together, and every now and then made a little scene when one insisted that the other should listen to what he was saying.

Suddenly Mrs. Crowley threw up her hands with a gesture of dismay.

' Oh, how stupid of me! ' she cried. ' I quite forgot to tell you why I telegraphed to you the other day.'

' I know,' he retorted.

' Do you? Why? '

' Because you're the most disgraceful flirt I ever saw in my life,' he answered promptly.

She opened her eyes wide with a very good imitation of complete amazement.

' My dear Mr. Lomas, have you never contemplated yourself in a looking-glass? '

' You're not a bit repentant of the havoc you have wrought,' he cried dramatically.

She did not answer, but looked at him with a smile so entirely delightful that he cried out irritably:

' I wish you wouldn't look like that.'

' How am I looking? ' she smiled.

' To my innocent and inexperienced gaze very much as if you wanted to be kissed.'

' You brute! ' she cried. ' I'll never speak to you again.'

' Why do you make such rash statements? You know you couldn't hold you tongue for two minutes together.'

'What a libel! I never can get a word in edgeways when I'm with you,' she returned. 'You're such a chatterbox.'

'I don't know why you put on that aggrieved air. You seem to forget that it's I who ought to be furious.'

'On the contrary, you behaved very unkindly to me a month ago, and I'm only here to-day because I have a Christian disposition.'

'You forget that for the last four weeks I've been laboriously piecing together the fragments of a broken heart,' he answered.

'It was entirely your fault,' she laughed. 'If you hadn't been so certain I was going to accept you, I should never have refused. I couldn't resist the temptation of saying no, just to see how you took it.'

'I flatter myself I took it very well.'

'You didn't,' she answered. 'You showed an entire lack of humour. You might have known that a nice woman doesn't accept a man the first time he asks her. It was very silly of you to go to Homburg as if you didn't care. How was I to know that you meant to wait a month before asking me again?'

He looked at her for a moment calmly.

'I haven't the least intention of asking you again.'

But it required much more than this to put Julia Crowley out of countenance.

'Then why on earth did you invite me to tea?'

'May I respectfully remind you that you invited yourself?' he protested.

'That's just like a man. He will go into irrelevant details,' she answered.

'Now, don't be cross,' he smiled.

'I shall be cross if I want to,' she exclaimed, with a little stamp of her foot. 'You're not being at all nice to me.'

He looked at her thoughtfully for a moment, and his eyes twinkled.

'Do you know what I'd do if I were you?'

'No, what?'

'Well, *I* can't suffer the humiliation of another refusal. Why don't you propose to me?'

'What cheek!' she cried.

Their eyes met, and she smiled.

'What will you say if I do?'

'That entirely depends on how you do it.'

'I don't know how,' she murmured plaintively.

'Yes, you do,' he insisted. 'You gave me an admirable lesson. First you go on your bended knees, and then you say you're quite unworthy of me.'

'You are the most spiteful creature I've ever known,' she laughed. 'You're just the sort of man who'd beat his wife.'

'Every Saturday night regularly,' he agreed.

She hesitated, looking at him.

'Well?' he said.

'I shan't,' she answered.

'Then I shall continue to be a brother to you.'

She got up and curtsied.

'Mr. Lomas, I am a widow, twenty-nine years of age, and extremely eligible. My maid is a treasure, and my dressmaker is charming. I'm clever enough to laugh at your jokes and not so learned as to know where they come from.'

'Really you're very long winded. I said it all in four words.'

'You evidently put it too briefly, since you were refused,' she smiled.

She stretched out her hands, and he took them.

'I think I'll do it by post,' she said. 'It'll sound so much more becoming.'

'You'd better get it over now.'

'You know, I don't really want to marry you a bit. I'm only doing it to please you.'

'I admire your unselfishness.'

'You will say yes if I ask you?'

'I refuse to commit myself.'

'Obstinate beast,' she cried.

She curtsied once more, as well as she could since he was firmly holding her hands.

'Sir, I have the honour to demand your hand in marriage.'

He bowed elaborately.

'Madam, I have much pleasure in acceding to your request.'

Then he drew her towards him and put his arms around her.

'I never saw anyone make such a fuss about so insignificant a detail as marriage,' she murmured.

'You have the softest lips I ever kissed,' he said.

'I wish to goodness you'd be serious,' she laughed. 'I've got something very important to say to you.'

'You're not going to tell me the story of your past life,' he cried.

'No, I was thinking of my engagement ring. I make a point of having a cabochon emerald: I collect them.'

'No sooner said than done,' he cried.

He took a ring from his pocket and slipped it on her finger. She looked from it to him.

' You see, I know that you made a specialty of emeralds.'

' Then you meant to ask me all the time? '

' I confess it to my shame: I did,' he laughed.

' Oh, I wish I'd known that before.'

' What would you have done? '

' I'd have refused you again, you silly.'

Dick Lomas and Mrs. Crowley said nothing about their engagement to anyone, since it seemed to both that the marriage of a middle-aged gentleman and a widow of uncertain years could concern no one but themselves. The ceremony was duly performed in a deserted church on a warm September day, when there was not a soul in London. Mrs. Crowley was given away by her solicitor, and the verger signed the book. The happy pair went to Court Leys for a fortnight's honeymoon and at the beginning of October returned to London; they made up their minds that they would go to America later in the autumn.

' I want to show you off to all my friends in New York,' said Julia, gaily.

' Do you think they'll like me? ' asked Dick.

' Not at all. They'll say: That silly little fool Julia Crowley has married another beastly Britisher.'

' That is more alliterative than polite,' he retorted. ' On the other hand my friends and relations are already saying: What on earth has poor Dick Lomas married an American for? We always thought he was very well-to-do.'

They went into roars of laughter, for they were in that state of happiness when the whole world seemed the best of jokes, and they spent their days in laughing at one another and at things in general. Life was a pleasant thing, and they could not imagine why others should not take it as easily as themselves.

They had engaged rooms at the *Carlton* while they were furnishing a new house. Each had one already, but neither would live in the other's, and so it had seemed necessary to look out for a third. Julia vowed that there was an air of bachelordom about Dick's house which made it impossible for a married woman to inhabit; and Dick, on his side, refused to move into Julia's establishment in Norfolk Street, since it gave him the sensation of being a fortune-hunter living on his wife's income. Besides, a new house gave an opportunity for extravagance which delighted both of them since they realised perfectly that the only advantage of having plenty of money was to spend it in unneccessary ways. They were a pair of light-hearted children, who refused firmly to consider the fact that they were more than twenty-five.

Lady Kelsey and Lucy had gone from the River to Spa, for the elder woman's health, and on their return Julia went to see them in order to receive their congratulations and display her extreme happiness. She came back thoughtfully. When she sat down to luncheon with Dick in their sitting-room at the hotel, he saw that she was distubed. He asked her what was the matter.

'Lucy has broken off her engagement with Robert Boulger,' she said.

'That young woman seems to make a speciality of breaking her engagements,' he answered drily.

'I'm afraid she's still in love with Alec MacKenzie.'

'Then why on earth did she accept Bobbie?'

'My dear boy, she only took him in a fit of temper.

When that had cooled down she very wisely thought better of it.'

' I can never sufficiently admire the reasonableness of your sex,' said Dick, ironically.

Julia shrugged her pretty shoulders.

' Half the women I know merely married their husbands to spite somebody else. I assure you it's one of the commonest causes of matrimony.'

' Then heaven save me from matrimony,' cried Dick.

' It hasn't,' she laughed.

But immediately she grew serious once more.

' Mr. MacKenzie was in Brussels while they were in Spa.'

' I had a letter from him this morning.'

' Lady Kelsey says that according to the papers he's going to Africa again. I think it's that which has upset Lucy. They made a great fuss about him in Brussels.'

' Yes, he tells me that everything is fixed up, and he proposes to start quite shortly. He's going to do some work in the Congo Free State. They want to find a new waterway, and the King of the Belgians has given him a free hand.'

' I suppose the King of the Belgians looks upon one atrocity more or less with equanimity,' said Julia.

They were silent for a minute or two, while each was occupied with his own thoughts.

' You saw him after Lucy broke off the engagement,' said Julia, presently. ' Was he very wretched? '

' He never said a word. I wanted to comfort him, but he never gave me a chance. He never even mentioned Lucy's name.'

'Did he seem unhappy?'

'No. He was just the same as ever, impassive and collected.'

'Really, he's inhuman,' exclaimed Julia impatiently.

'He's an anomaly in this juvenile century,' Dick agreed. 'He's an ancient Roman who buys his clothes in Savile Row.'

'Then he's very much in the way in England, and it's much better that he should go back to Africa.'

'I suppose it is. Here he reminds one of an eagle caged with a colony of canaries.'

Julia looked at her husband reflectively.

'I think you're the only friend who has stuck to him,' she said.

'I wouldn't put it in that way. After all, I'm the only friend he ever had. It was not unnatural that a number of acquaintances should drop him when he got into hot water.'

'It must have been a great help to find someone who believed in him notwithstanding everything.'

'I'm afraid it sounds very immoral, but whatever his crimes were, I should never like Alec less. You see, he's been so awfully good and kind to me, I can look on with fortitude while he plays football with the Ten Commandments.'

Julia's emotions were always sudden, and the tears came to her eyes as she answered.

'I'm really beginning to think you a perfect angel, Dick.'

'Don't say that,' he retorted quickly. 'It makes me feel so middle-aged. 'I'd much sooner be a young sinner than an elderly cherub.'

Smiling, she stretched out her hand, and he held it for a moment.

'You know, though I can't help liking you, I don't in the least approve of you.'

'Good heavens, why not?' he cried.

'Well, I was brought up to believe that a man should work, and you're disgracefully idle.'

'Good heavens, to marry an American wife is the most arduous profession in the world,' he cried. 'One has to combine the energy of the Universal Provider with the patience of an ambassador at the Sublime Porte.'

'You foolish creature,' she laughed.

But her thoughts immediately reverted to Lucy. Her pallid, melancholy face still lingered in Julia's memory, and her heart was touched by the hopeless woe that dwelt in her beautiful eyes.

'I suppose there's no doubt that those stories about Alec MacKenzie were true?' she said, thoughtfully.

Dick gave her a quick glance. He wondered what was in her mind.

'I'll tell you what I think,' he said. 'Anyone who knows Alec as well as I do must be convinced that he did nothing from motives that were mean and paltry. To accuse him of cowardice is absurd—he's the bravest man I've ever known—and it's equally absurd to accuse him of weakness. But what I do think is this: Alec is not the man to stick at half measures, and he's taken desperately to heart the maxim which says that he who desires an end desires the means also. I think he might be very ruthless, and on occasion he might be stern to the verge of brutality. Reading between the lines of those letters that Macinnery sent to the *Daily Mail,* I have wondered if Alec, finding that someone must be sacrificed, didn't deliberately choose George Allerton because he was the least useful to him and could be best spared. Even in small undertakings like that there must be some men who are only food for powder. If Alec had found George worthless to him, no consideration for Lucy would have prevented him from sacrificing him.'

' If that were so why didn't he say it outright? '

' Do you think it would have made things any better? The British public is sentimental; they will not understand that in warfare it is necessary sometimes to be inhuman. And how would it have served him with Lucy if he had confessed that he had used George callously as a pawn in his game that must be sacrificed to win some greater advantage? '

' It's all very horrible,' shuddered Julia.

' And so far as the public goes, events have shown that he was right to keep silence. The agitation against him died down for want of matter, and though he is vaguely discredited, nothing is proved definitely against him. Public opinion is very fickle, and already people are beginning to forget, and as they forget they will think they have misjudged him. When it is announced that he has given his services to the King of the Belgians, ten to one there will be a reaction in his favour.'

They got up from luncheon, and coffee was served to them. They lit their cigarettes. For some time they were silent.

' Lucy wants to see him before he goes,' said Julia suddenly.

Dick looked at her and gave an impatient shrug of the shoulders.

'I suppose she wants to indulge a truly feminine passion for making scenes. She's made Alec quite wretched enough already.'

'Don't be unkind to her, Dick,' said Julia, tears welling up in her bright eyes. 'You don't know how desperately unhappy she is. My heart bled to see her this morning.'

'Darling, I'll do whatever you want me to,' he said, leaning over her.

Julia's sense of the ridiculous was always next door to her sense of the pathetic.

'I don't know why you should kiss me because Lucy's utterly miserable,' she said, with a little laugh.

And then, gravely, as she nestled in his encircling arm:

'Will you try and manage it? She hesitates to write to him.'

'I'm not sure if I had not better leave you to impart the pleasing information yourself,' he replied. 'I've asked Alec to come here this afternoon.'

'You're a selfish beast,' she answered. 'But in that case you must leave me alone with him, because I shall probably weep gallons of tears, and you'll only snigger at me.'

'Bless your little heart! Let us put handkerchiefs in every conceivable place.'

'On occasions like this I carry a bagful about with me.'

## XX

In the afternoon Alec arrived. Julia's tender heart
was touched by the change wrought in him during the
three months of his absence from town. At the first
glance there was little difference in him. He was still
cool and collected, with that air of expecting people to
do his bidding which had always impressed her; and
there was still about him a sensation of strength, which
was very comfortable to weaker vessels. But her sharp
eyes saw that he held himself together by an effort of
will, and it was singularly painful to the onlooker.
The strain had told on him, and there was in his haggard eyes, in the deliberate firmness of his mouth, a
tension which suggested that he was almost at the end
of his tether. He was sterner than before and more
silent. Julia could see how deeply he had suffered, and
his suffering had been greater because of his determination to conquer it at all costs. She longed to go
to him and beg him not to be too hard upon himself.
Things would have gone more easily with him, if he
had allowed himself a little weakness. But he was
softer too, and she no longer felt the slight awe which
to her till then had often made intercourse difficult.
His first words were full of an unexpected kindness.

'I'm so glad to be able to congratulate you,' he said,
holding her hand and smiling with that rare, sweet
smile of his. 'I was a little unhappy at leaving Dick;
but now I leave him in your hands I'm perfectly con-

tent. He's the dearest, kindest old chap I've ever known.'

'Shut up, Alec,' cried Dick promptly. 'Don't play the heavy father, or Julia will burst into tears. She loves having a good cry.'

But Alec ignored the interruption.

'He'll be an admirable husband because he's been an admirable friend.'

For the first time Julia thought Alec altogether wise and charming.

'I know he will,' she answered happily. 'And I'm only prevented from saying all I think of him by the fear that he'll become perfectly unmanageable.'

'Spare me the chaste blushes which mantle my youthful brow, and pour out the tea, Julia,' said Dick.

She laughed and proceeded to do as he requested.

'And are you really starting for Africa so soon?' Julia asked, when they were settled around the tea-table.

Alec threw back his head, and his face lit up.

'I am. Everything is fixed up; the bother of collecting supplies and getting porters has been taken off my shoulders, and all I have to do is to get along as quickly as possible.'

'I wish to goodness you'd give up these horrible explorations,' cried Dick. 'They make the rest of us feel so abominably unadventurous.'

'But they're the very breath of my nostrils,' answered Alec. 'You don't know the exhilaration of the daily dangers, the joy of treading where only the wild beasts have trodden before.'

'I freely confess that I don't want to,' said Dick.

Alec sprang up and stretched his legs. As he spoke all signs of lassitude disappeared, and he was seized with an excitement that was rarely seen in him.

'Already I can hardly bear my impatience when I think of the boundless country and the enchanting freedom. Here one grows so small, so mean; but in Africa everything is built to a nobler standard. There the man is really a man. There one knows what are will and strength and courage. You don't know what it is to stand on the edge of some great plain and breathe the pure keen air after the terrors of the forest.'

'The boundless plain of Hyde Park is enough for me,' said Dick. 'And the aspect of Piccadilly on a fine day in June gives me quite as many emotions as I want.'

But Julia was moved by Alec's unaccustomed rhetoric, and she looked at him earnestly.

'But what will you gain by it now that your work is over—by all the danger and all the hardships?'

He turned his dark, solemn eyes upon her.

'Nothing. I want to gain nothing. Perhaps I shall discover some new species of antelope or some unknown plant. I may be fortunate enough to find a new waterway. That is all the reward I want. I love the sense of power and the mastery. What do you think I care for the tinsel rewards of kings and peoples!'

'I always said you were melodramatic,' said Dick. 'I never heard anything so transpontine.'

'And the end of it?' asked Julia, almost in a whisper. 'What will be the end?'

A faint smile played for an instant upon Alec's lips. He shrugged his shoulders.

'The end is death. But I shall die standing up. I shall go the last journey as I have gone every other.'

He stopped, for he would not add the last two words. Julia said them for him.

'Without fear.'

'For all the world like the wicked baronet,' cried the mocking Dick. 'Once aboard the lugger, and the gurl is mine.'

Julia reflected for a little while. She did not want to resist the admiration with which Alec filled her. But she shuddered. He did not seem to fit in with the generality of men.

'Don't you want people to remember you?' she asked.

'Perhaps they will,' he answered slowly. 'Perhaps in a hundred years, in some flourishing town where I discovered nothing but wilderness, they will commission a second-rate sculptor to make a fancy statue of me. And I shall stand in front of the Stock Exchange, a convenient perch for birds, to look eternally upon the shabby deeds of human kind.'

He gave a short, abrupt laugh, and his words were followed by silence. Julia gave Dick a glance which he took to be a signal that she wished to be alone with Alec.

'Forgive me if I leave you for one minute,' he said.

He got up and left the room. The silence still continued, and Alec seemed immersed in thought. At last Julia answered him.

'And is that really all? I can't help thinking that at the bottom of your heart there is something that you've never told to a living soul.'

He looked at her, and their eyes met. He felt suddenly her extraordinary sympathy and her passionate desire to help him. And as though the bonds of the flesh were loosened, it seemed to him that their very souls faced one another. The reserve which was his dearest habit fell away from him, and he felt an urgent desire to say that which a curious delicacy had prevented him from every betraying to callous ears.

' I daresay I shall never see you again, and perhaps it doesn't much matter what I say to you. You'll think me very silly, but I'm afraid I'm rather—patriotic. It's only we who live away from England who really love it. I'm so proud of my country, and I wanted so much to do something for it. Often in Africa I've thought of this dear England and longed not to die till I had done my work.'

His voice shook a little, and he paused. It seemed to Julia that she saw the man for the first time, and she wished passionately that Lucy could hear those words of his which he spoke so shyly, and yet with such a passionate earnestness.

' Behind all the soldiers and the statesmen whose fame is imperishable there is a long line of men who've built up the empire piece by piece. Their names are forgotten, and only students know their history, but each one of them gave a province to his country. And I too have my place among them. Year after year I toiled, night and day, and at last I was able to hand over to the commissioner a broad tract of land, rich and fertile. After my death England will forget my faults and my mistakes; and I care nothing for the flouts and gibes with which she has repaid all my pain, for I have added another fair jewel to her crown. I don't want rewards; I only want the honour of serving this dear land of ours.'

Julia went up to him and laid her hand gently on his arm.

'Why is it, when you're so nice really, that you do all you can to make people think you utterly horrid?'

'Don't laugh at me because you've found out that at bottom I'm nothing more than a sentimental old woman.'

'I don't want to laugh at you. But if I didn't think it would embarrass you so dreadfully, I should certainly kiss you.'

He smiled and lifting her hand to his lips, lightly kissed it.

'I shall begin to think I'm a very wonderful woman if I've taught you to do such pretty things as that.'

She made him sit down, and then she sat by his side.

'I'm very glad you came to-day. I wanted to talk to you. Will you be very angry if I say something to you?'

'I don't think so,' he smiled.

'I want to speak to you about Lucy.'

He drew himself suddenly together, and the expansion of his mood disappeared. He was once more the cold, reserved man of their habitual intercourse.

'I'd rather you didn't,' he said briefly.

But Julia was not to be so easily put off.

'What would you do if she came here to-day?' she asked.

He turned round and looked at her sharply, then answered with great deliberation.

'I have always lived in polite society. I should never dream of outraging its conventions. If Lucy happened to come, you may be sure that I should be scrupulously polite.'

' Is that all? ' she cried.

He did not answer, and into his face came a wild fierceness that appalled her. She saw the effort he was making at self-control. She wished with all her heart that he would be less brave.

' I think you might not be so hard if you knew how desperately Lucy has suffered.'

He looked at her again, and his eyes were filled with bitterness, with angry passion at the injustice of fate. Did she think that he had not suffered? Because he did not whine his misery to all and sundry, did she think he did not care? He sprang up and walked to the other end of the room. He did not want that woman, for all her kindness, to see his face. He was not the man to fall in and out of love with every pretty girl he met. All his life he had kept an ideal before his eyes. He turned to Julia savagely.

' You don't know what it meant to me to fall in love. I felt that I had lived all my life in a prison, and at last Lucy came and took me by the hand, and led me out. And for the first time I breathed the free air of heaven.'

He stopped abruptly, clenching his jaws. He would not tell her how bitterly he had suffered for it, he would not tell her of his angry rebelliousness because all that pain should have come to him. He wanted nobody to know the depths of his agony and of his despair. But he would not give way. He felt that, if he did not keep a tight hold on himself, he would break down and shake with passionate sobbing. He felt a sudden flash of hatred for Julia because she sat there and watched his weakness. But as though she saw at what a crisis of

emotion he was, Julia turned her eyes from him and
looked down at the ground. She did not speak. She
felt the effort he was making to master himself, and she
was infinitely disturbed. She wanted to go to him and
comfort him, but she knew he would repel her. He
wanted to fight his battle unaided.

At last he conquered, but when he spoke again,
his voice was singularly broken. It was hoarse and
low.

' My love was the last human weakness I had. It was
right that I should drink that bitter cup. And I've
drunk its very dregs. I should have known that I
wasn't meant for happiness and a life of ease. I have
other work to do in the world.'

He paused for a moment, and his calmness was re-
stored to him.

' And now that I've overcome this last temptation I
am ready to do it.'

' But haven't you any pity for yourself? Haven't
you any thought for Lucy? '

' Must I tell you, too, that everything I did was for
Lucy's sake? And still I love her with all my heart
and soul.'

There was no bitterness in his tone now; it was gentle
and resigned. He had, indeed, won the battle. Julia's
eyes were filled with tears, and she could not answer.
He came forward and shook hands with her.

' You mustn't cry,' he said, smiling. ' You're one of
those persons whose part it is to bring sunshine into the
lives of those with less fortunate dispositions. You
must always be happy and childlike.'

' I've got lots of handkerchiefs, thanks,' she sobbed,
laughing the while.

' You must forget all the nonsense I've talked to you,' he said.

He smiled once more and was gone.

Dick was sitting in his bedroom, reading an evening paper, and she flung herself sobbing into his arms.

' Oh, Dick, I've had such a lovely cry, and I'm so happy and so utterly wretched. And I'm sure I shall have a red nose.'

' Darling, I've long discovered that you only weep because you're the only person in the world to whom it's thoroughly becoming.'

' Don't be horrid and unsympathetic. I think Alec MacKenzie's a perfect dear. I wanted to kiss him, only I was afraid it would frighten him to death.'

' I'm glad you didn't. He would have thought you a forward hussy.'

' I wish I could have married him, too,' cried Julia. ' I'm sure he'd make a nice husband.'

# XXI

THE days went by, spent by Alec in making necessary preparations for his journey, spent by Lucy in sickening anxiety. The last two months had been passed by her in a conflict of emotions. Love had planted itself in her heart like a great forest tree, and none of the storms that had assailed it seemed to have power to shake its stubborn roots. Reason, common decency, shame, had lost their power. She had prayed God that a merciful death might free her from the dreadful uncertainty. She was spiritless and cowed. She despised herself for her weakness. And sometimes she rebelled against the fate that crushed her with such misfortunes; she had tried to do her duty always, acting humbly according to her lights, and yet everything she was concerned in crumbled away to powder at her touch. She, too, began to think that she was not meant for happiness. She knew that she ought to hate Alec, but she could not. She knew that his action should fill her with nameless horror, but against her will she could not believe that he was false and wicked. One thing she was determined on, and that was to keep her word to Robert Boulger; but he himself gave her back her freedom.

He came to her one day, and after a little casual conversation broke suddenly into the middle of things.

'Lucy, I want to ask you to release me from my engagement to you,' he said.

Her heart gave a great leap against her breast, and she began to tremble. He went on.

'I'm ashamed to have to say it; I find that I don't love you enough to marry you.'

She looked at him silently, and her eyes filled with tears. The brutality with which he spoke was so unnatural that it betrayed the mercifulness of his intention.

'If you think that, there is nothing more to be said,' she answered.

He gave her a look of such bitterness that she felt it impossible to continue a pretence which deceived neither of them.

'I'm unworthy of your love,' she cried. 'I've made you desperately wretched.'

'It doesn't matter about me,' he said. 'But there's no reason for you to be wretched, too.'

'I'm willing to do whatever you wish, Bobbie.'

'I can't marry you simply because you're sorry for me. I thought I could, but—it's asking too much of you. We had better say no more about it.'

'I'm very sorry,' she whispered.

'You see, you're still in love with Alec MacKenzie.'

He said it, vainly longing for a denial; but he knew in his heart that no denial would come.

'I always shall be, notwithstanding everything. I can't help myself.'

'No, it's fate.'

She sprang to her feet with vehement passion.

'Oh, Bobbie, don't you think there's some chance that everything may be explained?'

He hesitated for a moment. It was very difficult to answer.

' It's only fair to tell you that now things have calmed down, there are a great many people who don't believe Macinnery's story. It appears that the man's a thorough blackguard, whom MacKenzie loaded with benefits.'

' Do *you* still believe that Alec caused George's death? '

' Yes.'

Lucy leaned back in her chair, resting her face on her hand. She seemed to reflect deeply.

' And you? ' said Bobbie.

She gave him a long, earnest look. The colour came to her cheeks.

' No,' she said firmly.

' Why not? ' he asked.

' I have no reason except that I love him.'

' What are you going to do? '

' I don't know.'

Bobbie got up, kissed her gently, and went out. She did not see him again, and in a day or two she heard that he had gone away.

Lucy made up her mind that she must see Alec before he went, but a secret bashfulness prevented her from writing to him. She was afraid that he would refuse, and she could not force herself upon him if she knew definitely that he did not want to see her. But with all her heart she wanted to ask his pardon. It would not be so hard to continue with the dreary burden which was her life if she knew that he had a little pity for her. He could not fail to forgive her when he saw how broken she was.

But the days followed one another, and the date

which Julia, radiant with her own happiness, had given her as that of his departure, was approaching.

Julia, too, was exercised in mind. After her conversation with Alec she could not ask him to see Lucy, for she knew what his answer would be. No arguments would move him. He did not want to give either Lucy or himself the pain which he foresaw an interview would cause, and his wounds were too newly-healed for him to run any risks. Julia resolved to take the matter into her own hands. Alec was starting next day, and he had promised to look in towards the evening to bid them good-bye. Julia wrote a note to Lucy, asking her to come also.

When she told Dick, he was aghast.

' But it's a monstrous thing to do,' he cried. ' You can't entrap the man in that way.'

' I know it's monstrous,' she answered. ' But that's the only advantage of being an American in England, that one can do monstrous things. You look upon us as first cousins to the red Indians, and you expect anything from us. In America I have to mind my p's and q's. I mayn't smoke in public, I shouldn't dream of lunching in a restaurant alone with a man, and I'm the most conventional person in the most conventional society in the world; but here, because the English are under the delusion that New York society is free and easy, and that American women have no restraint, I can kick over the traces, and no one will think it even odd.'

' But, my dear, it's a mere matter of common decency.'

' There are times when common decency is out of place,' she replied.

'Alec will never forgive you.'

'I don't care. I think he ought to see Lucy, and since he'd refuse if I asked him, I'm not going to give him the chance.'

'What will you do if he just bows and walks off?'

'I have his assurance that he'll behave like a civilised man,' she answered.

'I wash my hands of it,' said Dick. 'I think it's perfectly indefensible.'

'I never said it wasn't,' she agreed. 'But you see, I'm only a poor, weak woman, and I'm not supposed to have any sense of honour or propriety. You must let me take what advantage I can of the disabilities of the weaker sex.'

Dick smiled and shrugged his shoulders.

'Your blood be upon your own head,' he answered.

'If I perish, I perish.'

And so it came about that when Alec had been ten minutes in Julia's cosy sitting-room, Lucy was announced. Julia went up to her, greeting her effusively to cover the awkwardness of the moment. Alec grew very pale, but made no sign that he was disconcerted. Only Dick was troubled. He was obviously at a loss for words, and it was plain to see that he was out of temper.

'I'm so glad you were able to come,' said Julia, in order to show Alec that she had been expecting Lucy.

Lucy gave him a rapid glance, and the colour flew to her cheeks. He was standing up and came forward with outstretched hand.

'How do you do?' he said. 'How is Lady Kelsey?'

'She's much better, thanks. We've been to Spa, you know, for her health.'

Julia's heart beat quickly. She was much excited at this meeting; and it seemed to her strangely romantic, a sign of the civilisation of the times, that these two people with raging passions afire in their hearts, should exchange the commonplaces of polite society, Alec, having recovered from his momentary confusion was extremely urbane.

' Somebody told me you'd gone abroad,' he said. ' Was it you, Dick? Dick is an admirable person, a sort of gazetteer for the world of fashion.'

Dick fussily brought forward a chair for Lucy to sit in, and offered to disembarrass her of the jacket she was wearing.

' You must make my excuses for not leaving a card on Lady Kelsey before going away,' said Alec. ' I've been excessively busy.'

' It doesn't matter at all,' Lucy answered.

Julia glanced at him. She saw that he was determined to keep the conversation on the indifferent level which it might have occupied if Lucy had been nothing more than an acquaintance. There was a bantering tone in his voice which was an effective barrier to all feeling. For a moment she was nonplussed.

' London is an excellent place for showing one of how little importance one is in the world. One makes a certain figure, and perhaps is tempted to think oneself of some consequence. Then one goes away, and on returning is surprised to discover that nobody has ever noticed one's absence.'

Lucy smiled faintly. Dick, recovering his good-humour, came at once to the rescue.

' You're overmodest, Alec. If you weren't, you might be a great man. Now, I make a point of telling my friends that I'm indispensable, and they take me at my word.'

' You are a leaven of flippancy in the heavy dough of British righteousness,' smiled Alec.

' It is true that the wise man only takes the unimportant quite seriously.'

' For it is obvious that one needs more brains to do nothing with elegance than to be a cabinet minister,' said Alec.

' You pay me a great compliment, Alec,' cried Dick. ' You repeat to my very face one of my favourite observations.'

Julia looked at him steadily.

' Haven't I heard you say that only the impossible is worth doing? '

' Good heavens,' he cried. ' I must have been quoting the headings of a copy-book.'

Lucy felt that she must say something. She had been watching Alec, and her heart was nearly breaking. She turned to Dick.

' Are you going down to Southampton? ' she asked.

' I am, indeed,' he answered. ' I shall hide my face on Alec's shoulder and weep salt tears. It will be most affecting, because in moments of emotion I always burst into epigram.'

Alec sprang to his feet. There was a bitterness in his face which was in odd contrast with Dick's light words.

' I loathe all solemn leave-takings,' he said. ' I prefer to part from people with a nod or a smile, whether I'm going for ever or for a day to Brighton.'

' I've always assured you that you're a monster of inhumanity,' said Mrs. Lomas, laughing difficultly.

He turned to her with a grim smile.

' Dick has been imploring me for twenty years to take life flippantly. I have learnt at last that things are only grave if you take them gravely, and that is desperately stupid. It's so hard to be serious without being absurd. That is the chief power of women, that life and death for them are merely occasions for a change of costume, marriage a creation in white, and the worship of God an opportunity for a Paris bonnet.'

Julia saw that he was determined to keep the conversation on a level of amiable persiflage, and with her lively sense of the ridiculous she could hardly repress a smile at the heaviness of his hand. Through all that he said pierced the bitterness of his heart, and his every word was contradicted by the vehemence of his tortured voice. She was determined, too, that the interview which she had brought about, uncomfortable as it had been to all of them, should not be brought to nothing; characteristically she went straight to the point. She stood up.

' I'm sure you two have things to say to one another that you would like to say alone.'

She saw Alec's eyes grow darker as he saw himself cornered, but she was implacable.

' I have some letters to send off by the American mail, and I want Dick to look over them to see that I've spelt *honour* with a u and *traveller* with a double l.'

Neither Alec nor Lucy answered, and the determined little woman took her husband firmly away. When they were left alone, neither spoke for a while.

' I've just realised that you didn't know I was coming to-day,' said Lucy at last. ' I had no idea that you were being entrapped. I would never have consented to that.'

' I'm very glad to have an opportunity of saying good-bye to you,' he answered.

He preserved the conversational manner of polite society, and it seemed to Lucy that she would never have the strength to get beyond.

' I'm so glad that Dick and Julia are happily married. They're very much in love with one another.'

' I should have thought love was the worst possible foundation for marriage,' he answered. ' Love creates illusions, and marriage destroys them. True lovers should never marry.'

Again silence fell upon them, and again Lucy broke it.

' You're going away to-morrow?'

' I am.'

She looked at him, but he would not meet her eyes. He went over to the window and looked out upon the busy street.

' Are you very glad to go?'

' You can't think what a joy it is to look upon London for the last time. I long for the infinite surface of the clean and comfortable sea.'

Lucy gave a stifled sob. Alec started a little, but he did not move. He still looked down upon the stream of cabs and 'buses, lit by the misty autumn sun.

' Is there no one you regret to leave, Alec?'

It tore his heart that she should use his name. To hear her say it had always been like a caress, and the word on her lips brought back once more the whole agony of his distress; but he would not allow his emotion to be seen. He turned round and faced her gravely. Now, for the first time, he did not hesitate to look at her. And while he spoke the words he set himself to speak, he noticed the exquisite oval of her face, her charming, soft hair, and her unhappy eyes.

' You see, Dick is married, and so I'm much best out of the way. When a man takes a wife, his bachelor friends are wise to depart from his life, gracefully, before he shows them that he needs their company no longer.'

' And besides Dick? '

' I have few friends and no relations. I can't flatter myself that anyone will be much distressed at my departure.'

' You must have no heart at all,' she said, in a low, hoarse voice.

He clenched his teeth. He was bitterly angry with Julia because she had exposed him to this unspeakable torture.

' If I had I certainly should not bring it to the *Carlton Hotel*. That sentimental organ would be surely out of place in such a neighbourhood.'

Lucy sprang to her feet.

' Oh, why do you treat me as if we were strangers? How can you be so cruel? '

' Flippancy is often the only refuge from an uncomfortable position,' he answered gravely. ' We should really be much wiser merely to discuss the weather.'

' Are you angry because I came? '

' That would be very ungracious on my part. Perhaps it wasn't quite necessary that we should meet again.'

' You've been acting all the time I've been here. Do you think I didn't see it was unreal, when you talked with such cynical indifference? I know you well enough to tell when you're hiding your real self behind a mask.'

' If that is so, the inference is obvious that I wish my real self to be hidden.'

' I would rather you cursed me than treat me with such cold politness.'

' I'm afraid you're rather difficult to please,' he said.

Lucy went up to him passionately, but he drew back so that she might not touch him. Her outstretched hands dropped powerless to her side.

' Oh, you're of iron,' she cried pitifully. ' Alec, Alec, I couldn't let you go without seeing you once more. Even you would be satisfied if you knew what bitter anguish I've suffered. Even you would pity me. I don't want you to think too badly of me.'

' Does it much matter what I think? We shall be five thousand miles apart.'

' You must utterly despise me.'

He shook his head. And now his manner lost that affected calmness which had been so cruelly wounding. He could not now attempt to hide the pain that he was suffering. His voice trembled a little with his great emotion.

' I loved you far too much to do that. Believe me, with all my heart I wish you well. Now that the first bitterness is past I see that you did the only possible thing. I hope that you'll be very happy. Robert Boulger is an excellent fellow, and I'm sure he'll make you a much better husband than I should ever have done.'

Lucy blushed to the roots of her hair. Her heart sank, and she did not seek to conceal her agitation.

' Did they tell you I was going to marry Robert Boulger? '

' Isn't it true? '

' Oh, how cruel of them, how frightfully cruel! I became engaged to him, but he gave me my release. He knew that notwithstanding everything, I loved you better than my life.'

Alec looked down, but he did not say anything. He did not move.

'Oh, Alec, don't be utterly pitiless,' she wailed. 'Don't leave me without a single word of kindness.'

'Nothing is changed, Lucy. You sent me away because I caused your brother's death.'

She stood before him, her hands behind her back, and they looked into one another's eyes. Her words were steady and quiet. It seemed to give her an infinite relief to say them.

'I hated you then, and yet I couldn't crush the love that was in my heart. And it's because I was frightened of myself that I told Bobbie I'd marry him. But I couldn't. I was horrified because I cared for you still. It seemed such odious treachery to George, and yet love burnt up my heart. I used to try and drive you away from my thoughts, but every word you had ever said came back to me. Don't you remember, you told me that everything you did was for my sake? Those words hammered away on my heart as though it were an anvil. I struggled not to believe them, I said to myself that you had sacrificed George, coldly, callously, prudently, but my love told me it wasn't true. Your whole life stood on one side and only this hateful story on the other. You couldn't have grown into a different man in one single instant. I've learnt to know you better during these three months of utter misery, and I'm ashamed of what I did.'

'Ashamed?'

'I came here to-day to tell you that I don't understand the reason of what you did; but I don't want to understand. I believe in you now with all my strength. I believe in you as better women than I believe in God. I know that whatever you did was right and just—because you did it.'

Alec looked at her for a moment. Then he held out his hand.

' Thank God,' he said. ' I'm so grateful to you.'

' Have you nothing more to say to me than that? '

' You see, it's come too late. Nothing much matters now, for to-morrow I go away for ever.'

' But you'll come back.'

He gave a short, scornful laugh.

' They were so glad to give me that job on the Congo because no one else would take it. I'm going to a part of Africa from which Europeans seldom return.'

' Oh, that's too horrible,' she cried. ' Don't go, dearest; I can't bear it.'

' I must now. Everything is settled, and there can be no drawing back.'

She let go hopelessly of his hand.

' Don't you care for me any more? ' she whispered.

He looked at her, but he did not answer. She turned away, and sinking into a chair, began to cry.

' Don't, Lucy,' he said, his voice breaking suddenly. ' Don't make it harder.'

' Oh, Alec, Alec, don't you see how much I love you.'

He leaned over her and gently stroked her hair.

' Be brave, darling,' he whispered.

She looked up passionately, seizing both his hands.

' I can't live without you. I've suffered too much. If you cared for me at all, you'd stay.'

' Though I love you with all my soul, I can't do otherwise now than go.'

' Then take me with you,' she cried eagerly. ' Let me come too.'

' You!'

' You don't know what I can do. With you to help me I can be very brave. Let me come, Alec.'

' It's impossible. You don't know what you ask.'

' Then let me wait for you. Let me wait till you come back.'

' And if I never come back?'

' I will wait for you still.'

He placed his hands on her shoulders and looked into her eyes, as though he were striving to see into the depths of her soul. She felt very weak. She could scarcely see him through her tears, but she tried to smile. Then without a word he slipped his arms around her. Sobbing in the ecstasy of her happiness, she let her head fall on his shoulder.

' You will have the courage to wait?' he said.

' I know you love me, and I trust you.'

' Then have no fear; I will come back. My journey was only dangerous because I wanted to die. I want to live now, and I shall live.'

' Oh, Alec, Alec, I'm so glad you love me.'

Outside in the street the bells of the motor 'buses tinkled noisily, and there was an incessant roar of the traffic that rumbled heavily over the wooden pavements. There was a clatter of horses' hoofs, and the blowing of horns; the electric broughams whizzed past with an odd, metallic whirr.

THE END

# FINE WORKS OF FICTION AVAILABLE IN QUALITY PAPERBACK EDITIONS FROM CARROLL & GRAF

☐ Asch, Sholem/THE APOSTLE $10.95
☐ Asch, Sholem/MARY $10.95
☐ Asch, Sholem/THE NAZARENE $10.95
☐ Asch, Sholem/THREE CITIES $10.50
☐ Ashley, Mike (ed.)/THE MAMMOTH BOOK OF SHORT HORROR NOVELS $8.95
☐ Asimov, Isaac et al/THE MAMMOTH BOOK OF GOLDEN AGE SCIENCE FICTION (1940) $8.95
☐ Babel, Isaac/YOU MUST KNOW EVERYTHING $8.95
☐ Balzac, Honoré de/CESAR BIROTTEAU $8.95
☐ Balzac, Honoré de/THE LILY OF THE VALLEY $9.95
☐ Bellaman, Henry/KINGS ROW $8.95
☐ Bernanos, George/DIARY OF A COUNTRY PRIEST $7.95
☐ Brand, Christianna/GREEN FOR DANGER $8.95
☐ Céline, Louis-Ferdinand/CASTLE TO CASTLE $8.95
☐ Chekov, Anton/LATE BLOOMING FLOWERS $8.95
☐ Conrad, Joseph/EASTERN SKIES, WESTERN SEAS $12.95
☐ Conrad, Joseph/SEA STORIES $8.95
☐ Conrad, Joseph & Ford Madox Ford/THE INHERITORS $7.95
☐ Conrad, Joseph & Ford Madox Ford/ROMANCE $8.95
☐ Coward, Noel/A WITHERED NOSEGAY $8.95
☐ Dalby, Richard/VICTORIAN GHOST STORIES $9.95
☐ Delbanco, Nicholas/GROUP PORTRAIT $10.95
☐ de Maupassant, Guy/THE DARK SIDE $8.95
☐ de Montherlant, Henry/THE GIRLS $11.95
☐ Dos Passos, John/THREE SOLDIERS $9.95
☐ Durrell, Laurence/THE BLACK BOOK $7.95
☐ Feuchtwanger, Lion/JEW SUSS $8.95
☐ Feuchtwanger, Lion/THE OPPERMANNS $8.95
☐ Fisher, R.L./THE PRINCE OF WHALES $5.95
☐ Fitzgerald, Penelope/THE BEGINNING OF SPRING $8.95
☐ Fitzgerald, Penelope/INNOCENCE $7.95
☐ Fitzgerald, Penelope/OFFSHORE $7.95
☐ Fitzgerald, Penelope/INNOCENCE $7.95
☐ Flaubert, Gustave/NOVEMBER $7.95
☐ Fonseca, Rubem/HIGH ART $7.95
☐ Forster, E.M./GREAT NOVELS OF E.M. FORSTER $13.95
☐ Fuchs, Daniel/SUMMER IN WILLIAMSBURG $8.95
☐ Gold, Michael/JEWS WITHOUT MONEY $7.95
☐ Gorky, Maxim/THE LIFE OF A USELESS MAN $10.95

☐ Greenberg & Waugh (eds.)/THE NEW ADVENTURES
OF SHERLOCK HOLMES $8.95
☐ Greene, Graham & Hugh/THE SPY'S BEDSIDE BOOK $7.95
☐ Greenfeld, Josh/THE RETURN OF MR. HOLLYWOOD $8.95
☐ Hamsun, Knut/MYSTERIES $8.95
☐ Hardinge, George (ed.)/THE MAMMOTH BOOK OF
MODERN CRIME STORIES $8.95
☐ Hawkes, John/VIRGINIE: HER TWO LIVES $7.95
☐ Higgins, George/TWO COMPLETE NOVELS $9.95
☐ Hugo, Victor/NINETY-THREE $8.95
☐ Huxley, Aldous/ANTIC HAY $10.95
☐ Huxley, Aldous/CROME YELLOW $10.95
☐ Huxley, Aldous/EYELESS IN GAZA $9.95
☐ Ibañez, Vincente Blasco/THE FOUR HORSEMEN OF
THE APOCALYPSE $8.95
☐ Jackson, Charles/THE LOST WEEKEND $7.95
☐ James, Henry/GREAT SHORT NOVELS $12.95
☐ Jones, Richard Glyn/THE MAMMOTH BOOK OF
MURDER $8.95
☐ Just, Ward/THE CONGRESSMAN WHO LOVED
FLAUBERT $8.95
☐ Lewis, Norman/DAY OF THE FOX $8.95
☐ Lowry, Malcolm/HEAR US O LORD FROM HEAVEN
THY DWELLING PLACE $9.95
☐ Lowry, Malcolm/ULTRAMARINE $7.95
☐ Macaulay, Rose/CREWE TRAIN $8.95
☐ Macaulay, Rose/KEEPING UP APPEARANCES $8.95
☐ Macaulay, Rose/DANGEROUS AGES $8.95
☐ Mailer, Norman/BARBARY SHORE $9.95
☐ Maugham, W. Somerset/THE EXPLORER $10.95
☐ Mauriac, François/THE DESERT OF LOVE $6.95
☐ Mauriac, François/FLESH AND BLOOD $8.95
☐ Mauriac, François/WOMAN OF THE PHARISEES $8.95
☐ Mauriac, François/VIPER'S TANGLE $8.95
☐ McElroy, Joseph/THE LETTER LEFT TO ME $7.95
☐ McElroy, Joseph/LOOKOUT CARTRIDGE $9.95
☐ McElroy, Joseph/PLUS $8.95
☐ McElroy, Joseph/A SMUGGLER'S BIBLE $9.50
☐ Mitford, Nancy/DON'T TELL ALFRED $7.95
☐ Moorcock, Michael/THE BROTHEL IN ROSENSTRASSE $6.95
☐ Munro, H.H./THE NOVELS AND PLAYS OF SAKI $8.95
☐ Neider, Charles (ed.)/GREAT SHORT STORIES $11.95
☐ Neider, Charles (ed.)/SHORT NOVELS
OF THE MASTERS $12.95
☐ O'Faolain, Julia/THE OBEDIENT WIFE $7.95
☐ O'Faolain, Julia/NO COUNTRY FOR YOUNG MEN $8.95
☐ O'Faolain, Julia/WOMEN IN THE WALL $8.95
☐ Olinto, Antonio/THE WATER HOUSE $9.95
☐ O'Mara, Lesley/GREAT CAT TALES $9.95

□ Pronzini & Greenberg (eds.)/THE MAMMOTH BOOK OF
   PRIVATE EYE NOVELS                                $8.95
□ Rechy, John/BODIES AND SOULS         $8.95
□ Rechy, John/MARILYN'S DAUGHTER     $8.95
□ Rhys, Jean/AFTER LEAVING MR. MACKENZIE   $8.95
□ Rhys, Jean/QUARTET                 $6.95
□ Sand, George/MARIANNE             $7.95
□ Scott, Evelyn/THE WAVE             $9.95
□ Sigal, Clancy/GOING AWAY           $9.95
□ Singer, I.J./THE BROTHERS ASHKENAZI     $9.95
□ Taylor, Elizabeth/IN A SUMMER SEASON    $8.95
□ Thornton, Louise *et al.*/TOUCHING FIRE     $9.95
□ Tolstoy, Leo/TALES OF COURAGE AND CONFLICT  $11.95
□ van Thal, Herbert/THE MAMMOTH BOOK OF
   GREAT DETECTIVE STORIES            $8.95
□ Wassermann, Jacob/CASPAR HAUSER       $9.95
□ Wassermann, Jacob/THE MAURIZIUS CASE   $9.95
□ Weldon, Fay/LETTERS TO ALICE         $6.95
□ Werfel, Franz/THE FORTY DAYS OF MUSA DAGH  $13.95
□ West, Rebecca/THE RETURN OF THE SOLDIER   $8.95
□ Winwood, John/THE MAMMOTH BOOK OF SPY
   THRILLERS                           $8.95

Available from fine bookstores everywhere or use this coupon for ordering.

Carroll & Graf Publishers, Inc., 260 Fifth Avenue, N.Y., N.Y. 10001

Please send me the books I have checked above. I am enclosing $_____
(please add $1.00 per title to cover postage and handling.) Send check
or money order—no cash or C.O.D.'s please. N.Y. residents please add
8¼% sales tax.

Mr/Mrs/Ms _____

Address _____

City _____ State/Zip _____

Please allow four to six weeks for delivery.